CHILD KILLER

A DI OCTAVIAN novel

by
Hester Keegan

CHILD KILLER

A DI Octavian novel by Hester Keegan ©

Published by Bronwyn Editions UK

via Amazon KDP 2022

ISBN: 9798844368769

Cover design by Kathleen Tuguyen

A legal deposit copy has been sent to the British
Library

Excerpt from DI Octavian's novel

Fucking Americans.

Arsyanendra Raja began to run through the gloomy and dusty concrete shell of the warehouse building, skipping over wires, avoiding pillars with exposed steel bars, going around upturned desks. It was difficult to run quickly, being weighed down with a packet of legal documents, an umbrella and a silver ice bucket, thankfully minus the Krug champagne bottle and crystal flutes, but still with ice and water sloshing all over him.

A siren sounded. That was the second one.

Fucking Americans.

He had a sweat on.

Go to the light, Arsyanendra, he told himself. Must go quicker.

He ran through a section of offices. A rat scuttled across his path, on its own route out. Finally, he scooted outside through an opening in the wall that used to contain a door. The rain on his face was a Godsend. He kept running, through a post-apocalyptic canyon of abandoned buildings, their broken windows looking down mockingly at his flight.

Another siren. He wondered what that meant? Was that the last one?

He got clear of the concrete monstrosity and stumbled over grassy wasteland, his Gucci shoes squelching in the mud. His black waistcoat and white shirt were quickly drenched in rainwater, not to mention the ice water and quite a lot of perspiration. He could see safety. Human beings were there, in an elevated position, framed against the Jakarta skyline. But they were not concerned for his safety. Nobody was waving him on or rushing to help him. They were chatting amicably and laughing, sheltered beneath golf umbrellas.

He kept moving. He was quite fit, so didn't start puffing and blowing, halfway across the wasteland. Then he heard the boom, boom, boom, boom of controlled explosions going off behind him. Despite himself, he glanced back, seeing the building start to come down, top to bottom, and then he was forced to the ground, engulfed in a massive cloud of dust, with concrete and metal shrapnel bouncing around him in a cacophony of noise.

When it was all over, and he could see again, and get to his feet, he did a mental check on his faculties. He was okay. He had all his limbs. But his entire front was caked in mud. The building was no longer there, and the rain suddenly stopped, the sun appeared, and he felt reborn. 'Fucking Americans,' he said out loud.

The humans were descending from the viewing platform, and heading towards a fleet of Bentley Continentals and Mercedes vehicles, with waiting chauffeurs. He straggled in after them. He stood and looked at them all – had his recent near-death experience not impacted on them in the slightest? His employer, Margo Lipman, was talking in English to her Indonesian solicitor, and then joking with business associates. She was one of those mature women who still carried with them the remembrance of great beauty when younger; the kind that attracts a billionaire husband. She wore a black coat with feathers around the collar, and big knee-high boots, with dangling gold earrings, which looked like the scaffolding needed to keep her facelift attached.

She glanced back at him with a mixed expression of confusion and annoyance, as if to question where on earth he had gotten to. A solicitor's clerk, a fellow Indonesian, looked at him with sympathy as he came to take the documents from him, which mercifully were quite clean. Raja (he thought of himself as Raja, when on duty) had been sent back for the forgotten legal forms, and "Raja, don't forget the ice bucket, it's an antique."

Raja took a moment to himself, breathing deeply. He should quit. Really, he should, but they paid him double what he would get anywhere else, and he was leaving soon, anyway – he wanted his bonus and reference. He had arranged the visit to the warehouse, it was part of his job, after all – the warehouse being the first property bought by Margo's recently deceased husband for his Asian portfolio. It had been due for demolition before Margo decided to liquidate all the assets, and the buyers were happy for it to be gone. The meeting (all Margo's meetings require champagne) was just a sentimental setting for Margo as final details were ironed out. Nobody bothered to tell him that the demolition had been brought forward twenty *four hours, in order to provide a little entertainment.*

He couldn't swear at them again, as the eldest daughter was approaching him. She was tall and sexy, with very straight black hair, and a wide mouth that surely made every man think inappropriate thoughts about her. She was called London Lipman, and she was twenty-four years old. She was dressed in a tight designer grey sweater and dark trousers, and had similar earrings to her mother. 'Raja,' she said. None of the family could pronounce his first name, so they all called him Raja. Whenever Margo addressed him, it was in that particular tone of voice from the English TV dramas she had watched: Carson, Benton, Phillips. None of them ever knew that Raja actually meant King.

He turned his face towards London. She didn't even glance at his filthy front.

'Raja, you're not going to be late to the airport, are you?'

'No, Miss London.'

'I do hope not.'

Her "friends" were coming in for a Halloween party, before going on to Bali.

More vacuous, rich Americans, mostly from Los Angeles: models, failed basketball players, unknown actors, children of millionaires. Raja would look first to see if the plane had gone down somewhere between Honolulu and Soekarno-Hatta, before hiding his disappointment and getting into character to welcome them all.

ONE

Ezi Pardi was thoroughly enjoying his civil engineering course at Manchester University. He was normally quite a solitary person, but had managed to make some new friends in his host country. He had seen a little of the city, done the stadium tour at Old Trafford, and was compiling a list of his favourite takeaways and coffee shops.

One dark early evening in winter, he was on Oxford Road, heading for some fish and chips. He stepped into the pungent, brightly lit shop and got into the queue of students and older locals. He was still enjoying the novelty of using pounds and pence. As always, there seemed to be some idiot with a cardboard box ordering twenty portions, which caused grumblings in the queue. Ezi looked at the people: a little old woman who had probably lived around Fallowfield or Rusholme all her seventy-five years, a young professional guy in a smart grey coat and beanie hat, two cute Asian girl students who he unfortunately didn't know, and a local white girl who seemed to have her pajamas on, given what was showing below her stained coat. People came in behind him, as the man at the counter finally paid and left, but Ezi didn't look back, he just shuffled along the tiled wall.

Then four English lads entered the chippy; scruffy, tracksuit bottoms barely covering their bellies, hoodies up, swaggering, noisy. Clearly, they didn't care much for queueing and took the front place. The old lady tutted. The local white girl was a little more forceful in her disapproval.

'Wait your turn, you fucking wankers.'

She was ignored and the biggest member of the crew ordered four portions of chips. Not wanting any trouble, the girl behind the counter just got on with it.

Ezi was not particularly insulted; back home, politeness was not a big thing. He stood quietly watching them. He assessed them as out-of-shape wide-boys, but they could still cause mayhem. Ezi, unusually for an Asian, was taller and bigger than any of them, but he had not been to the gym for a year. Anyway, he was in no rush, he would wait for the morons to get their chips and move on.

But the leader seemed to want Ezi to be offended. He kept looking back at him. He had a touch of acne around his unshaven chin. He was an unpleasant individual.

'You upset?' he asked Ezi.

Ezi was surprised at how the question was asked in such a nice way. 'No.'

'I think you are, mate. Say what's on your mind.'

'Nothing is on my mind.'

Another member of the gang turned, holding his chips. 'What's this fucker want?'

'He's giving us grief.'

The girl spoke up again, 'Leave him alone, you knobheads.'

The shop owner shouted from where he was frying fish. 'Oi! No trouble. Out.'

'We doing this inside or out?' the main thug asked Ezi.

'Outside, I suppose.'

Ezi's heart rate remained the same. He saw that it was going to happen, whether he wanted it to or not, and he was fine with it. His expression had not changed throughout the brief but nasty incident; something that made at least two of the gang wonder if this guy was more than he looked. Maybe he was into Taekwondo, UFC cage fighting or something.

The four lads walked outside – two putting their chip packets on top of a bin. They fanned out. Ezi followed. He stepped down onto the pavement and looked around the horrible group. His limbs were loose, he was ready to respond to wherever the attack started. It came quickly from the two to the left, with a punch and a kick. Ezi punched back successfully, causing a squirt of blood to fly through the air and the man to squeal, but the kick really hurt him. The main thug stepped in with a flurry of punches, left, right and an uppercut. Ezi hit him back hard. Then they were all at him, in nervous spurts of violence in case he was that surprise package. But Ezi Pardi had no particular fighting skills and, well, basically, they beat the crap out of him.

TWO

Half English, half Indonesian, Detective Inspector Tony Octavian, of the Greater Manchester police, was born in the city of Yogyakarta (or Jogjakarta, as it was commonly known). He grew up in south Manchester, the son of an Indonesian father who loved any country except his home one, and an English mother who adored everything about Indonesia, apart from the corrupt police and the mosquitoes, in no particular order.

They had lived in a leafy area of Didsbury, while his father worked as a GP, and his mother a teacher. That was how the pair had originally met, with Jane Hornsby teaching English in Jogja (as it was also known), and meeting the handsome Doctor Ridho Octavian at a party. For the sake of Tony and his sister, Intan, they had shared their time between the two countries; and while Tony felt more English, Intan identified more with South East Asia.

A serious student, the police service had always fascinated Tony Octavian, so, after college, he had started with the Metropolitan Police Service (London-based relatives had always been nagging him that he needed to head south for a career). His had been a meteoric career, possibly aided by his Muslim ethnicity, but his arrest record and conduct had been exceptional. Now thirty-six, it was his wife, Charlotte, who hankered for the less mental North West of England, especially as their first child arrived. With his parents currently in the Indonesian capital of Jakarta, Octavian and Charlotte might have enjoyed a quiet family life, but a never-ending stream of Indonesian relatives kept their spare room filled.

They had settled in the town of Altrincham, to the south of Manchester, which was acceptable, geographically, for his work, and just needed a brief motorway journey every morning. It was a lovely estate, and Charlotte had quickly made new friends, and re-established old ones. An architect, on maternity leave, she was a happy wife and mother, and Octavian adored her to bits.

DI Octavian's domestic situation was the topic of conversation, one morning, as he was in Stockport town centre with his Detective

Sergeant, Phil Knowles. Octavian stood and looked about him, seeing office buildings and the massive Victorian railway viaduct, as Knowles changed a puncture on their VW Golf. Knowles was puffing and blowing and swearing.

'Is this a rank thing, Boss?'

Octavian laughed. 'No, Phillip, this is a you were driving at the time of the puncture thing.'

Octavian stepped a few yards away to a sign that read: River Mersey. He looked with disinterest at the sluggish water, which he guessed was nearly at its furthest point away from Liverpool. He was dressed in a sharp blue suit, with very white shirt. He was well-built, very handsome, with jet black hair swept back over his head.

'It was the missus who moved you up here, wasn't it, Boss? If you don't mind me asking?'

'Yes, she's from the village of Lymm. London got too much for her.'

'Yes, I can imagine it would.'

'But if you think London is busy, you should see Jakarta.'

With a final grunt, Knowles tightened the last wheel nut and put the flat tyre and the tools into the boot.

'Before the puncture, Boss, you were going to tell me about your new book.'

Octavian's hobby was writing fiction novels. Not crime ones, more about love, adventure, with the occasional zombie apocalypse. So far, he had about twenty standard rejection emails from literary agents, or had been ignored by them, but he was not disheartened – he remembered that in the old days, writers used to wallpaper their toilets with rejection letters.

'This one is about an Indonesian butler to a rich obnoxious American family in Jakarta, as they are about to leave for LA. They set off on their superyacht for Hawaii but get shipwrecked on a desert island. Have you ever heard of a film called The Admirable Crichton?'

Knowles' eyes glassed over; he had only been trying to be polite. 'No, Boss.'

'It's a role reversal. The butler becomes the king of the island.'

'What, and then he gets his pick of the women?'

Octavian grimaced. 'Something like that.'

Octavian's phone rang and he took the call. Knowles heard Peel Hall Park mentioned.

'A suspicious death,' Octavian said to Knowles, putting his phone away. 'Peel Hall Park, let's go.'

'Really? That's a bit close to home.' They got into the Golf and set off quickly, with Octavian driving.

It was a quick burn down the M56 motorway to Wythenshawe, which happened to be the area of Manchester that they were based out of. Over the radio, Knowles found out that the incident involved a crossbow. They parked opposite the local shops and walked into the park. To their left was an island with a moat and stone bridge, from the days when a medieval manor house had once stood on the site. Octavian was amazed and disgusted that there were two men actually sat fishing into the filthy moat.

The incident was on the far side of the park, beyond the new tennis courts that nobody ever used, where they could see several police cars and SOCO vehicles parked on the pathway, with two PCs taping off the wooded area.

Detective Constable Shirley Speight approached them from a long way away through the trees. Octavian saw that her blonde hair was in a ponytail and her strong physique was dressed smartly in a black trouser suit, with a maroon cardigan. He compared her to Knowles with his bad brown suit, loose kipper tie that screamed that he wanted to stay a detective sergeant forever, and shoes of the style that Octavian remembered his father wearing in the 1990's.

'Where are you coming from?' Knowles asked Speight, with familiarity. 'Needed a pee, or something?'

'No, my gran used to have one of those houses. I was having a nosy about.'

'Morning, Shirley,' said Octavian.

'Morning, Boss. Just over here. Young male. Found by a dog walker. It's a shocker.'

Knowles began to tuck his trouser legs into his white socks, much to the amazement of Octavian and Speight.

'Last time I was in a wood,' explained Knowles, 'I got a tick running up and down my legs.'

Speight rolled her eyes, and then the three of them walked along a hardened earth footpath before stepping into the undergrowth.

'Shirley,' whispered Knowles. 'Can you imagine the route the tick had to take to get from one leg to the other?'

'I can, and I pity the poor creature.'

SOCO people, in the all-encompassing white suits, were underway with their work; two of them putting up their forensic tent. The police forensic pathologist was already on scene. Octavian found himself faced with a dead boy, perhaps fifteen years old, who was pinned to a tree with a crossbow bolt through his mouth.

'Any ID?' he asked Speight.

'Yes, Boss. A library card. Steven McLaughlin. Fourteen. Local boy.'

'A crossbow. Jeez. You know, if kids are going to mess about with crossbows, then the woods are the best place for it. But he's in his school uniform, and it's very early.'

Octavian exchanged nods with Doctor Neil Shevington. The doctor had a presence about him, like a Shakespearean actor. All three police officers stared at the man, in case he suddenly set forth with a burst of *Hamlet*.

'Hello again,' said Dr Shevington to Octavian, warmly, as if they were at a cocktail party. 'Our first proper job together, DI Octavian. How are you settling in, back up here in Grimsville?'

'I'm liking it, Dr Shevington. Until I see things like that.'

'Yes, yes, indeed. Very recent. I'd say within the last two hours. Anticipating your first question, the force of the bolt suggests it was fired from at least ten feet away. I'm not an expert but I did archery at Uni.' He laughed. 'As a hobby, not a course, you understand. One should assume it was pure chance that it entered through the mouth.'

Octavian looked again at the horrible sight and then stepped away to speak to his officers.

'No CCTV as we walked across. I'm assuming there are none on any entrances. Shirley, check with the houses around the ways in. And the shops. Is this the right route from home to school?'

'I would say so, Boss,' answered Speight.

'So, might be random,' mused Knowles. 'He wasn't coming to meet someone he knew.'

'I walked to school with mates,' said Octavian. 'So maybe something stupid happened by accident. Philip, get the dog walker's statement, and arrange for us to see the victim's school Head. Me and Shirley will try to see the family. Then we can check the friends' lockers, before splitting up to speak to them. Where's DC Datta?'

'The dentist, Boss,' said Speight.

Knowles made the sound of a dentist drill.

'Philip, tell uniform I want a thorough search between here and the school. Shirley, let's go.'

The McLaughlin family home was one of those new-build semis, where the detached garage is closer to someone else's house, and with one neighbour's window overlooking their back garden. Octavian noticed these things, being married to an architect – he guessed that the designer of the estate didn't live in a house that was overlooked. The thing he most despised was when the grasping bastards crammed an extra floor into the roofspace of an apartment building – and nobody should ever mention to him those church conversions where your living room window is a thigh-high curve of stained glass.

'Ready, Boss?'

Speight had realized that her new boss had a habit of daydreaming. Wasn't he a writer, or something? So far, she had nothing but good things to say about the way he worked, his firm but friendly style of leadership, but he seemed a deep one. From day one, she had also tried to ignore the fact that he was fucking gorgeous. She stepped up to the McLaughlin house and rang the doorbell.

Twenty minutes later they exited, both feeling quite unhappy, and with their mouths tasting of badly made tea. It had been the usual distressing situation; disbelief and wailing from the mother, and grim silence from the father. Both Octavian and Speight had come to the conclusion that neither parent had anything to hide. They came out of the house with a recent photo of Steven McLoughlin, the statement that he had not a care or enemy in the world, and that his mates lived on the other side of school, so he always walked there on his own.

Speight's mobile was ringing. They paused while she took the call. Then she looked very seriously at Octavian.

'Another one?' he asked.

THREE

Octavian drove Speight in his Golf, travelling fairly quickly. They actually drove past the Wythenshawe police station, then headed through Northenden and headed along Palatine Road, going towards Manchester city centre. They stopped short of traffic chaos at a junction, seeing police vehicles and ambulances. A traffic officer was trying to keep rubbernecking drivers moving along. Octavian and Speight parked up and walked over – SOCO were yet to arrive, and there was a body on the ground, covered over but with a trickle of blood heading into a drain. A mangled bicycle lay nearby. From a different road, Knowles was delivered by a police car and he jogged to catch up with them.

'Why are we here?' asked Knowles, puffing from even that short run. 'It's an RTC, isn't it?'

'Another child, Phil,' replied Octavian.

'Oh, crap.'

A different traffic officer recognized Knowles and Speight. He paid attention to the new face in the middle, assuming he was the man in charge.

'This is DI Octavian,' introduced Speight.

'Sir,' said the traffic officer. 'Witnesses say it was a deliberate hit and run. Boy was on a bicycle. The vehicle was a black SUV, possibly a Mercedes.'

'Thank you.'

The SOCO vehicle arrived, followed by Dr Shevington in his BMW X5, doing a royal wave towards Octavian.

Octavian and his colleagues waited for the forensic team to take charge of the scene before they wandered over, making sure to stay back, not wanting to cross-contaminate with their earlier park visit.

'Doctor,' said Octavian.

'Busy morning, DI Octavian.' Dr Shevington stood back from his initial inspection. 'Approximately fifteen years old. Male. Crush injuries conducive with a road collision. There's nothing to give identification at this stage.'

Octavian had the briefest glimpse at the mess, nodded his thanks and returned to the others, who then set off to speak to the witnesses.

Knowles glanced about him, at the nearby pub, MOT garage and a line of local shops. There was an old building with big blue letters on the side that read dentist. Standing at the upper floor window, in medical gown, in the middle of dental treatment, was DC Aamina Datta. She and Knowles shared a comical set of gestures. He was amazed and amused to see her there, but he controlled himself out of respect for the crime scene. He gave her one more "well, you're there, we're here, what can we do?" gesture, then got on with seeing his witness.

When Octavian had first found out that he would be based out of Wythenshawe police station, he had mixed thoughts on it – it was convenient to get to, but was in a sprawling, rough area. Of course, most parts of Manchester were somewhat rough, but he just grew up not liking Wythenshawe very much. He and Charlotte drove past the station one day, just to have a look at it. Charlotte thought it looked like a lower league football stadium stand, with its curved roof. It was red brick above pale brick, with blue window frames, containing a lot of glass which would afford Octavian quite a view out over Wythenshawe itself.

The small incident room was upstairs: desks, computers, phones, white boards, on which so far was the photograph of Steven McLaughlin and a big question mark for the boy killed on Palatine Road. The view was from the back, actually, over the vehicle compound and then the Wythenshawe Forum building, which had a library and swimming pool. Beyond that was the Civic Centre shopping precinct.

Knowles entered the room with his coffee, to be faced with the bizarre sight of Octavian taking a knee in front of Datta, staring into her wide-open mouth.

'Yes, that's a fabulous crown, Aamina,' announced Octavian, standing. 'But I bet a few slivers will slice off it before it settles down.'

Datta looked horrified. 'Huh?'

Speight trailed in after Knowles and took her seat. The only other person there was DC Beth McAlister, who was on light duties following an injury caused by a drunk driver during an arrest, and she was proving to be a wonderful IT officer. Octavian found her to be reliable and a massive help to the team. He started the meeting by looking to her, while tapping a marker pen on to the question mark.

'Beth, stay on top of recent missing persons and responses to news reports on the Palatine Road incident. We need to know who this is. If he's a pal of Steven McLaughlin...'

Knowles sat at his desk. 'SOCO found nothing between the woods and the school, Boss.'

'Right, Steven's pals live the other side of the school, but we still need to see them.'

Speight raised a hand. 'The school Head says we can see him anytime.'

'We'll go there next. We need to know if Steven had any worries, and about the mates. Phil: crossbows. What's that all about? Is there a club for that? Has anyone got form for misuse? Can we speak with a specialist? Someone who knows where they can be bought, etc.'

Knowles acknowledged his task.

'Aamina, I want you to find out about the McLaughlin family. You take it easy, this afternoon, you've had major work done. Shirley, let's go.'

Octavian and Speight exited his Golf and walked towards the large glass entrance to the school. They passed a group of girl pupils in their purple uniforms, all with their skirts hitched up, one of whom was doing a long, slow spit onto the floor, much to Speight's horror.

They entered, spoke to a receptionist, and were invited to sit and wait on a leather couch for a few minutes. Several male pupils passed by, all in need of a haircut, much to Octavian's distaste.

'Have you been here before, Shirley?'

'While at school. We came here to play a netball match. It had a very different reputation, back then. The new man we are here to see has very liberal attitudes. Apparently, he gets good results, though. Here he comes now.'

Head Teacher, Simon Hulme, bounded over to them, his hair split down the middle like an Afghan hound. He was early thirties, fairly handsome, friendly and open to them. Octavian was just pleased that the man didn't spit on the floor.

'Sorry to keep you waiting,' said Hulme. 'Ofsted on the phone. Simon Hulme. Head.'

Octavian did the introductions, and then they were invited through to Hulme's office, offered seats.

'I know why you're here, of course,' said Hulme, reaching his chair and almost sat cross-legged on it.

Octavian immediately asked about Steven McLaughlin.

'I don't recall any interaction with him at all. A perfectly regular student. Happy, as far as I knew.'

'We would like a list of his close friends here,' said Octavian. 'With home details.'

'Of course.'

Speight handed Hulme one of her business cards, before checking a text from McAlister on her phone.

'If you could get that information to my colleague within the hour,' said Octavian. 'Then some officers will be back to look in the relevant lockers.'

Speight showed Octavian the text, which identified the Palatine Road victim as a Tom Walsh. He looked back at Hulme. 'Is Tom Walsh a student here?'

Simon Hulme looked about him as he thought. 'I don't believe so. Let me go check.' He got up and popped his head out of the room to consult with his secretary. She checked her computer, and then he retook his seat. 'No Tom or Thomas Walsh at my school. By the way, is it true that a crossbow was used? That's the gossip on the grapevine.'

'Because of your position here,' said Octavian, 'I feel that I can confirm that to you, Mr Hulme. But please don't quote me, especially to the press.'

'Of course not.'

'Well, that's all for now, Mr Hulme.'

Octavian and Speight took their leave of Hulme with handshakes, all round. Out of the office, Octavian paused at the secretary.

'What time did you first see Mr Hulme this morning?'

She was startled, at first. 'Oh, we arrived together at seven. What I mean is, we got here at the same time.'

Outside, walking towards the Golf, Octavian frowned at a cold wind coming right into their faces. 'I spoke to my sister this morning. It's thirty-three degrees in Jakarta today.'

Speight desperately needed a holiday. 'Sounds amazing.'

'Our Mr Hulme is certainly different, Shirley. He didn't express any sadness over Steven McLaughlin's death. And I thought schools closed for the day when there's a student death?'

'At least we know the Palatine Road victim didn't go here.'

'Could still be connected to Steven, though.'

Octavian stopped dead, then looked back. He then returned towards the school, making a puzzled Speight trail on behind. Parked in the Head Teacher bay was a black Mercedes SUV. Octavian and Speight shared a look, before circling the vehicle. There was not a scratch on it. Inside was just the usual detritus of empty McDonalds bags and magazines. The only thing in the window was a school parking badge.

'There would have to be some damage,' said Octavian. 'After what was done to the bicycle.'

'I'm pretty sure of that. Unless it was somehow just tyre and then the underneath.'

Octavian took out a small torch and looked at the underside of the Mercedes.

'How does it look?'

He jumped up. 'Like it's still in the showroom. Let's go. But run a check on our hippy Head. He wouldn't be the first teacher to get into something with young people.'

Back in the incident room Octavian was pointing at a photograph of Tom Walsh.

'Tom Walsh is confirmed as the Palatine Road victim. Fifteen years old. Lived with just his mother in nearby Northenden. Aamina, you please go and ask the McLaughlins if Steven knew this Tom Walsh.'

Datta nodded, then spoke from her notes, 'Gary McLaughlin, the father, used to cultivate and deal cannabis. Nothing else, apart from a bit of shoplifting when he was a teenager. Seems to be quite a regular family.'

'Okay. Beth, I want to know more about the background of Head, Simon Hulme. Phil?'

'I've found the main man for crossbows. He runs courses. He's a licensed firearms keeper. He also provides props for TV dramas. Name of John Paterson. He's coming in to see you tomorrow.'

'That's good work, Phil.'

'He'd have come today, Boss, but he's in York, killing Vikings.'

FOUR

Octavian's home in Altrincham was a three-storey townhouse, built in the Georgian style. It was semi-detached, but large, and the garden was a curving corner plot. Charlotte's Mini sat on the drive. He parked beside it and headed in. He entered the hall. There was a genuine red and white Indonesian flag hanging on the wall, below the stairs. He was disappointed not to receive his usual welcome home kiss. 'Darling, are you home?'

A male voice called playfully from the kitchen, 'I'm here, honey.'

A teenaged, Indonesian male stepped into the hall. Octavian grinned at his nephew.

'Delighted to see you, as always, Ezi, but I think I need my wife.'

'I believe Charlotte and Jack are next door, gossiping.'

'Have you had a good day today? Did you go to uni?'

'Yes. I feel much more educated. I'm cooking.'

Octavian joked, 'The least you can do for your bed and board.'

Ezi returned to the stove, as Charlotte came in, carrying baby, Jack. They kissed, and he relieved her of their son for a cuddle. He looked lovingly at Charlotte. She had thick black hair and black eyes – Asian traits, but she was fully English. At university together, she had joked that he subconsciously wanted to fall in love with an Asian girl. He replied that he'd had all the Asians, and the blondes, before she showed up.

'You're so beautiful,' he told her.

'You say that every day.'

'You're beautiful every day.'

'Are you hungry? (it was a silly way they had to say hungry) Go and have your shower.'

'Whatever Ezi is cooking today smells wonderful.'

'I *know*. He can never, ever, go back to Indonesia.'

Octavian kissed his son's head, handed him back, and went to hit the shower.

The pool club was in the centre of Stockport. A fairly disreputable establishment, it was near to both Knowles' house and Speight's flat, so they occasionally headed there to wind down, especially when they had two dead boys on their hands. Knowles and his wife were living together but separated, in all but name. They were the classic "ships that passed in the night" as Maria Knowles was a nurse, doing shifts. The Covid experience had dulled her life spirit, and she had never liked his job – the early years of worry had turned into recent years of apathy. Shirley Speight was between dickhead boyfriends at the moment. Her flat was nice, spacious, above a Bookmakers, so, quiet at night.

Knowles got the pints in at the bar. They seemed to know everybody there, and he nodded at a prolific burglar, and connected fists with a passing off-duty solicitor.

'DS Woolaston is in, I see,' said Speight. 'Are you going to take him on at pool again?' Knowles put on his fighting face. 'I will, if he asks. Nobody beats Philip Knowles twenty-four times in a row!'

'What's your plan for beating him?'

'I'll destroy his concentration.'

'And how are you going to do that?'

'I thought I would dive headfirst into the pack as he's about to break.'

Speight laughed. They sat down at the bar. He was lost in melancholia for a moment and she was eyeing up a new, handsome face, playing the quiz machine.

'Who's that?' she asked Knowles.

He looked across. 'I spy a stranger. Shall I throw him out?'

'He's really cute. So, Phil, do you think we've got a killer of children and young people on our hands?'

'Too early to say, but I'm bothered by it, Shirley. I think more are coming.'

She sipped her pint of lager and sadly hmmmed her agreement.

Beth McAlister drove her beloved Fiat Cinquecento home to Cheadle, one of the more affluent areas of south Manchester. She had only just started driving again, after a drunk driver sent her cartwheeling one night. After a short hospital stay and intense physiotherapy, she was almost back to who she had been before the incident.

Her fella was away on a course, but her mother happened to be visiting from

Staffordshire – the two events a coincidence, not deliberately arranged. McAlister was welcomed by mum's Yorkshire terrier, Susie, and thankfully there was a meal underway on the stove.

'You all right, mum?'

'Hello, dear. Had a good day? Mind you, I saw the local news. That's just terrible, that is.'

'Yes, we're on that.'

'You stay safe, of course.'

'With my bad back I'm mainly in the office.'

Mrs Enid McAlister was up north to visit old friends, really, so it was quite all right that Beth couldn't take time off to be with her. They would have a nice evening and watch some TV with a bottle of wine. She was widowed, so often stayed with one of her three children, although she much preferred son, Stuart's place, down in St Ives, Cornwall.

'Is Ian back tomorrow, dear?'

'Should be, yes.'

'I'll get away in the morning, then. Let you two have your peace.'

'Is everyone all right? All the old girls?'

'Yes, still the same.'

'I'll shower before we eat.' She carefully picked up the dog and looked it right in the eyes. 'You coming in with me? Shower.' It growled its unhappiness at that very idea, so she laughed, put it down and went upstairs.

Aamina Datta drove an old Mazda 6, with a different coloured driver's door, which she thought gave it personality, but which her colleagues thought just looked chavvy. She lived in a rented, pebble-dashed terraced house in Woodhouse Park (a short walk from work) with her boyfriend, Taheer, because it was near to his workplace. He was a fireman, or more accurately a firefighter, but she preferred the old term.

In the early evening gloom, she pulled onto the lit station forecourt. Shifts were changing. She stood out from the car, and a few firemen cheerfully waved when they recognized her. She smiled and waved back. Taheer came jogging out, soon after. Datta's eyes widened, as they always did, to see his muscular build within its tee-shirt, and his cool work pants almost falling down because he had shaken off his braces; boots, crewcut, cheeky smile, the works. He lifted her off the ground as they kissed.

'Oh, I'm sorry,' he said, putting her down and gently cupping her jaw. 'Are you sore from the dentist, baby?'

'A little, still.'

'I'll look after you, I promise. Let me drive. Let's get you home.'

He dumped his gear in the back and took charge of the driving. Datta settled into the passenger seat, enjoying his hand on her thigh, between gear changes.

'Can you eat, baby?'

'I think so.'

'I'll cook us something nice. You can just relax all evening, I'll massage your feet, I'll caress your hair, and we can postpone the anal sex.'

She screamed with laughter. 'Taheer! You're so bad.'

FIVE

The following morning, in the police station's reception area, Octavian was chatting with friendly Bill Fitzgerald, one of the civilian staff members who manned the front desk. The greying, pot-bellied Fitzgerald was a big *Warrington Wolves* rugby league fan, and had quickly got into the habit of telling Octavian about the latest match he had attended, and even some bamboozling transfer gossip. Octavian had initially wondered what made Fitzgerald believe he was a rugby league fan, and suspected that DS Knowles had something to do with it.

Octavian watched Speight and Datta putting on their coats, about to leave to go straight off to see Steven McLaughlin's friends. The lockers at the school had been checked by Uniform the previous afternoon, with nothing found. McAlister came in.

'About the teacher, Boss,' said McAlister. It was not unusual for her to do some work from home. 'A spotless background.'

'Oh, right, Beth. Thank you.' He got Speight's attention. 'Don't forget to drop the name of Tom Walsh into the conversation when you see the boys.'

'Will do, Boss.'

Bill Fitzgerald wanted his attention again, indicating that a man had just walked in to see him. Octavian turned to be faced with a middle-aged man in corduroy trousers and a scruffy, loose-knit jumper, with a manila folder under his right armpit. He sported black framed, old-style glasses that reminded Octavian of an actor he had recently seen in a black and white Ealing comedy. He guessed that it was the crossbow expert. 'Mr Paterson?'

'Yes. Detective Inspector Octavian?'

Handshakes.

'Good to meet you. Thank you for coming in. Please come through. I'm getting coffee, can I offer you something?'

'Coffee would be lovely, thank you.'

Octavian got them settled down in one of the interview rooms. It was a completely boring room with no strange smell and no graffiti, whatsoever.

'Terrible news yesterday,' said John Paterson. 'I know Peel Hall Park quite well. I'm guessing a crossbow was used?'

'You guess correctly, Mr Paterson. I hear you do re-enactments. I bet that's fun?'

'It is, yes. I like the medieval the best. All that chainmail and broadswords shenanigans.'

'I have an interest in the English Civil War times, myself. The Roundheads and Cavaliers. Anyway, the reason for asking you here, I was just wondering where someone gets a crossbow? Are there clubs, like for archery?'

'Oh, they are perfectly legal, at the moment. Age permitting, of course.' He drank some coffee, seemingly pleased to have the chance to expound on one of his favourite things in life. 'Anyone can order one from the internet. Just the budget decides the quality, of course. As for clubs, I only know one, based in the Congleton area. It's run by a couple of re-enactors. I think the members are regular, working people; a doctor, factory workers, a farmer. I suppose they started with archery before moving on to crossbows.'

Octavian brought out a clear evidence bag, which contained the bolt that killed Steven

McLaughlin. 'Is that for any particular weapon?'

'Oh, no, I think that's pretty standard.'

Paterson opened his manila folder and brought out photographs of crossbows for Octavian to examine. 'Some examples for you. And, actually, I have a letter from the Congleton club, if you care to visit. There's the address.'

'Thank you. Have you ever known a crossbow murder before, Mr Paterson?'

'I recall a couple, down the years. Loner types going on the rampage. There was one in Liverpool, and another near to Preston.'

'Do you know of any individual who owns one of these weapons? Perhaps they shouldn't, in your opinion?'

John Paterson had a long think. 'No, I don't think I currently know of anybody I would feel uncomfortable about them having a crossbow.'

'Last question. I've seen a crossbow loaded in Robin Hood films. Are they easy to load? Does it take a strong man to get the string back? Or could a child or a slight woman do it?'

'Modern compound-bows are not that hard to cock. Never seen a woman interested in crossbows, though. Archery, yes, of course.'

'Well, that's been very helpful, Mr Paterson. Thank you for your time.'

'My pleasure. I only wish the circumstances were different. If you need to have a go on a crossbow, you're welcome at my place.'

'Thank you, I'll keep that in mind. Let me show you out.'

They stood and shook hands again.

Octavian watched John Paterson walk away to where he had parked a Mitsubishi Shogun, and then he jogged up the stairs to the incident room, and was immediately accosted by Knowles.

'Boss, reports are back on the mobiles of both our victims. Usual teenage nonsense. Nothing of interest. Steven McLaughlin was texting some girl called Lucy, for what that's worth.'

Octavian sat down and Knowles continued.

'There is a local man who was charged with firing a crossbow out of his bedroom window. Lives nearby, in Brownley Green. Uniform are trying to track him down, as we speak. Be nice to know where he was yesterday morning.'

McAlister spotted DCI Ian Horsefield entering the room. 'Heads up, Boss.'

Octavian and Knowles were about to get up to face their "guvner".

'Please don't get up, I'm not royalty,' said Horsefield, planting his feet wide and crossing his arms over his waistcoat. He was a tall man, greying and balding, but still handsome, though he would be anonymous in a crowd.

'The powers that be are frightened of a serial killer, I have to tell you. So, here I am, telling you. We have a teenager shot dead, just now in Heywood. Now, I wouldn't automatically link it to yesterday, but local officers attempted to stop a black Mercedes SUV in the area. No number plate.'

Octavian and Knowles did then get to their feet.

'We should go to that,' said Octavian, feeling his blood stir.

'Of course. Ask for a DI Cowfield. I shit you not. I absolutely shit you not. Cowfield. What kind of a name is that?'

It was an immense strain for Knowles to keep his face straight as he looked at Horsefield.

'Okay, Sir,' said Octavian.

Octavian virtually pushed Knowles out of the room.

It was about twenty motorway miles to Heywood; an old cotton town, north of Manchester. Octavian drove fast, but it still felt to Knowles that they were almost in Yorkshire, by the time they got there.

'I've never been here before,' said Octavian.

'I can't actually think of any reason to come here.'

Octavian drove down a High Street that was as soulless as any northern town. He took an instant dislike to Heywood; not because there was anything wrong with it, just that it was stuck out in the hills and there was nothing pleasant or uplifting about it. He followed his SatNav and they parked on a red-brick terraced street, as near to the police crime scene tape as possible.

Octavian showed his warrant card to a bored Police Community Support Officer, manning the perimeter, and asked for DI Cowfield.

'Coming over now, Sir,' said the PCSO.

'Thank you.'

DI Cowfield broke the rule: that you could wear a bad suit and a wide tie and still progress up from detective sergeant. His two main features were a big belly and a really friendly smile. He raised the blue and white tape and shook their hands at the same time. A welcome and introductions were concluded as they walked up the street.

'The victim's family is known for drug dealing,' stated Cowfield. 'So that's my first impression. But you think there's a connection with your horrible day yesterday?'

Octavian was the one having the conversation. 'Well, mention of the SUV.'

'I'll get the patrol car footage to you. The Merc flew off through a school zone and then went off-road, just around the corner from here. No rear number plate.'

'If we get a look at it, we might be able to match some marks or stickers. Who is your victim?'

They stood to watch the investigation proceeding.

'Shotgun at point-blank range,' said Cowfield. 'Fourteen. Mohammad Asif. I knew him. Bloody gobby, but not such a bad kid. Mental to do this to him.'

'The family drug dealing; local or spread out a bit?'

'I would say very local. I've never heard anything about Warrington in connection with this family. I think it might be a coincidence.'

'You're probably right. It's just, you know, the victim ages, and within two days. And the Merc.'

'We're still looking for it. It might pop up somewhere while you're still here.'

'Thank you for seeing us. We'll step out.'

They shook hands goodbye, and Octavian and Knowles returned to the Golf.

'Probably is a coincidence,' said Knowles. 'We're a long way away here, Boss.'

'Something is niggling me about a connection, Phil. Let's find a café for a snack. Maybe the Mercedes will reappear.'

Knowles was always ready for something to eat. They found a decent café on the High Street, for iced buns and coffee. Octavian took the moment to text his love to Charlotte.

Knowles took the moment to wonder if his wife had paid the gas bill. Nothing transpired any further with the case, and they left Heywood while it was still morning.

SIX

There was now a photo of Mohammad Asif on the white board, alongside Steven McLaughlin, Tom Walsh, and the crossbow examples, donated by John Paterson. Octavian pointed from his seat.

'Mohammad Asif, shot dead this morning in Heywood. He's on our board because of his age, the timing of his murder and the fleeing SUV at the scene. I'll keep in touch with Heywood to see if their investigation comes up with anything. Shirley, how did it go with the friends?'

'Aamina and I agree that the three friends are idiots. They appreciate that their friend died but they were all still joking around. They were baffled by any mention of a crossbow. And nobody knew a Tom Walsh.'

Knowles shifted his weight, making his chair creak. 'Getting more random by the minute.'

McAlister said, 'I'm waiting for a list of Mercedes SUVs registered in the North West.

Oh, but now we have the footage from Heywood.'

They all jumped up to gather around and watch the patrol car images of the fleeing SUV. It only lasted twenty seconds and the rear of the vehicle could not have been more anonymous. They sat back down, disappointed.

A fresh-faced young police constable came nervously into the incident room.

'Oh, hello, what does Work Experience want?' asked Knowles.

The PC's name was Lewis Green, an athletic local boy. The females in the room looked up at him and instantly wanted to be his mummy. Octavian looked, and thought that there was a ridiculous amount of gear attached to the man's hi-vis vest: taser, cuffs, radio, ID lanyard, video camera, utility pockets, PAVA spray, Royal British Legion poppy (even though it was April).

'Sorry, Sir,' interrupted PC Green, addressing Octavian. 'DS Knowles wanted to know when we had found Alan Hallworth.'

'Who's he?' asked Octavian.

'The local man with the record for public order offences, to do with crossbows.'

'Oh, him! Thank you, PC..?'

'Green, Sir.'

'Thank you, PC Green. Put him in an interview room, I'll be right down.'

Green lingered, looking slightly embarrassed. 'We haven't exactly got him, Sir. We just know where he is.'

Knowles laughed and clapped his hands together, loving that.

Octavian led Knowles, Speight, Datta and Green out to the police station steps. Bill Fitzgerald looked on from the door. Across the road were a couple of local press photographers getting shots of the man leading the new murder investigation, but Octavian was not interested in them. Everyone watched agog as a man passed by on an e-scooter, laughing his head off at the police.

'Alan Hallworth, Sir,' introduced Green, almost apologetically.

'I gather as much, PC Green.'

The e-scooter went around the block, through the Forum, and then returned to pass again, with Alan Hallworth giving them the v-sign.

'Knock him off,' suggested a less than impressed Knowles.

'If only we could,' replied Octavian.

A laughing crowd of shoppers started to gather to watch the entertainment. Octavian disappeared into the building for a few minutes, during which time Alan Hallworth continued to circle the police station, becoming quite the local celebrity, even blowing kisses to the crowd. Octavian came back with a Stinger stop-stick. Just before the e-scooter came around again, he deployed it across the road. Alan Hallworth inadvertently rode over it, puncturing both tyres. He started to slow along the street, with the crowd cheering and several police constables comically running after him.

Octavian entered the interview room to see a sullen Alan Hallworth. He sat down across the table from the man. Octavian had seen dozens of these losers. Hallworth looked gaunt and pale, which possibly hinted towards drug use. He had a ferrety nose and unkempt hair. Although he was clean, there was a cheap aftershave aroma about him.

'I want compensation for my tyres,' sneered Hallworth.

Hearing that, Octavian looked up and shared a moment of mirth with PC Green, who was the uniform presence, standing against the far wall.

'It's not even insured. It's gone, forget it.' Octavian's face brightened; bad cop, good cop, in the same person. 'Thank you for coming in for interviewing, anyway, Mr Hallworth. I'm DI Octavian.'

Octavian proceeded to caution Alan Hallworth.

Hallworth rocked in his chair. 'What is this?'

'Can I ask where you were this morning?'

'You can ask.'

'Where were you yesterday morning?'

'I don't remember.'

'Well, I'll come back to that. Do you still own a crossbow?'

'Listen, I know the McLaughlin boy was killed with a crossbow. It wasn't mine. I sold mine, over a year ago.'

'Can you prove that you sold it?'

'No. Go and look for it at my house. You won't find it. Bloody hell, wait a minute, you don't think I killed Steven McLaughlin, do you?'

'How do you know the boy?'

'Through his dad. The pub, and football. Can I have a smoke?'

'You can have a smoke as soon as you leave. Do you know anybody else who owns a crossbow?'

At the very suggestion that he would ever give a name to the police, Hallworth made a snorting sound through his nose.

'Mr Hallworth, come on, all joking aside, I'm trying to find the murderer of at least two children. It's a murder investigation. So, stop messing about. Tell me where you were yesterday morning, and tell me the name of anybody you know who has a crossbow.'

Straight from seeing Alan Hallworth, Octavian was accosted by DCI Horsefield in the corridor.

'Tony, worrying now. Reports of another killing, in Chorlton-cum-Hardy. This looks to be escalating. Do you want more help?

'More people are always welcome, Sir.'

'I think DS Williams is free. She's dealt with a few child deaths. Tony, the Press will soon be getting into a frenzy over this. Do you want to put out a statement?'

'Not yet, Sir.'

'Okay, if you're sure.'

Octavian went upstairs.

'Boss,' called McAlister. 'I have the list of registered keepers for Mercedes SUVs in the North West.'

'Right, Beth, try to make sense of it. Compare the nearest with criminal records. Everyone else, listen up. We have another one. Let's go. It's Chorlton-cum-Hardy.'

The team grabbed their coats and followed Octavian out.

Knowles nudged Datta. 'Chorlton-cum-Hardy. What a name.'

'Do you realise that you're a bit odd, the way you point out names?'

'Odd in what way? Odd like the way doubles players in tennis have to touch hands after every point?'

'Yes, odd like that.'

SEVEN

The team looked out at the sprawling Southern Cemetery, in passing, and then found the murder scene on a normal suburban road in dire need of resurfacing. Their cars bobbled along the cracking tarmac before finding places to park. Light rain had begun to fall.

Octavian went to see the victim's body inside the SOCO tent (without getting so close as to need a white paper suit) and then spoke with a gaggle of local officers and medical officials, including Dr Shevington, again, before walking back to update his team.

'Fifteen. Name of Englebert Dox.'

Knowles almost fell down. 'Englebert Dox, Boss? Is that a wind-up?'

Datta looked sideways at Knowles.

'That's his name,' continued Octavian. 'Shirley, Aamina, all these houses for CCTV, please. Surely, we have the killer on camera.'

Speight and Datta set off.

'Single shot to the back of the head,' Octavian told Knowles. 'Then a double-tap to the chest.'

'Double-tap? You mean like in the movies? A professional hit?'

Octavian shivered, glad he had his coat on. "Roll on summer" was a phrase that his father was often heard to say. 'More like someone playing the professional hitman.'

'Why the young age for the victims? That's what puzzles me. A loser who missed out on his childhood, perhaps?'

'Who knows? But if we include the Heywood killing, then he has at least two firearms, as well as the crossbow.'

'But he was happy to use the Merc on Palatine Road. So, it's not just for the fun of shooting. It must be drugs. These kids must owe someone for something.'

'Drug dealers don't murder their young customers, Phil. They would give them a slap. Maybe demand they do some county lines work for their debt. I'm wondering why it's all coming along in this sudden spurt.'

'He wants to get as many in before being caught, perhaps.'

Datta returned. 'Boss. A neighbour has something ready for us.'

They were happy to get out of the rain, but then found themselves crammed into the overly warm lounge of an elderly resident. Knowles found himself standing with his face between a deer's head, mounted on the wall, and an urn, on a shelf. He considered moving away, but then put up with it. Octavian thanked the elderly neighbour, and declined tea, all round. The man set his home security CCTV footage playing on his TV screen.

'When I realized the police were here, I looked at this.'

'Did you hear anything at the time, Sir?' asked Octavian.

'I'm afraid not, no.'

They watched a view of the front driveway, which took in the pavement. A young male walked past. A few seconds elapsed before another figure ran in the same direction. It looked male, slim and hooded.

'Male. Looks early twenties,' said Knowles.

'He comes running back in a second,' said the elderly neighbour.

They waited, and saw the hooded figure run back through the shot.

'Can we pause that as he passes?' asked Octavian.

The elderly man was a wizard on the remote control and had it stopped in the right place for them. Unfortunately, the figure's face was slightly downward facing. It was not the best image, and the man wore a surgical face mask.

'Is he white?' Octavian asked his team.

'Possibly,' replied Speight. 'Or Asian. Certainly not black. Slim, perhaps six-foot, early twenties, I guess.'

Octavian nodded for Datta to secure the footage. He thanked the neighbour, and he stepped outside, happy for the cool air and to feel the rain on his face again.

That evening, at the house in Altrincham, Octavian bounced a big foam ball off the belly of his laughing son, Jack, on the rug in the lounge. Charlotte came in to happily watch for a minute or two, before she straddled her husband. They had a moment where she sensed his stress and tried to share it.

'I love you,' she said.

'I love you more.'

'Come on, dinner's ready. Go get Ezi away from those books.'

She got to her feet, lifted Jack up and left the room with him. Octavian hauled himself off the floor and walked slowly across to the study. Ezi looked up at him from the desk. Octavian leant on the doorframe.

'Ezi, have you seen anything of England, since you've been here?'

Ezi paused, having good comic timing. 'I went to Blackpool, that time.'

'So, you did,' laughed Octavian. 'That's enough for anybody. Dinner's ready.'

'Oh, right, thank you.'

After dinner, Octavian retired to his office area, in the heated, carpeted conservatory, where the previous home owner's Covid lockdown bar had once been. Now it was where Octavian had his computer to write his novels. On one wall was a cartoon of a cat in an Indonesian police cap. He settled in with his coffee and was soon tweaking his recently finished novel of time-travel love and mystery. It was inspired by his recent interest in Family History, and had characters time-travelling back to see, and help, the ancestors who interested them the most: the man who fell on hard times after the Great War, the family in

Lincolnshire who tried to stay out of the Workhouse, the girl who vanished from the census records and was believed murdered by her common-law husband. Then, he opened his new novel, the one about the Indonesian butler in Jakarta, and happily moved it forward a couple of chapters. After thinking more about the overall plot, he relaxed back, and checked his emails. Surprisingly there were none that were work related; just *Screwfix* offering him a fantastic deal, *Amazon* saying his order had been dispatched, and something dodgy that needed to be immediately deleted without being opened. There was also a reply from a London agent about his time-travel novel submission. His heart quickened with hope. Probably as all writers did, Octavian scanned it quickly to gather that it was, of course, in the negative, and then read it properly: a standard, polite note about the work not being suitable for them, but that it was only a subjective opinion and he should keep trying elsewhere. Over the years, both a policeman and as a man, Octavian had been stabbed, punched, pushed down a flight of stairs, had a lit cigarette put out on his bare chest, cheated on by partners, betrayed by friends; the usual stuff of life. But he was always surprised how having his writing rejected hurt the most – in a deep, deep place.

EIGHT

Raja watched Margo Lipman and her solicitor enter the house. Margo's other two offspring were discussing how to salvage the rest of their wasted morning. The very attractive man was called Rome: a feckless, total waste of privileged space. He was twenty-two, and something in the model world. He had modelled as a teenager, and now he was looking to become a manager. He was in designer jeans and a very flimsy white tee-shirt with holes that had been strategically planned and each costing about fifty dollars. His hair was gorgeous, thick, light brown and swept back, shaved at the sides. There was just a little bit of stubble around his mouth and chin. He was certainly interesting to look at, as long as he didn't say anything.

With him, looking more sulky than usual, was nineteen-year-old Harper Lipman. Her hair was as black and straight as her sister, but cut shorter. She had the glow of young beauty, and ruined it completely with her spoilt attitude. She was supposedly in education, but Raja had lost track of her latest course. The family joke was that she had been conceived in the back of a limousine as it passed through a boring Mid-West town, and so she had ended up with a more sensible name. The two of them went off to their own quarters.

Raja had the luxury apartment above one of the garages. He clattered up the metal stairs to shower and put on a new uniform. While he was there, he sent a text to his partner to say he was safe. He giggled at putting a little mystery into the message, but he would explain it all, that evening. The early demolition of the warehouse would be all over the news.

He grabbed a snack and milk from the fridge while he made sure he was composed, as he usually needed to be. He checked himself in a mirror. Twenty-nine years old, short black hair, and fairly handsome. Perhaps, a result of his more exciting youth spent in the Indonesian army, he was a little too well-built to be a butler/concierge. He smiled; his gayness would always compensate and make him the reliable, quiet force behind the family power. A text came in from his boyfriend, Ari, demanding to know what he meant. Had there been another car accident? What happened at the warehouse thing? Raja video-called, and got to see his handsome, policeman boyfriend.

'They only demolished it early. It got a bit wild for a minute.'

'But you're safe?'

'Yes, honey. I can't stop to chat. See you tonight.'

'I'm going to get them investigated if they broke any safety rules.'

'Baby, they'll be forever back in LA next month. You can't extradite them. I'll be free of them.'

'Unless they double your wages. You'll leave me for that job, I'm sure.'

'Never. Come with me, anyway. LA, baby!'

'Pffft! LA.'

Raja ended the call. He walked over to the main house, entering through the kitchen (a proper chef's kitchen). Cook, Mr Roberts, who was a mature Englishman, welcomed him and tried to force a cup of Yorkshire tea onto him. Roberts had been the Lipman's personal chef for nearly two decades, but he still longed for home. He ate as well as all chefs, but somehow managed to stay slim. His ex-wife used to be with the family, too, but had escaped the "cult" a few years earlier – they still talked, and maybe would retire together to a cottage in Cheshire, if LA ever became too much for him.

'I can't stop, Mr Roberts. I'm off to the airport. Is everything good in your world?'

'Yes, Raja. All the usual stress. I could do without this Halloween thing, given that I'm trying to pack before I'm forced onto the high seas. Book me a ticket, while you're there.'

'Again?' He laughed. 'Is it Manchester airport?'

'Please.'

He laughed again, and went through to check whether Margo wanted anything. She dismissed him. So, he checked his Rolex watch. Time to go get the party guests from the airport.

Raja owned a BMW e-scooter for when he was off-duty. It was mainly matt grey, with an orange seat, and he loved it to death. That evening, he bobbed in and out of the crazy Jakarta traffic to get to Ari's apartment. All around him, car horns were blaring, and there was the ubiquitous motorbike carrying an entire family, as well as the cat.

He parked in the underground car-park and rode the lift up. It was one of those old cage lifts that you had to pull the grill shut first, and it always made him giggle at the novelty of it. His boyfriend was cooking, when he entered the apartment. They kissed. Raja flopped down on a chair to happily watch the cooking process. Ari wore a Marks and Spencer apron, from their one trip to England together. He moved from side to side, flamboyantly tending each dish. Raja liked Ari very much and admired him greatly. They were too similar for there to be true love, he felt. They had three good days, one argument, then another three good days. Ari had a crew cut and a day's manly stubble on his chin. They kept smiling at each other. Their relationship was not a big secret, but they kept their lives as private as possible. They often talked about living abroad, one day, in order to have total freedom from the strictness of Indonesian society.

'Catch any bad guys today?' Raja asked.

'Now, you know, we take the long, measured approach to that kind of thing. So, tell me what happened today.'

Raja told him, with Ari shaking his head throughout.

'Arsyanendra!!! They're less caring than Dutch colonialists. I'll be glad when they quit Indo. I don't know how you stomach them?'

'I didn't tell you, Margo has bought a beach house on Malibu Road. The price is twenty million dollars.'

Ari's eyes went to the heavens. 'Nobody should be in a position to be able to do that. Anyway, enough of them. Let's eat.'

They enjoyed their meal, before washing up together. Then they settled down to watch a movie. Inevitably, the conversation returned to the Lipman family, with Raja mentioning the upcoming Halloween party.

'Maybe I will get a costume,' mused Ari. 'And come along to see it all for myself.'

'You know how balloons are banned these days? Well, they made me get a balloon roof for the pool.'

'A balloon roof? What's that?'

'Thousands of balloons tied together and arching over the swimming pool. Black and red ones, of course, for the Halloween element.'

'Those absolute fuckers!'

They both laughed hysterically and fell into one another.

'I should bust them just for that,' continued Ari.

Raja giggled. 'I love how you say bust them. You wouldn't say that at work. I collected some guests from the States today. The usual D'Shawns and cokehead models.'

'They flew the Pacific Ocean for a Halloween party?'

'No, they are all off to Bali, before the family wave goodbye to Indo. That's why the children are here. They have no interest in Margo's business dealings.'

'Good riddance to them all, that's what I say. I'm still not happy about you going on the yacht to America. Yes, it's a super yacht, but surely flying is better.'

'She hates flying. Anyway, baby, I see Margo back to LA, and then my contract is up. Hopefully, I can find a less extreme place for my next job.'

'There will be drugs at this party?'

'Yes.' Raja laughed, throwing his head back. 'What time will the raid be?'

Harper Lipman sat by the pool to breakfast and text on her iPhone, irritated that the balloon arch for the Halloween party was making her have a minor agoraphobic panic attack. She considered cutting it loose, and making the staff do it all over again later, but Rome was approaching. Her brother was wearing just gold-coloured swimming trunks. She took a photo of him and sent it to her friend in England, with "wtf?"

Harper wore a tee-shirt and a traditional batik sarong that she had recently bought in the market. She had no intention of sunbathing, as Indonesian sun just killed her. Rome had one of his newly-arrived friends with him, and at least he was properly dressed in shirt, shorts and sandals. She checked him out over her Prada Havana sunglasses. The black hair was highlighted at the front. There was one ear stud, and he was very athletic. His shirt was just opened enough to hint at a really hard chest. She considered him to be gorgeous, but knew he was as gay as Rome.

'Halo, Harper,' called Harry Rashford, in his weird English accent. English, but from some far province, she guessed.

They both watched Rome dive into the pool.

'Halo?' she repeated back at him, nonplussed.

Harry was shocked at her stupidity. 'Halo is hello in Indonesian.'

'Don't be coming at me with that nonsense, English model person guy. It's too early. Sit. Have one of these things. I've no idea what they are but they are yummy.'

Harry tried one of the local pastry morsels.

'I'm messaging with one of your people,' she said.

'One of my people?'

'English. At least, she lives just outside London, not in Cornwallshire. I showed her your photo yesterday and she says you are fucking hot.'

'Thank her for me. Where exactly does she live?'

'Luton, I think.'

Harry laughed at that.

'Happy to be here, Harry?' asked Harper.

'I am, yes. It's hotter than the Valley. I'm melting. I suppose I will acclimatize just before we head back to the States. Do you like it here?'

'Not Jakarta. I love Bali, though. Oh, my God, what is she saying now?'

Harry watched Rome doing the backstroke while Harper read her text. The aquamarine water parted over Rome's smooth chest; quite a wonderful sight. A female staff member came to ask if he wanted a drink.

'Two beers, Ayu,' interjected Rome.

'Listen to this,' said Harper, crossing her legs. 'The earth spins at 24,000 miles an hour at the equator, in space. If it stopped suddenly, all the people in England would be thrown over to Asia. I could visit you without airfare.'

'I'm replying, "what about the people here in Asia?" That will get her. "Oh, good point," she says. "You'd all be in Mexico".'

Harry smiled as he sipped his beer. He was definitely gay, but he still admired Harper's legs as they emerged out of the sarong.

'That's a beautifully patterned sarong, Harper. I'll have to get my sister one before I leave.'

'Have one of mine, I bought six.'

'Thanks.'

She ended her messaging and looked at him. 'Are you sleeping with my brother?'

'No. We're just mates.'

Harry was quite taken aback. He was a confident guy who had no worries about relocating to Southern California for his career. But these Lipmans were something else. On a couple of occasions, Rome's behaviour had almost got them both hospitalized. He knew the fairly debauched reputations of London and Harper, and the mother was infamous for her tough business practices and wild parties, back in Los Angeles.

Rome came dripping out of the pool, finishing his morning beer. 'Harper, are you coming to the club with us tonight?'

'I wish I could, but I don't want to.'

'Okay. Come on, Harry, let's get some breakfast.'

Harry did as his friend bid him.

'See you, English Harry,' said Harper. 'Oh, the Halloween party, tomorrow night? What are you coming as?'

Harry was excited at her interest. 'A kind of blood-soaked Guy Fawkes.'

Harper took off her sunglasses, her slightly sweating, pristine brows crinkled. 'Who?'

NINE

Knowles entered the incident room noisily, banging the door with his hip. He was laughing to himself. 'Has anyone seen that new civilian worker on the front desk? Fuck me, that is rough. It shouldn't be allowed out in public.' He laughed some more, greatly tickled at his own story. 'I tell you, I've seen some sights in my time, but that is fucking horrible.'

Green laughed, Speight was amused, Datta was not amused, and DS Williams was quite shocked. Knowles was surprised to see the woman DS sitting there.

'Oh, hello, DS Williams. I'm glad you've joined us.'

Williams nodded curtly at him. 'DS Knowles.'

Williams went back to looking at something on the computer screen. Knowles grimaced at Speight, then moved away, towards Green, who was in plain-clothes. The young man had dark trousers with big pockets on the thighs, and a dark blue polo neck sweater – quite trendy. Knowles looked the young PC up and down.

'Did you want something?' Knowles asked Green.

'I've been assigned to this case.'

'Have you, indeed? Okay, for future reference, I like my coffee milky with two sugars.'

Octavian came in, and Williams rose to meet him. Octavian smiled broadly.

'Katie, hi! Great to have you on board. Your exceptional reputation precedes you.'

'Oh, I don't know about that. Thank you. I hope I can help. Shirley and Aamina have brought me up to speed.'

Octavian nodded at being happy with that. He had heard good things about Katie Williams. She was quite tall, well-built, from a junior athletics career, he seemed to remember hearing. Shoulder length brunette hair and piercing blue eyes, wearing a dark suit and flat shoes. He encouraged her to retake her seat. He sat, himself, and looked at the white board, which now had a murder scene image of Englebert Dox. Also, there was a CCTV still of the suspect.

'Katie, why don't you and Aamina go and see the Dox family? Local broke the news to them last night.' Williams nodded enthusiastically. 'Me and Phil will go and see this person that Alan Hallworth told us about. Shirley, you and Beth please keep trawling through the Palatine Road CCTV. If we can see the Merc, hopefully he didn't mask up until he went for Tom Walsh.'

Octavian bounced up when he realized that Green was there. He shook his hand. 'Green, welcome. Look into the Hallworth alibi.'

Green was chuffed to bits to have a task. 'Yes, Sir.'

A pack of Press and TV newsmen surrounded Octavian and Knowles as they left the station fifteen minutes later, shouting questions about the serial killer. They both gestured no comment, and got to the car-park.

They headed out into the Cheshire countryside towards the Handforth area, with Octavian driving. They passed under an extremely low plane, taking off from Manchester airport.

'You're very quiet,' commented Octavian, glancing to the side. 'What are you thinking about?'

'I was hoping for another puncture, Boss.' Octavian laughed. 'No, I found this snack the other day. It's popcorn but in crisp format. I was thinking about that; I'm hungry. They're awesome, and no chance of breaking a filling.'

'I'll look out for them, next time I'm in the supermarket.'

'You do that.'

It was a lovely day. Knowles had the window down a little way – it was sending a pleasant buzz through Octavian's ears. The road was clear and the Golf was always fun to drive.

'I bet you shop in Waitrose, in Altrincham, Boss?'

Octavian was mildly surprised that they were still discussing food. 'It has been known that I frequent that store.'

'You still got that student living with you?'

'Ezi, yes.'

'Isn't it a bit annoying?'

'No, I hardly see him. Actually, I've got an eighteen-year-old niece from Bali wanting to come over. Can you put her up?'

Knowles laughed raucously. 'I'll ask the wife.'

Octavian pulled onto a farm track, with the green tuft of grass running all the way down the middle. Ahead was a traditional farmhouse, a wooden barn that was painted black, and what looked like a log cabin farm shop, with cars parked in front of it. He took a parking place and they got out into the sunshine.

A fairly young farmer soon approached them. His most noticeable feature was a cracking set of sideburns that Knowles couldn't wait to tell the others about. He even considered sneaking a photo on his phone. The farmer wore green wellies, dirty jeans and a checked shirt, but also a baseball cap with the Australian-style flap down the back of his neck. Clearly, he was quite an individual. His name was Neil Ikin, and he didn't show any great enthusiasm, once Octavian made the introductions and flashed his warrant card.

'What do you want?'

'Is it true that you own a crossbow, Mr Ikin?'

'Who says that?' Neither policeman was forthcoming. 'Oh, right. Yeah, I do. It's somewhere in the house. I've not used it in years.'

'I'd like to see it,' said Octavian. 'Could I ask where you were on Wednesday morning?'

'Wednesday morning? I was here.'

'Can anyone confirm that?'

Neil Ikin sniffed, indicated the staff in the farm shop. Knowles wandered off to have a word with them about it.

'What do you drive, Mr Ikin?'

'Nothing at the moment. I'm on a ban, thank you very much. Sixty in a forty, at midnight. Ridiculous. I don't suppose you meant the tractor? On the property, of course.'

'Do you still own any road vehicle? I'll be checking.'

'No, I don't.'

'The crossbow, please?'

'You'd better come in then, I suppose.'

Back at the police station, Octavian took an evidence bag containing Neil Ikin's crossbow from the boot of the Golf. He looked earnestly at a sheepish Knowles who was cradling a packet of farm shop sausages.

'They talked me into it,' explained Knowles.

They entered the station through the back door. Horsefield looked out from his office. Knowles hid his sausages behind his back.

'We'll have to stop meeting like this, Tony,' joked Horsefield. 'There is something similar to what you're on, happening in the South East. Youngsters being targeted. I'm waiting to hear who's heading that up. I'll let you know.'

'I'm keen to speak with them, Sir.'

Octavian's phone rang and he excused himself from Horsefield.

'Yes, Katie?' he said into the phone. 'Right, we will come out to you.'

Local police, in their full body armour gear, were preparing to raid a house in the Whalley Range area of Manchester. Octavian, Knowles and Speight, all wearing stab-proof vests, passed through a crowd of interested students and walked up to Williams and Datta, who were similarly attired. Octavian noticed that the officer in charge of the big red battering ram was a fairly slight female, tattooed and physically fit, but it was something he had not seen before. Williams welcomed them with a smile.

'What's happening, Katie?' asked Octavian.

'So, Mrs Dox told us that her son had recently been beaten up and threatened by a David Davidson. He's got form for violence against the police. We think he's home in his flat right now. Mrs Dox said she thinks he drives a black vehicle.'

'David Davidson?' mused Knowles. 'Another good name.'

'Good, Katie,' continued Octavian. 'It's all yours.'

Datta spoke up, 'I've looked around, Boss. No obvious vehicle in the nearby streets. It could be garaged, of course.'

'Now you're here,' said Williams to Octavian. 'I'll give the order to go in.'

They watched the police team move along a first-floor walkway with a bulletproof shield carried before them. Octavian thought it was slightly over the top, but he watched closely as the small WPC wielded the big battering ram and obliterated the front door, first time; impressive. She stepped away and her colleagues stormed in, shouting introductions.

When the scene was secured, Octavian and his team went up. Octavian looked at the useless PVC door – many years of watching such raids had made him get a reinforced front door at home. David Davidson and a male friend, both handcuffed, both scruffy in tee-shirts and tracksuit bottoms, were sitting on the sofa, expressionless. Octavian looked about the room, which smelled musty, but did not speak to David Davidson. There was cannabis, drug paraphernalia and cash scattered around the grim room. He stepped back out onto the landing, where Datta soon joined him.

'Starting to search for weapons now, Boss. I found a key for a VW Touareg. Maybe that was what Mrs Dox meant.'

Octavian grimaced. 'Don't forget the other guy's details.'

Two local PCs brought out the docile-looking David Davidson, accepting of his situation. Suddenly in passing, he managed to land a horrible headbutt on Datta, who dropped like a stone. Octavian instantly sprang forward to sweep Davidson's legs away from him and pin him to the ground, with the PC's struggling to hold the now suddenly raging man. Other officers rushed in, allowing Octavian to roll away and check on Datta. She was okay, conscious, with a cut on her right eyebrow, which was already swelling up to the size of a golf ball. Speight ran over to slide down and get her legs under Datta's head to provide support.

'Let's have an ambulance, Shirley.'

Speight was already reaching for her mobile, doing just that. Octavian watched David Davidson have his legs bound, and a spit hood put on, before he was carried ranting downstairs to be put into the back of a police van.

After a trip to A&E, to be assessed and patched up, Datta returned to the station to show everyone that she was fine, but Octavian had already called Taheer to come and collect her. Datta was slightly embarrassed with all the fuss, but happy that her colleagues cared so much about her. Octavian was yet to meet Taheer, so they shook hands in reception and he told the firefighter to take care of Datta.

'You look after her,' he said earnestly to Taheer.

'I will do,' replied Taheer. 'It's good to meet you, DI Octavian. Aamina talks well of you.'

'I should think so, as well. But I'm serious, watch for the signs of concussion.'

Everyone stood in reception and watched Taheer help Datta down the front steps.

'Aw, they're so much in love,' purred Speight.

Knowles pulled a face expressing nausea at her, before heading back upstairs.

Williams touched Octavian's elbow to get his attention.

'Yes, Katie?'

'We have a videocall booked with Kent police.'

'Let's do it.'

Octavian was a bit of a technophobe, so he sat quietly in the interview room while Williams made the connection to down south.

'Best if you just do the talking,' said Williams. 'To save confusion.'

A ruddy-complexioned, cheery DI Anstead appeared on screen and smiled.

'Hi there! Paul Anstead of the Kent police.'

'Hello, Paul. Tony Octavian and my colleague, DS Katie Williams. Thanks for speaking with us.'

'No worries. I believe you've got a series of youngster killings. We have three so far.'

'Paul, any obvious links?'

'Absolutely not. Our victims have juvenile records for criminal damage, shoplifting and suchlike. But nothing serious. Just kids. A thirty-mile radius between them. I hear you have firearms being used, though. We have one knifing, one blunt trauma and one hit and run.'

'Any thoughts on the vehicle?'

'It happened at night. Forensics can only say it was a red vehicle. We have nothing; we're not happy. I don't think you and us are linked.'

'No, neither do I. Paul, let's keep in touch, in case anything makes itself clear.'

'Sure. Sorry to not be of much help. Okay? I'll go. I'll have to walk away from the desk as I have no idea about this zoom crap.'

Octavian laughed and Williams smiled.

'Me neither,' said Octavian. 'Thanks, Paul. Goodbye for now.'

Williams ended the call. The room was silent and cold again – like their case.

'He was a friendly chap,' said Williams.

Octavian grinned. 'People are nicer, down south.'

That brought a smirk from Williams.

'Now what?' she asked.

'Chat with our nice Mr Davidson. Ask why he threatened Englebert Dox.'

First, they returned back upstairs. The white board drew Octavian again, and everyone, took notice.

'We're struggling for suspects,' he announced.

'Doesn't seem random to me,' said Williams. 'Random is when somebody runs through a shopping precinct stabbing anyone they find. These are targeted. But they are not linked. Strange.'

'Surely, it's got to be drug related,' suggested Knowles. 'Of course, the families don't know, but maybe these boys were running for one gang, and another is trying to interrupt operations.'

Octavian pointed his favourite marker pen at Knowles. 'Phil, talk to the relevant department. Even a drug dealer will help if its innocent kids getting killed. Shirley, this crossbow club in Congleton. John Paterson, our helpful expert, vouched for the members, but go out there. Get a list of names, match them with Beth's Merc owners. Take Green with you for the experience.'

Speight glanced at Green, not sure she liked being teamed with a regular PC.

'It'll definitely be an experience, Green,' joked Knowles.

Green was pleased to be involved. He then remembered to speak up.

'The Alan Hallworth alibi is verified by four people.'

McAlister said, 'Boss, I have the CCTV images of the Merc driver earlier. Masked up already. Clearly not stupid. And David Davidson's solicitor is here.'

'Good timing. Shall we, Katie?'

TEN

Octavian closed the door after finishing interviewing David Davidson. He looked at Williams.

'That wasn't any help to us at all,' she said, quite frustrated, tugging at her high ponytail.

'I wasn't expecting anything more than no comment.'

She expelled a deep sigh. 'You think he's a coincidence?'

'I do. He fell out with Englebert over something and nothing. Made a few threats. But then someone else came for Englebert. There's nothing to link Davidson with Peel Hall Park, Palatine Road or Heywood.'

'Let him go?'

'Yeah. After he's been charged with the assault on Aamina.'

Speight and Green got out of her car in a semi-rural area of Congleton and looked at the scattering of old houses. One rickety chimney stack was actually showing heavy smoke, which was a surprise. Green pointed the way and they walked up a drive. They rang the doorbell but were called around to the side kitchen door. An elderly man by the name of Ernie Jolley looked out. His jeans were being kept up by red braces, over a large beer belly in a blue tee-shirt. He was trying to step into his trainers while listening to Speight introducing herself and Green.

'Police, you say?'

'It's just a routine enquiry, Mr Jolley,' said Speight. 'Can we have a chat about your crossbow club?'

He was a friendly pensioner. 'Oh, right, fine. You'd better come this way, then, officers.'

Speight and Green were led into a large building that had replaced the man's back lawn. There was some kind of mechanical project underway on work benches, as well as a section for storing archery and crossbow equipment. The walls were covered with advertisement and petroleum signs (clearly, he liked *American Pickers* on the TV). There were several large photographs of medieval re-enactment events, some with castles in the backdrop. On another wall hung a number of swords and pikes, which peaked Green's interest. It was warm and cosy in there.

'The place I spend most of my retirement. I'm not really into bowls or dominoes. Cup of tea? The kettle is recently boiled.'

Green would have preferred coffee, but Speight accepted tea for both of them. Green continued to look at the weapons while Ernie Jolley brewed up.

'Please, sit yourselves down,' said Jolley. 'Those seats are out of an Alpha Romeo Spider.'

Speight examined where she had just sat herself.

'Where are you based?' asked Jolley. Speight told him. 'Never been there, but I've heard of it, of course.'

'Don't make a special effort to visit.'

The tea was passed around and Jolley took a different style car chair. He was all ears, keen to know why he was being visited by the police.

'Mr Jolley...' started Speight.

'Ernie, please.'

'Ernie, we're just interested in your crossbow club. There's no suggestion that anything is wrong.'

'The club's not been active for about three years. We lost some members to Covid. I still do archery every Sunday. Archery is more popular, of course. We have an allocated section in the nearby park.'

'Is there anybody you know who still owns a crossbow?'

'Well, a couple of members borrowed my spare ones. But most will have one in their shed, or somewhere.'

Green asked, 'Ernie, do you do those re-enactment meetings?'

'I have done in the past. But all weapons there are decommissioned. Someone could run about with a crossbow but there won't be any firing going on.'

'Ernie,' said Speight, 'can we get a list of your members? And anybody who does the archery with you.'

'Has somebody done something bad?'

'No, it's just a string of a complex investigation.'

'Of course, I'll do that for you.'

They soon said a warm farewell to Ernie Jolley, and walked back to Speight's car. She scanned the sky, fearing rain for the drive back. Green was perusing the list of names on the list.

'DC Speight.'

'Hmmm? What?'

'I see the name Simon Hulme on here. Isn't that the Head teacher you went to see?'

ELEVEN

The Halloween party was completely blowing the minds of two members of Margo Lipman's yacht crew. Both were twenty years old: a Scot called Stevie McCoist, and an Englishman called Jack Nesbitt. They had found white boiler suits, down in the stores, which they had splattered liberally in red paint, and they both wore scary traditional Indonesian masks, with big teeth, which they had previously picked up in Bali. But they were staggered by the cornucopia of fabulously frightening costumes on show, or lack of costumes, in some cases. There were rabid zombies, killer nurses, orange-jacketed hunters with arrows through their blood-soaked heads, ghosts trailing literally six feet of real metal chains, and a black-shrouded witch who kept dropping little glass balls that let off a mini-smoke bomb around her. Also, there was a stunning blonde model in a bikini, with fantastic make-up on one shoulder that made it appear that she had been bitten by a shark.

And the music was pumping, and the light show was illuminating the mansion and the grounds, and they were drinking some unknown cocktail. Their masks turned to each other and they were both giggling underneath.

They had cruised with Mrs Lipman, and the younger Lipmans; they knew Rome Lipman the best. Then, of course, there was London, and her wild student younger sister, Harper. But they couldn't recognize the famous girls, anyway, even though they had been advised not to make idiots of themselves with them.

'Oh, look at this,' said Jack, nudging his friend.

A bloodied mortuary assistant was actually pushing a naked woman (in flesh-coloured leotard) on a gurney, while they were both drinking alcohol through rubber tubing. They were being applauded for their efforts, and Stevie and Jack enthusiastically joined in.

Through the library window, Raja watched the same scene, and shook his head and smiled. These people. He had just been to check the front gate, where Paddy Finucane, Margo's bodyguard when she was in Asia, and *some hired staff were still admitting ticketed guests. Raja was hungry. He didn't drink alcohol. He wasn't in any kind of costume, but he was glad that the night had started well. He wondered if he had missed anything. They couldn't possibly run out of booze or food. The family doctor was actually at the party, somewhere. And there was even a zombie lifeguard watching the shenanigans in the pool (Margo didn't want the bad press of a drowning, at one of her famous parties).*

He spotted Margo, with some of her Jakarta socialite friends, all in various, less-outrageous, costumes. There were Indonesian people, Chinese, Singaporeans, one or two ex-pat Westerners. He recognized most of them. They seemed to be chatting very happily.

Raja continued to scan the party. A tortured Guy Fawkes was pouring wine down the throat of a zombie Cardinal Wolsey: Rome Lipman and his English buddy Harry Rashford, surrounded by dancing friends. Raja shuddered to think what they would get up to in Bali. He turned away and headed to the kitchen, hoping to be fed by Mr Roberts. He was welcomed by the cook and allowed to snack to his heart's content, while trays of food were going out with the hired waiters.

'Right, panic over,' said the sweating Mr Roberts. 'Forget my airline ticket, Raja. I need a nice ocean cruise.'

'One week, Mr Roberts, and you'll be on your way to Honolulu.'

'Is it going all right, out there?'

'It's marvellous. I've not spotted London or Harper yet.'

'Perhaps they are powdering their noses, if you know what I mean.'

Raja feigned shock.

'I'm going to text my man. Catch you later.'

'Okay. Say hello to Ari from me.'

'I will do.'

Raja found sanctuary in the snooker room. The snooker table had already been taken down and sold. Raja stood with one foot in the indentation of where a table leg had once been, as he texted Ari. No reply forthcoming, so he assumed that Ari was busy working. He looked out the front window of the property, seeing Paddy Finucane smoking with his staff. A yellow Humvee arrived. Then Raja saw London head down the drive to meet it. She was dressed as a pirate, with tricorn hat, red jacket, sword belt, hotpants and fishnet stockings, made with large gaps. Raja couldn't decipher the Halloween element, but she looked stunning.

He wondered who was arriving in the Humvee. A couple of Heavies got out first and spoke with Finucane. Lots of man hugging going on. So much testosterone, smiled Raja. London seemed excited. She was steepling her fingers in front of her face. Raja hoped it wasn't a new boyfriend and she would announce tomorrow that she was staying in Jakarta. The ensuing shitstorm would be unpleasant and hard to resolve. Was it somebody famous? The man exited the Humvee like he was on coke, about to wave at the crowd outside a movie premiere. He was famous, but not to the Western eye; he was an up-and-coming Indonesian actor. London jumped into his arms, wrapping her fishnet-clad legs around him, kissing him.

The man's name was Rafael Putra Bagaskara. He was in casual clothes, and wore a black bandana. Do-rag? thought Raja.

He walked as if his trainers had no laces in them. Soon they were out of Raja's view.

'Shitstorm,' said Raja, as he left the snooker room.

The party finally slowed its momentum. People were drunk, well-fed, danced out. It had been a wild success. Margo and her circle of friends were indoors. Raja looked out from a different window. He had just spoken to Ari on the phone, and his boyfriend was going to bed, lucky man.

Raja finally noticed the Indonesian crew of Margo's yacht. Their costumes were very normal, probably hired, rather than designed. They were getting what was probably their second or third helping from the barbecue, and they were goggle-eyed to see London Lipman hanging off Rafael Putra Bagaskara.

Suddenly Raja saw a disturbance out of the corner of his eye. Within a melee of costumed guests, he could clearly make out Harper Lipman punching a girl in the face. Not just hitting or slapping, but punching with lefts and rights, from her boxercise routines, with the girl recoiling each time, unable to defend herself, and finally she was unconscious before she vanished into the shrubbery. Harper was going in after the girl, until Paddy Finucane managed to get there to lift her off the ground, howling like a wild animal, and carry her into the house. Other guests rushed to the aid of the battered and bleeding girl. Whatever had she said to provoke that?

TWELVE

Octavian and Charlotte were having a meal out together, for a change, at a cosy Italian restaurant in Altrincham town centre. He was clean shaven and casually dressed in a black polo shirt and jeans. His hair was newly slicked back, and he liked how his wife had done her own hair, tucked behind her right ear, but down over the left.

'There was an earthquake today?' she informed him.

'Really? Off the coast of Indonesia?'

'No, here.'

'*Here*?'

'Yes, only a tiny one, so the news said. I did see a pencil move on the table, though.'

'I'm sorry I missed it.'

They smiled at one another.

'How's your food?' she asked. 'Are you not hungry?'

'I'm hungry. The food's good.'

'You're quite pensive tonight, darling.'

'I'm sorry, sweetheart.'

'Is it a bad investigation?'

'You remember my first case, after we moved here? That was a simple murder over a debt. The forensic evidence was like a trail of breadcrumbs through the forest. I think this new one is going to be very bad. I'm sorry.'

'Don't be sorry. You don't regret transferring, do you?'

'Of course not. It was a knife murder a day, down in London. And besides, I would live anywhere as long as it was with you.'

Charlotte almost cried with joy at hearing him say that.

'So sweet,' she said. 'Thank you.'

'Unless it's Scotland. I draw the line at Scotland.'

From the restaurant, they took a walk in the pleasant sunshine of a Spring evening, before getting a taxi home.

'We're a bit late,' said Charlotte, as they entered the house.

Octavian kissed her on the left ear. They walked into the lounge, to find Charlotte's mum, Joan, playing chess with Ezi. Both had a mug of hot chocolate and marshmallows in front of them.

'Well, this is cosy,' said Charlotte, smiling.

'Oh, hello,' replied Joan. 'You two are back early. I'm involved in this battle with Ezi. You know, I didn't know Indonesians could be so smart.'

Octavian grinned at hearing that comment from his mother-in-law.

'Is Jack okay?' asked Charlotte.

'Fast asleep, darling,' replied Joan. 'I keep checking on him.'

Ezi made a move on the board, saying to Joan, 'Checkmate.'

Joan threw up her hands, and everyone laughed. Octavian wondered if Ezi timed his strike for just as they got home.

Early the next morning, Octavian and Speight walked up the drive of Head teacher, Simon Hulme's home in Burnage. They looked at his Mercedes SUV in passing. Speight rang the bell, but Octavian noticed that Hulme was gardening at the side of the house, so he nudged Speight's elbow and they drifted around. Hulme sprang up and came towards them in his Wellington boots and scruffy gardening clothes, carrying a pair of secateurs.

'Careful, I have a taser,' joked Octavian.

Hulme giggled, out of politeness.

'Sorry to bother you at home, Mr Hulme,' continued Octavian. 'We were passing. Just one more question, if you don't mind.'

'No problem at all, Detective Inspector.'

'Congleton crossbow club. You didn't tell us you were a member.'

'Should I have done? Oh, of course. I haven't been for, wow, three years, at least. I don't own a crossbow. Never have. I used the group leader's spare. It was only a passing phase. I've done skydiving and potholing since then.'

'Have you, indeed? Wow. Okay. Right. We just wondered, that's all. Enjoy your gardening. Sorry to have disturbed you.'

'That's all right.'

Octavian and Speight retraced their steps down the drive.

'Skydiving and potholing,' mimicked Speight.

Entering the incident room, Octavian was delighted to see Datta sitting there at her desk, and enquired how she was. She smiled shyly.

'Bruised but fine, Boss.'

He looked at her a little dubiously but had to accept what she said. Williams went to brew up for everyone. McAlister passed Octavian a print-out. He sat down near his disappointing white board and perused the piece of paper.

'The revised list of young men who own a Mercedes SUV,' said McAlister. 'The nearest is Altrincham.'

'Altrincham? Great. The killer is probably my bloody neighbour. It'll be the one building an extension for the last three months.'

'Of course, that doesn't include the Head of the first victim's school, because he is mid-thirties.'

They looked at each other, as if telepathically going through the details of Simon Hulme, the Mercedes not having a scratch on it, the lack of any link to other victims, the man being in school at the time of the first murder.

Octavian ran his fingers through his hair. He looked about the room, something niggling away at him. Green walked in, and nodded politely as Williams asked if he wanted tea. Knowles arrived, nodding at Octavian.

Octavian had to get up and walk about. Everyone looked at him. 'Katie!'

Williams hurried over from the small kitchen area, teabag poised on teaspoon. 'Yes?'

'The Mercedes on Simon Hulme's drive. Something was wrong with it.'

'Such as?'

'I don't know. Finish the tea.'

He sat back down, deflated. Everyone in the room felt the anti-climax. Williams hurried back to finish brewing up, then encouraged everybody to grab their mugs. After that, she took her seat and watched Octavian thinking.

Octavian clicked his fingers. 'On the drive, it didn't have the school parking sticker in the window that it had at the school.'

Williams hunched forward. 'Meaning?'

'Meaning, he's got two identical Mercedes SUV's. If he ran over Tom Walsh, he could have any scratches and dents sorted out, while he switches to the other Merc.'

All the team gathered around, keen.

'What about Steven McLaughlin?' asked Knowles.

'He could have sneaked out on foot. Nobody monitors a Head Teacher at school. It's just assumed that they are there, all the time, in charge.'

'So, do we get a warrant to search his house?' asked Williams.

'If he is our man,' said Octavian. 'There's not going to be any crossbow or firearm at his property. But we might find some link to the victims.'

'Could we let him run?' asked Knowles. 'See what he does next?'

'What if he kills another child?' asked Datta. 'I think we have to move now.'

Knowles was prepared to argue. 'What if we turn up nothing at his house? We're showing our hand, then. We've no DNA, no witnesses, and the Chorlton-cum-Hardy killer is not him. He'll just stop what he's doing and we're screwed.'

'Aamina's right,' said Octavian, after a moment. 'We'll put surveillance on him, overnight, and go in at dawn tomorrow. Agreed?'

Everyone agreed; Knowles lastly. He put an arm over Green's shoulder. 'No sleep for you, sunshine.'

It transpired that Simon Hulme was in all night. Octavian sent a bleary-eyed Green home to bed; then gave the order to move.

A surprised and sleepy Hulme, alongside his wife, Ann, opened the front door to Williams and Speight, showing their warrant cards and a search warrant. Octavian lingered at the bottom of the drive, surrounded by a squad of officers climbing from their van.

The search progressed as the sun rose over Burnage. Octavian thought it was going to be a lovely day again. Hulme and his wife retreated to the back garden as the dark shapes of the police moved by all the windows of their home. After a while, Octavian walked over to them.

'Mr Hulme, the key to your garage, please.'

Looking like a docile Afghan hound, no longer bouncy and happy as he had been at school, Hulme leant into his kitchen and retrieved the key, which Green politely took from him. The detached garage was on an angle to the drive. For a change of scene, the Hulmes followed the police and stood watching as Green opened the garage door. Octavian and Williams peered in at the other black Mercedes.

'Identical registration to the one on the drive,' Williams noted to Octavian.

'Indeed.'

The front of the Mercedes was facing outwards, with no sign of damage or of recent restoration work. Knowles joined them.

'The house seems clear,' Knowles said.

Octavian stepped around the corner of the garage to where Hulme was standing.

'Mr Hulme, we will be taking away both vehicles for forensic examination. Could you tell me why do you have two vehicles with identical number plates?'

Simon Hulme looked highly embarrassed, almost like a pupil who had been caught cheating in an exam. 'Because... we don't like paying two lots of road tax and insurance.'

Octavian could only stand there, chewing his bottom lip. It seemed to be another dead end.

THIRTEEN

Octavian drove home for lunch, which was a very rare thing for him to do. To his surprise, he stumbled across a Baby and Toddler group picnicking on his back lawn. He found his nicest smile for Charlotte's friends, who were happy to see him. Most fancied him, or so Charlotte had said in the past. 'Hello, ladies. Please don't mind me. I just popped home for a spot of lunch.'

He sought sanctuary in the kitchen and began making a cheese and pickle sandwich. Charlotte stepped into the kitchen carrying Jack and he kissed them both.

'Are you okay, baby?' she asked. 'Pleasant surprise.'

'I'm okay.'

She could see that he was not his usual self. 'You know you can share it with me.'

He pulled an expression to say that he must keep his work stress away from his home life. They cuddled for a moment until his phone rang. Charlotte kissed his cheek and went back to her gathering.

The call was from Williams, alerting him to another youth murder. He noted the address on a shopping list pad. His stomach didn't want anything to eat, suddenly, but he knew he would be starving later, so he made his sandwich, sat down at the kitchen table and took fifteen minutes over it, with a bottle of *Coke Zero*.

Then Octavian drove to the Prestwich area, north of the city; specifically, to where two modern residential tower blocks stood. In no way did they resemble the old-style concrete council estate flats, but to Octavian, as he drove near, they did seem to have outside walkways between the apartments. There was a communal area between the two buildings, which contained a playground, bench seating and, currently, about nine police and SOCO vehicles. 'Jesus,' he said to himself – it was virtually the entire sub-division fleet. He parked alongside the BMW X5 that he believed belonged to Dr Shevington. He got out, locked his Golf and craned his neck to look up at both buildings, before seeing Datta striding out to meet him.

'Aamina.'

'Boss. Another crossbow killing. A girl, this time.'

'A girl? Damn it. Tell me this building has good CCTV.'

They started to walk over.

'It does, Boss. But maybe we won't be looking at it.'

'Why is that?'

The communal entrance door was propped open with a chair. A PC stood there. Octavian looked at the CCTV cameras as he stepped inside, and then let Datta take him up in the lift.

'Name is Lily Bowden,' reported Datta, as they trundled upwards. 'Sixteen. Mother reported the incident.'

They came out onto a draughty walkway. Knowles was standing there, talking to a uniformed officer.

'That's their flat, to the left,' explained Datta. 'But we go round this way.'

'Where's the mother now?'

'Downstairs talking with DS Williams.'

They turned the corner, to see SOCO officers working on the thin walkway. Dr Shevington stepped past Octavian to allow him room to take a look. It was shockingly gruesome, first to see all the blood that had spurted up a door and then flowed onto the floor, then the bolt buried deep into the thin neck of the victim, who was a slender black girl in a pale blue tracksuit, with white trainers.

Dr Shevington stated the obvious. 'Crossbow shot to the neck.'

The two professional men shared a moment of mutual disbelief.

'Entered on a slightly downward trajectory,' continued Dr Shevington.

'Which means?'

'Which means, I think it came from over there.'

Dr Shevington pointed at the other tower block, perhaps eighty yards away, on a slight angle. Octavian stared, aghast.

'You're not serious?' he asked Dr Shevington.

Dr Shevington performed a dramatic silence in reply.

Octavian stepped away. He patted Knowles on the shoulder in passing, then went back down alone. He walked across to the other building and entered through another propped open door (Health and Safety would be spitting feathers). Speight met him.

'Uniform have found where it was fired from, Boss.'

'How can they tell?'

'A resident challenged our killer. Saw him run for the stairs with the weapon. Baseball cap and facemask again, apparently.'

Octavian moved towards the lift.

'Oh, the lifts are out,' said Speight. 'It's only thirteen floors. I've got Green with the Caretaker, by the way, looking though CCTV. It might give us something new.'

They took the stairs and arrived on the thirteenth floor, both slightly out of breath. They passed a PC who suddenly tried not to look bored. Octavian took in the view of fields and houses, which the other tower's walkway didn't offer, then he looked across at the crime scene.

'We've cleared out the residents on this floor, but SOCO haven't been up here yet. Not much point, really.'

'Shirley, look at that distance. And it's been windy all day. I don't believe that shot. The odds are worse than for the JFK shooting.'

'JFK shooting?'

He looked at her in astonishment. 'The shooting of the US President in Dallas in 1963.'

'Oh, yeah, that. Maybe he thought he would just give it a go, and got lucky.'

'But why not wait for a better time? He found Steven McLaughlin alone in the woods. But he takes on this miracle shot.'

'Boss, I think we're in trouble with this one.' She put a hand on a hip. 'There's just nothing to go on.'

'Get together with DS Williams. Usual questions to try to find a connection. Then, once we are back at base, I think we have to start working our way through the Mercedes owners.'

'Let's pray we get a break.'

They went back down to the foyer, where Green met them, with his notebook at the ready. Octavian felt guilty that the young man looked like he had only had an hour's sleep.

'On the CCTV I saw the suspect arriving at 08:45 hrs and again, leaving, at 09:10 hrs,' began Green. 'I could not see the suspect's face. He did look very similar to the Chorlton cum Hardy suspect.'

'How did he get in?' asked Octavian.

'He entered the building as a resident exited. Then left by pushing that red button, there.'

'Was he wearing gloves?'

'I don't know, Sir.'

Octavian waited while Green returned to the Caretaker's office. He was back almost immediately.

'No gloves, Sir.'

All three of them turned slowly to look at the big red exit button on the wall.

'Not much chance of a print,' said Speight, curling her upper lip.

'You never know,' replied Octavian. 'Depends how many times it's been pushed today. Green, guard that button until I send SOCO over.'

'Yes, Sir.'

Octavian and Speight left the building, and headed back over to the first tower block.

'I'll speak to SOCO about that button,' said Speight.

They got there just as Williams and a female PC were caringly guiding the victim's mother out to a police car, to move her away from the distressing scene, perhaps to see a doctor. Octavian and Speight respectfully stepped back to give the tragic woman all the space she required. Octavian looked at her, trying not to stare. She was a black woman, perhaps his age, in a white Puffa jacket with jeans and brown boots. Despite the appalling circumstances, it was impossible not to notice that she was a very beautiful woman. Octavian suddenly did a double-take. He *knew* her. He knew her from a completely different phase of his life. She was called Kezia. She was his first ever girlfriend, the love of his life, before Charlotte appeared on the scene. He was stunned. He almost said her name, before he managed to control himself in his professional capacity.

Kezia briefly stopped walking, as her mind was going into overdrive. Williams waiting, understanding that the woman needed a moment. Then Kezia freaked out at the world, flailing her hands in despair. Unfortunately, a finger caught Williams in an eye, causing her to cry out and flinch away. Instantly, Kezia was terribly apologetic. Speight rushed to aid Williams.

Octavian stepped in. 'I'm DI Octavian. Where is it you need to go?'

The female PC said, 'She wanted to go to her sister's, Sir.'

'Let me drive you.'

Kezia looked at him through her puzzled, tear-stained despair. Perhaps he should have stepped away, not become involved, but it had been an instinctive reaction to seeing an old friend in distress. Williams and Speight looked on (with three eyes), both more than a little surprised at Octavian's intervention.

FOURTEEN

Knowles and Speight settled at their regular place at the bar in the Stockport pool club. Datta had been talked into joining them, as Taheer was working a night shift at the fire station, and a shyly quiet Green was also present.

'Are you old enough to drink?' Knowles asked Green.

'That's very good of you, DS Knowles. Thank you, I'll have a pint of lager.'

They all laughed. Knowles ordered, with an orange juice for Datta.

'Shall we get a table and shoot some pool?' asked Knowles.

'You only want to play because DS Woolaston's not in.'

Knowles got the attention of a staff member to get a table.

'Who's DS Woolaston?' Green asked Speight.

'His nemesis.'

They moved to a table and Knowles racked the balls.

'Can you play, Green?' asked Knowles.

'A little.'

Knowles broke off, but failed to pot a ball. 'Fuck!'

'Phil!' admonished Speight. 'There's a lady present.'

'Who? Where?'

'Aamina.'

Speight sat alongside a grinning Datta on a raised sofa. They watched Green chalking his cue with great care and attention.

'I have a really bad feeling for this case,' said Speight.

'Me, too,' said Knowles. 'Just don't say it in front of the Boss.'

'I already have.'

They then watched on spellbound as Green proceeded to pot everything in sight.

DS Katie Williams lived with her property developer husband, Tim, in a detached extended bungalow that backed onto the Bridgewater Canal, in the Stockton Heath area of Warrington. It was definitely not overlooked, which would have pleased Octavian.

Classical music was playing on the radio in one part of the house, while her son, Ben, and his girlfriend had very different music playing in the conservatory, while they appeared to be doing their homework. Williams took two glasses of wine through to the study, where Tim had brought some work home. He paused to accept his glass and caress the back of her left thigh as she passed. She leant on a cabinet and watched her slightly older, greying, handsome man, with his work shirt a little unbuttoned and a pen behind his right ear, making him look like a very posh builder. He grinned at her. She tried to smile through her tiredness.

'You need an early night, chicken,' he said. 'Are you still re-running the day?'

'Somewhat, yes.'

'Forget it for now. What's on TV tonight? Are we continuing our series? Or can I watch the test match cricket from the West Indies?'

'You can watch the cricket, if you like.'

'Ooh, you are tired, giving in so easily.' He stood up to take her into an embrace.

'Sorry, Tim, I shouldn't bring things home. Especially not something involving young people.'

'Katie, I've always been ready to listen to you. I knew what I was getting into.'

He kissed her forehead and then she rested her head on his chest.

In the incident room, the white board now contained photographs of Steven McLaughlin, Tom Walsh, Mohammad Asif, Englebert Dox and Lily Bowden. Octavian stood looking at it, especially the photo of a smiling Lily, with (pixelated out) school pals around her. If things had turned out differently, he mused, he could have been looking at his own daughter. In his mind, he returned to the previous day, for the hundredth time.

Kezia had recognized him instantly, though thankfully not said his name out loud. She just needed to be with her sister and her family. Williams had taken a statement, and not been able to contact any relatives to come to the location. Octavian had taken charge of the moment, much to the consternation of Williams. He had driven Kezia the mile or so to her sister's home, which was the worst journey of his life – he felt dreadful, so he could only imagine the depths of misery that she was enduring.

Kezia was still Kezia Garswood. Now thirty-six, and, up close, Octavian could see, as with himself, the lines around the eyes and the maturing in the skin, from the absolutely clear smoothness of their teenage dating, to the texture of a grown woman who had seen life. Her daughter, Lily, had taken her father's name, but the father was not around much anymore.

The crying had been replaced by a deep silence. Octavian knocked on the sister's door but got no response, so they waited in the Golf. Apparently, the sister was due home any time soon. Octavian had his training, but was so conflicted with his feelings that he could barely think; they had once known true, first love. A school love story in Didsbury. There had been plans, there had been great fun, virginities lost to each other. But then, of course, they changed a little, grew up, met different types of people, went to different colleges, and drifted apart. Occasionally, though, he had thought back to her, over the years. Wondered what had become of her.

'My son,' she had whispered. 'He's at school at the moment.'

'Plenty of time.'

A woman was approaching the house. Octavian had forgotten that Kezia had a sister.

'Let me speak to her,' he had said.

'Yes. Thank you, Tony. So strange to see you again, like this.'

'You just sit quietly. I'll bring her to you. Then we'll get you inside.'

He had taken out his warrant card and approached the sister, who he recalled being called Emma. From then he was not needed; Kezia was taken into the house by her sister. The sister had assured him that all the family would come together immediately. She thanked him. He stepped away. Kezia tried to smile her thanks to him and then she was into the house. Octavian drove back to the crime scene, full of strange emotions.

FIFTEEN

Octavian should have immediately sought out a meeting with DCI Horsefield, to make him aware of this conflict of interest with the mother of a victim. But Horsefield was not in, anyway. Octavian left it. These things happened from time to time. So, he carried on.

He felt as sad for Lily Bowden as he would have done for a stranger. Of course, wanting a resolution now included his feelings for Kezia. He would keep seeking that breakthrough.

It was McAlister who disturbed his reverie. 'Yes, Beth?'

'There were no viable prints on the exit button in that tower block. And everyone has a list of Mercedes drivers to visit. Here are yours.'

He had told Horsefield recently that he liked being hands-on, but maybe going around checking cars was a bit below his rank. He accepted the list with a thank you; it would get him out of the station, if nothing else.

'Oh, traffic are still on the look-out for our vehicle,' continued McAlister. 'That list of people from the Congleton crossbow club: nobody under thirty, and none are the registered keeper of a Mercedes.'

He nodded. He saw Knowles enter the room.

'Phil, you ready?'

'Always ready, Boss.'

As they went to leave, Octavian looked at Green. 'Green, come with us.'

Green was out of his chair like a crossbow shot.

Wythenshawe sits to the south of all the other areas of Manchester, and is mainly surrounded by beautiful Cheshire countryside and some nice towns, such as Wilmslow, Hale and Cheadle. Octavian drove them out of the police station compound in his Golf. It was not far to the village of Gatley, just over the main Kingsway that went into the city centre. Knowles complained about "bloody cyclists", but then he was looking out at the nice semi-detached homes of Gatley.

'I like Gatley,' commented Knowles. 'It's got a nice ambience. But absolutely nothing happens here.'

Octavian found the address they were after and they parked on a wide road lined with expensive houses and magnificent trees that the local council were yet to decide to butcher. They approached a 1930's property that could do with a lick of paint and the paving slabs on the drive levelling.

'But this must be the scruffiest house in posh Gatley,' said Knowles.

There was no response to the doorbell, so they wandered around the side of the house. It was a big plot, but completely full up. They looked at a mouldy old caravan, with flat tyres, and a vehicle hidden under a tarpaulin. Knowles lifted the tarp to reveal an authentic US Army jeep, which delighted both himself and Green, both. Knowles touched the white star on the bonnet and Green played gently with the thin steering wheel, both briefly taken back to their childhoods.

There were dogs running loose, but they were friendly. Green lingered at the front to play with them, while Octavian and Knowles pressed on in the search of human life.

'Hello!?' called Octavian.

The back garden looked like a dump. There were several pebble-dashed outbuildings with corrugated iron roofs, before a more cultured long lawn went off towards several archery targets. Octavian began to sense that something was not quite right, but then a teenaged boy, perhaps sixteen, showed his head out of one of the buildings. He looked nerdy and shy, resenting the interruption.

'Can I help you?'

Octavian flashed his warrant card. 'I'm DI Octavian of Greater Manchester police. We're looking for Mr Paterson. There's no problem. We're just taking up his invitation to come and chat about weapons.'

'I'm his son, Lee Paterson. He's just popped to the shops. He'll be back in a minute.'

'Okay, we'll just hang about.'

'That's fine. I'll get back to my studies.'

'Yes! Very wise.'

Lee Paterson withdrew his head.

'I bet the neighbours don't like living next to a tip like this,' said Knowles.

'I suppose every area has an eccentric family.'

Octavian watched Green still playing with the dogs, then he drifted down the garden. He looked in to where Lee Paterson was studying. It was very organized, with computers and work desks.

'A nice set-up you've got here, Lee.'

Lee Paterson looked up nervously. Octavian could tell that the youth's reticence was because he was a deep kid, not because he disliked the police.

'Thank you,' said Lee Paterson. 'I'm hoping to get good grades so I can go to college to study to be an architect.'

'No way!? My wife is an architect. She's on maternity leave, at the moment. She's very talented.'

Lee Paterson was suddenly extremely interested in that, and his mood opened up to the policeman. He swivelled on his chair. 'Please, sit down.'

Octavian stepped inside and found a stool to sit on.

'Where did she study?'

'She studied at one of the Stockport colleges, and then Taiwan, would you believe? Her friend went there, so she followed.'

'Taiwan used to be called Formosa.'

'I believe you're right.'

'I'm hoping to study in America soon. I don't know where yet. Any state would be brilliant. Even in the middle of the country.'

'Good for you. I'm looking forward to telling her about you tonight. She'll be so pleased.'

Lee Paterson smiled nervously. 'Give her my regards. As one colleague to another.'

Octavian smiled at the interesting kid.

Knowles was calling.

'Probably my dad back. I said he wouldn't be long.'

Octavian stood. 'Well, best of luck with your studies, Lee.'

'Thank you.'

Octavian stepped back outside. It was, in fact, John Paterson. He was happy to see them, going around shaking hands, while his dogs bounced at his legs.

'I had something to ask you,' explained Octavian.

'Oh, okay. Fine. Cup of coffee first?'

'Sure.'

They gathered into John Paterson's kitchen and sat down while he made the coffee. Octavian saw that the kitchen décor had not changed since the 1970's, down to the blue linoleum flooring, with holes in it, although the gas cooker and white goods were up to date.

In the brief period of quiet, Octavian realized that he was thinking about a young Kezia Garswood, walking with him in a park in Didsbury, without a care in the world. Seeing her pale jeans and orange waistcoat, and her dazzling smile and pure skin. And then they were making love in his room...

John Paterson carried cups to them and they all thanked him. John Paterson took a seat.

'Oh, sorry,' he said, jumping back up to fetch a plate of digestive biscuits.

Knowles's face lit up, expressing *digestives, I should think so*, and he helped himself.

'I spoke with your son before you arrived,' said Octavian. 'He wants to be an architect. I was telling him my wife is an architect.'

'Is she, indeed? Marvellous. We're saving up so he can go to an American college.'

'Yes, he said. Oh, sorry, let me introduce my colleagues properly. DS Knowles and PC Green.'

Knowles nodded with his mouth stuffed with biscuit.

'Yes, very proud of Lee,' continued John Paterson. 'He doesn't waste much of his time with silly hobbies. Anyway, you said you had a question for me?'

'Yes, we've had another incident involving a crossbow.'

'Oh, dear.'

'It's just that the shot was over eighty feet, probably in windy conditions. I just wanted to get your thoughts on that.'

'Quite extraordinary.'

'Does that suggest an expert?'

'It does and it doesn't. An expert could make that shot. But so could anyone, if they have a scope attached.'

'Oh! A scope. I hadn't thought of that.'

After they had finished their tea, they returned to the garden. John Paterson disappeared into one of his sheds for a moment.

'You ate all the biscuits,' Green accused Knowles.

'I didn't.'

'You did.'

'I wasn't consciously aware of doing that.'

John Paterson reappeared carrying a selection of crossbows, which he passed out.

'All safe,' he assured them. 'Detective Inspector, there's the one with the scope I mentioned.'

Octavian handled the modern weapon; then looked through the scope at one of the archery targets, down the bottom of the garden.

'Detective Sergeant Knowles first,' decided John Paterson, who clearly liked being an organizer.

They moved into position at the top of the firing range.

'What's at the bottom of the garden?' asked Knowles.

'An impenetrable banking of soil. Don't worry. Unless you fall over, you're not going to hit any residents of Gatley.'

'I wouldn't put it past me.'

John Paterson cocked the crossbow. He made sure Knowles was steady on his feet. Knowles put the crossbow up to his shoulder and aimed. John Paterson loaded the bolt and tapped Knowles on the shoulder, like it was a bazooka. Knowles let fly, but the bolt went weakly to the grass at the side of the target.

John Paterson cocked Green's crossbow. Green took it very seriously. Once the bolt was settled in place he aimed with great care. He fired and hit the outer ring of the target. Octavian laughed with delight and patted Green on the back. Knowles was playfully exasperated. John Paterson encouraged Green to try again. Green had a second go, and again hit the target.

Then John Paterson put Octavian in position and loaded for him. Octavian aimed and fired, but his bolt hit one of the legs of the target, which he was quite satisfied with.

'Try the one with the scope,' suggested John Paterson.

The crossbow with the scope was put into Octavian's hands. John Paterson loaded while Octavian focused through the scope. He took his time, fired, and hit the target. Everyone laughed and he was congratulated.

'With the scope it's less challenging, certainly,' said Octavian.

Knowles then had a go on the crossbow with the scope, and still missed the target. John Paterson commiserated with him.

'What's that other crossbow?' asked Knowles.

'Oh, that's a replica wooden one. It's a French one from the Battle of Crecy.'

'The Battle of Crecy? Right.'

John Paterson cocked the wooden crossbow by putting his foot on it and drawing back the string. Knowles had the first go. He aimed and fired and nobody saw where the bolt went.

'Bullseye?' laughed Knowles.

There was a pause.

'Oh, there it is,' said John Paterson. 'In the far corner.'

Green took the next turn. Once it was loaded, he aimed and fired, hitting the bullseye. Octavian and John Paterson were delighted for him. Knowles was pleased for the young man, but pretended to be gutted.

They took their leave of John Paterson. Octavian looked in on Lee Paterson and exchanged waves. Then they left Gatley.

Returning to the station, they stopped their cheery banter before passing through a few members of the Press, which had become less of a scrum. In the reception, Octavian was surprised to find a serious looking Horsefield waiting for him. 'Sir?'

'Tony, your wife is here to see you. She's in my office.'

Octavian rushed straight there. Charlotte stood as he entered. Jack was not with her, and he felt a deep dread flood through his body. 'Charlotte, what are you doing here? Is anything wrong? Is Jack okay?'

Charlotte was quite weepy. 'Jack's fine.'

Octavian gasped with relief. He moved forward to embrace her. 'Then what is it? Why are you here? What's wrong?'

'Tony, it's your father.'

SIXTEEN

Octavian guided Charlotte through to the staff rest area for another cup of tea (Horsefield had looked after her with tea and his best biscuits). They sat and held hands across the table.

'When did he die?' he asked her.

'Yesterday. I'm so sorry, Tony.'

Octavian was processing it. 'Right.'

The death of a parent was an inevitability of life, of course, but Octavian had never actually thought about it.

'Ezi's looking at flights, as we speak,' said Charlotte.

Octavian thought of his mother, and of travelling home, but then he realized that he was in the middle of a very difficult murder inquiry.

'You should ring your sister in Jakarta.'

Octavian gulped down a mouthful of tea and looked at the clock on his phone, which always told him the time in both England and Jakarta, Indonesia.

'I'll ring soon,' he said.

They clasped their hands tighter.

'Where's Jack?'

'He's with my mother. I was at John Lewis in Heald Green with Becky when Intan rang me. That's why I came straight over here.'

'Is Becky still with you?'

'Yes, she's walking around the Civic Centre shops.'

'That'll be an experience for her. You and her get home safe, please. I won't be late tonight.'

'Okay, darling.'

His mind was a whirl. 'So, what are we thinking..?'

'I'll come with you, if that's what you want. My mother will have Jack. Or you and Ezi go. I don't know what's for the best.'

'I don't want you to leave Jack yet. Especially not for a quick visit for a funeral. Me and Ezi will go. Is that all right?'

'Yes, of course, dear.'

He walked her out to reception. They shared a look of love.

'I won't kiss you, baby,' he told her. 'Because of the press people looking in. But I love you so very much.'

'I love you, too.'

She wondered whether to make a light-hearted comment.

'What?' he asked.

'I feel like you're releasing me on police bail.'

It made him smile. 'You're as guilty as sin.'

They waved as if they were associates, and he watched her skip down the front steps. He jogged upstairs and watched her cross the Forum car-park in search of her friend.

Octavian stayed on top of his grief, his father constantly on his mind, and spent his afternoon checking Mercedes SUVs and their owners. Nothing came of it. He checked in with the team, doing the same task, but nobody had anything for him. Then he went in to see Horsefield.

Octavian drove home. Although his mind was in a fog, he found himself chatting with a couple of neighbours, who were half-jokingly annoyed that builders were still working on a nearby property. 'Fifteen skips they've had,' complained the husband, grinning. Octavian agreed that it had been going on for too long. 'It didn't take fifteen skips to originally build the thing,' continued the neighbour. Octavian managed to politely excuse himself and went into his house. Charlotte greeted him with a soft cuddle.

'What's happening with work?' she asked.

'Horsefield is understanding about me going. Katie Williams will become deputy senior investigating officer.'

'Right.'

'Where's Ezi?'

'He's packing his suitcase.'

'Are we sorted for flights, then? When is it?'

'You both have to be at Manchester airport at four o'clock tomorrow morning.'

'Oh, my God, 4 a.m. Did you or your mother volunteer to take us?'

She giggled. 'Taxi, silly.'

Nobody felt like cooking, so they ordered in pizza. Ezi went to bed at 9 p.m. Octavian packed his suitcase with the clothes and toiletries that Charlotte had decided upon, then went to check his emails: two more standard rejections from London literary agents. A couple of months ago, one agent had requested the full manuscript, but there had been no reply yet from that person. There was also a friend request on a family history site from someone who thought they might have the same ancestors as him. He would check that out when he had more time. He then sent an email to Williams, wishing her all the best while he was away, and promising to stay in touch. Before leaving the station, he had gathered his team to tell them what had happened, and that he would be absent for six or seven days. Everybody was extremely sorry for his loss, and they all said they would press on with the investigation.

He decided to turn in for the night. While doing his ablutions, his mind drifted onto Kezia, but he shook her out again. He never lay in bed mulling over his current cases, and determined not to think about his father yet, so was asleep before Charlotte finished watching her BBC police drama series and came up to bed.

Octavian's phone alarm woke him at 3 a.m. Charlotte was not beside him; clearly, she was in with Jack. Octavian showered and dressed very casually in navy blue sweater and jeans. He found his comfortable old *Nike* trainers for travelling in, then went downstairs, finding Ezi sitting eating cereal in the kitchen. Octavian made toast and coffee.

'I've packed that new box of *Yorkshire* tea, for mother,' said Ezi. 'You know how she likes it. Is that okay?'

'Of course. Are you ready for the long trip to Indo?'

'I think so. I like travelling.'

It was a lovely early morning. Charlotte hugged them both on the doorstep, demanding regular messages. Octavian kissed her. That morning she had a meeting with colleagues to "touch base" in anticipation for when her maternity leave came to an end.

'We'll discuss things when we get back,' said Octavian.

'Okay.'

'And have your friends around in the evenings. I don't like you being alone.'

'Okay. Travel safe. I'll watch your little plane icon on the *Kindle* screen.'

'That's tragic.'

He kissed her again, before joining Ezi in the waiting taxi, which swept away from the kerb. Within minutes they had jumped onto the M56 for the short burn up to the airport junction.

'Have you got your passport?' Octavian asked Ezi.

'I triple checked that I had. Have you?'

'Of course.' Octavian anxiously checked his pockets and was relieved to find it. 'See.'

Octavian paid off the taxi at the airport, while Ezi organized their luggage on the pavement. Then they headed into the terminal.

SEVENTEEN

Octavian and Ezi arrived at Soekarno-Hatta International Airport in Jakarta both in less than a fit state; Ezi even felt slightly dizzy. Neither liked eating on planes, so had only picked at the food they had been given. They collected their luggage and made their way out. After England, both had been expecting to be hit by a wall of heat, but they found that they adapted back to it quite naturally.

Ezi bought new SIM cards from a kiosk for their phones, and used his to order an *Uber*. Octavian texted Charlotte to say they had arrived safely. They sat down and waited at a bus stop for the Uber to come.

A smiling Octavian patted Ezi's left leg. 'We're home, Ezi, mate.'

'Yes. I'm thinking about my childhood, actually. Grandmother calling my name, or my dad driving me to school. Weird.'

'I don't think it's weird. It's nice memories.'

Shortly afterwards, a brown Toyota pulled up, with the driver speaking to Ezi through the open window, 'Ini sama mas Ezi ya?'

'Iya ini saya sendiri.'

The driver got out and put their luggage in the boot. Ezi slumped into the passenger seat, while Octavian got in the back. Thankfully, the driver didn't feel inclined to chat to them.

It took about half an hour to get to Intan's home. She and a few cousins met them at the gate. Intan actually ran a couple of feet in order to hug Ezi. Then she embraced her brother. She had the famous Octavian black hair, and wore glasses. She expressed sadness; not how she wanted to be reunited with her brother.

Children were playing in the compound, and neighbours were looking quizzically at the scene. Octavian hoped they wouldn't speak to him; he was too drained. Intan hugged him even more, as did his cousins, both male and female, and then they were taken in for some refreshments. The house smelled of Intan's cooking, which was extremely pleasant, but then he felt a wave of sadness, remembering all the places in the house that he had been with his father.

His mother was sitting in the cool lounge with relatives. He went immediately to hold her. He knelt by her side and they talked quietly. He apologized for not bringing

Charlotte and Jack, but she understood. She was so relieved that he had arrived safely.

Later, after food and drink, and catching up with the relatives, Intan sat with Octavian and asked him all about England, and how Charlotte and the baby were. He told her everything she wanted to know (although he was no help with the current goings-on in *Coronation Street*), and then she fell back into haranguing Ezi about his education again – he assured her that he was doing well at Manchester Uni. Thankfully, one of the family cats made an appearance across the white tiles.

'Ziggy!' Ezi scooped him into his arms, and Ziggy was happy to go with him to rest in his room. Nothing had changed in there. His bedsheets were freshly clean on. His posters had not been touched, especially his Manchester United one. None of his books had been moved. He put his shoes on the shelf and threw his socks in the basket. He put on some Taylor Swift music and lounged around, cuddling with Ziggy. The bed felt as great as it always had done. He was soon fast asleep.

Intan's husband, Doni, came home from work. Octavian stood to embrace the man.

Then they took coffee out to sit in the garden. That was where Octavian heard the details about his father's last day.

'I've always thought it was best to go quickly,' said Doni.

'I think the same. At least he had lived a full life, and he had all his marbles at the end.'

'You must be tired, Tony. Such a huge distance to travel. Are you staying long after the funeral?'

'Perhaps a couple of days. I have a big investigation on, at the moment.'

The funeral was the following day, but it passed Octavian by in a flash; too many people getting in his face, too much sadness. But he was supportive to his mother, and did his duty to the best of his ability. He thought a lot about his late father, throughout. Then they were back at the compound for food and for more people to ask him about England. He saw his mother chatting with Ezi, so moved across to them.

'Would you like England to be your permanent home?' asked a smiling Jane Octavian.

'I think I might like that, yes,' replied Ezi. 'I think I'll need a good job, though.'

'You could always join the British police,' she kidded.

Ezi laughed at the very thought. 'I doubt they would want me.' He looked up at Octavian, who squeezed his shoulder.

The next day allowed Ezi to be alone, and he borrowed a cousin's motorbike to get out and about. He stopped by some friends' houses, but they were either at work or college. He passed his old college, just to see it, then went off into the countryside, before returning when he got hungry. He bought some ketoprak, which is a vegetable, tofu and rice cake dish, served in a peanut sauce; he had missed that so much. He was happy enough to be back home, but he also wanted to be in Manchester again.

The few days in Indo flew by. He got to spend time with his old friends, and enjoyed his mother's cooking. He gave her the Yorkshire tea and she was very pleased.

'Not missing London?' Intan asked Octavian, at breakfast, on the third day.

'No, I think we are settled now in the North West.'

'I must go to England again soon.'

'You should.'

'Mother will probably want to return to England now.'

'I did think that. Good, I say, another babysitter.'

'What are your plans now? You know we want you to stay as long as you can.'

Actually, Octavian had been invited to Yogyakarta for a couple of days by one of his cousins at the funeral. The man was called Rangga, and he was one of those infamous Indonesian policemen, although Octavian could not imagine him taking a bribe. He told Intan and Ezi his plan to fly over to Jogja with Rangga, but be back in time to leave for Manchester.

'Oh, that'll be nice,' said Intan. 'You can see the old family home.'

EIGHTEEN

Octavian and cousin Rangga flew to Yogyakarta the following day. Rangga was not much of a talker, so Octavian was happy to rest and look out of the plane window. On arrival, Octavian breathed it all in, inordinately happy to be back in his beloved Jogja. He looked at everything and everyone on the taxi ride to Rangga's family home, right in the heart of the city, where a warm welcome awaited. Rangga's beautiful wife, Melati, was a well-known artist, so the house was filled with weird and wonderful paintings, of vibrant colours; dragons and lions and flowers and seascapes. It was hotter in Jogja, maybe 37 degrees, and Octavian felt it in his English genes, so he was happy to drink iced tea with his relatives on the covered back porch, watching their children playing in the walled garden.

Melati asked him specifically about London, rather than England in general, as she had ambitions to live and work there some day. Octavian told her all he knew, but he was not very well up on the art scene. He said he hoped to see one of her exhibitions in London, one day.

After a good night's sleep, and breakfast of porridge (rice, not oats, with gravy and crackers), Rangga took Octavian on a short walk to give him a tour of the police station. Octavian told him that it would take about three hours to walk to work for him in England.

Octavian knew the police station building well, but had never been inside before. It was in the famous Malioboro area, which had many shops and bars and was popular with Western tourists, some of whom he had spotted.

They headed in to Rangga's open-plan office, picking up some real Indonesian coffee along the way. Octavian was introduced to colleagues, who were all fascinated to have a real British policeman visiting. Two asked if he was there on an international case, and if they could be of any assistance. They laughed when he just said he had just come to see his city of birth again after many years away.

Rangga said he was sorry that his partner was not on that day to meet him, but he was keen to introduce him to his boss, and the senior man himself, identified by the epaulettes and badges on his grey shirt, came quickly into the room; but what Octavian saw was a hyperactive, highly-stressed man who was causing officers to get to their feet like a wave at sea, before they rushed out. Rangga became alarmed. 'Something's very wrong, Tony.'

'I gathered as much.'

The Police Chief reached their section, staring wide-eyed at Rangga and the stranger. 'Siapa sih ini?'

It was a foul-mouthed, no-nonsense enquiry about Octavian's identity. But the Police Chief went on quickly with himself, 'There's an on-going terrorist attack. It's very close. We are reacting to it now.'

'Right!' replied Rangga.

The Police Chief rushed away. Octavian was greatly alarmed at what he had just heard but his training kicked in, and he controlled his emotions, keen to help out.

'You'd better stay here, Tony.'

'Fuck that, Rangga! This is my city, too. I'm going with you.'

'Okay!'

They ran down the stairs, coming across organized panic taking place; bullet-proof vests going over heads, handguns being issued from the armoury. Rangga handed Octavian a vest, then stared at his cousin for a tense moment. 'I suppose you'll want a firearm?'

'Of course.'

Octavian was expecting a handgun, but what he got was a Pindad SS1 assault rifle. 'Holy fuck!' Then they actually put on army-style helmets, before following the rush of police officers out to the street.

Instantly, Octavian heard explosions in the near distance. Local pedestrians were running for their lives. Octavian and Rangga moved towards the danger, with Octavian keeping back and to the right of his cousin. The fleeing public became fewer and fewer, the nearer they got to the incident. Small arms fire crackled around the quiet streets.

Octavian saw his first civilian bodies on the ground; men, women and children. He was already keyed up, totally focused. In his peripheral vision he could make out Jogja police moving parallel to them. Another explosion came, sounding like the dull thud of a grenade, and then they made contact. Exactly as he would have imagined: two Asian youths, long hair, casually dressed, with backpacks, brandishing Kalashnikovs. Octavian and

Rangga both took a knee and engaged the figures. Rangga dropped his man, while Octavian only managed to squeeze off some rounds that destroyed the glass frontage of a clothes shop. The terrorist turned and returned fire at them, until Rangga fired again, hitting the youth in the legs, making him collapse. Other officers came forward at the side and poured bullets into both prone bodies, until there was no longer any movement.

Octavian and Rangga moved on. A shop worker was cowering behind a bus, his knees up to his chest. To their right, two female office workers fled, their hijabs fluttering in the air. More contact: bullets whistled past Octavian's head as he raised his weapon and fired at a Westerner with a Kalashnikov. Octavian was astonished to see the top of the blonde man's head pop off, as he was knocked down. Octavian engaged another Westerner terrorist, putting three rounds into the man's side, crumpling him into a grotesque heap on the ground.

A grenade exploded in a bus shelter, to their left, putting officers down. Blood turned their white shirts bright red. More fire was exchanged; then what appeared to be the last trio of attackers were running away, one of whom seemed to be wearing an out-of-date Manchester United shirt. Octavian, Rangga, and two other officers went in pursuit, firing as they moved. Octavian and Rangga took a moment behind an advertising hoarding, to reload and catch their breath. Octavian was sweating profusely. Out they went again, but then the local army were arriving in jeeps, between themselves and the fleeing terrorists. It was the time for Octavian and Rangga to stand down.

A grinning Rangga, not a bead of sweat on his brow, patted Octavian on the shoulder and they walked back the way they had come, seeing medical aid arriving for the wounded police officers. The man who had been hiding behind the bus was now filming on his phone. Before returning to the police station, Octavian and Rangga sat in a nearby park, helmets on their laps, simply to calm their heart rates and process what they had just gone through.

Octavian decided not to visit the old family home, under those circumstances, and returned to Jakarta on the next available flight, after first thanking Rangga and Melati for their hospitality.

His family were fully aware of the terrorist attack on Yogyakarta while he was in the city, but he said nothing about his part in it. They were just relieved that he had escaped it. His mother was particularly upset that she might have lost him, as well as her husband. That made Octavian think about his responsibilities towards Charlotte and Jack, but he would have done the same thing over, if he had to.

He Facetimed Charlotte, that evening. The attack was on the news in England. She simply expressed her love, and demanded that he leave Indonesia. But before he came home, Octavian borrowed brother-in-law Doni's car and set about visiting some of the locations in his Indonesian butler novel. He already knew all the places, but just wanted to refresh his memory. He went to the PIK district and chose a mansion for his American family, he picked a tower block where his main character lived, and he looked at all the municipal buildings. He had planned to go out to the docks to try to find some big yachts, but decided that he was too tired, so cut his research short.

And then it was time for him and Ezi to return to England. Another cousin drove them to the airport. They boarded the plane, not looking forward to the tortuously long flight. This time they were not able to secure seats next to each other.

'See you at Dubai,' said Ezi.

'Let's hope so.'

Ezi sat at the front of the plane. In the next seat was an elderly man, who he thought might be Indian or Pakistani. He was getting himself settled. Then, the other way, Ezi found a pretty Westerner girl joining their row. She was tanned and very casually dressed, and he assumed that she had been on a backpacking trip. As she reached into the overhead locker, he couldn't help but enjoy the sight of her toned midriff.

'Oh, hi,' she said to him, taking her seat, a bit flustered. 'I'm Poppy, from Leeds. Do you speak English?'

NINETEEN

Octavian was keen to get back to the murder investigation. He left Charlotte sleeping. He showered, dressed, breakfasted, and drove away from the house, having to wait as a sixteenth skip was delivered to the property that was having the extension built. Charlotte had brought up the subject of the terrorist attack again, and they had talked about it by text from Dubai, and then again on his return, but he had decided not to tell her about his personal involvement – he saw no reason to upset her about something that was now behind him.

He drove to Wythenshawe. Not much happened on his first day back on the investigation, good or bad. There were no developments with the search for the Mercedes, and no more children were murdered. All the team welcomed his return, but they could see he was tired and not yet back up to speed. Williams came to sit with him, to report on what had been happening while he was away; which was basically very little. They chatted about what else they could be doing, but she had nothing for him. He felt quite drained; the trip, the funeral, the incident in Yogyakarta. His stress with the case sat in the back of his mind (one compartment ahead of thoughts of Kezia).

Charlotte cooked their evening meal, that night, as Ezi was out somewhere.

'You didn't tell me Ezi met a girl on the flight back.'

'I didn't know that. Did he? We sat apart.'

'He's quite nervous about her. That's why he told me, I suppose.'

'Who is she?'

'Some girl from Yorkshire. Don't ask him about it, Tony. He's clearly embarrassed.'

'Okay. Wow. I'd better call my sister.'

'Why?'

'Get her to cancel his arranged marriage.'

She made a dismissive pffft noise.

'Sorry about the blandness of the food,' she joked, as they washed the pots. 'After Intan's amazing creations, no doubt.'

'Yes, it was a shock to come back to... whatever that was.'

She was playfully mortified, and they laughed, and he spun her around the kitchen with his hands wet from the sink.

'Tony! You're getting me all wet.'

'Wey-hey!'

She screamed with laughter. 'Aaaargh. Put me down.'

He put her down and they kissed with tenderness.

They settled themselves down, having their coffee in the lounge, watching ITV's quiz show, *The Chase*. Jack was happily in his play pen with them. Charlotte was seriously indignant when somebody had the gall to take the low money offer in the game. She didn't mention her meeting with colleagues, perhaps out of a sense of caring for his current difficult case, and the fatigue he must be feeling from the journey – they still had time to make decisions and arrangements.

TWENTY

The following morning, Octavian arrived at the incident room to find only McAlister sitting there. They exchanged pleasantries as he sat down with his coffee. Everybody else was already out, still checking Mercedes owners.

'Have a nice evening last night, Beth?'

'Yes, thank you. Me and Ian went to our regular yoga class.'

Octavian's face expressed surprise. 'He does yoga? That's an interesting fact for me to store away for use in the future.'

She smiled. Octavian drank his coffee.

Williams came in. She had something to say to Octavian, but she sat down at her desk, making him get up and walk over to her.

'Morning, Katie.'

'Morning, Boss. You saw in Kezia Garswood's statement she mentioned that Lily was having a dispute with another girl, over a boy. Well, that girl has finally got back to me, and I've arranged a meeting.'

'Okay. Take Green with you.'

She had been concerned that he would want to get involved personally; that was why she stayed away from McAlister.

'I'll be fine. I don't need Green.'

'Humour me, Katie. I've already had Aamina head-butted on this investigation. I'm feeling a bit protective towards my team at the moment. Besides, he's a prospect. It's good for him.'

'Very well.'

Williams let Green drive her in his Ford Focus. They headed to the Whitefield area of North Manchester, not far from Lily Bowden's flat in Prestwich. Williams noticed that the inside of the car was spotlessly clean. Not just a lack of any fast food detritus, but there was no dust in any of the plastic compartments, and when he squirted water on the windscreen and hit the wipers it was not, like with her car, resembling the work of a plasterer.

'Have you just had this valeted?' she asked.

He was fairly surprised by the question. 'No.'

They drove along. Green thought he should make some conversation but nothing interesting came to mind.

'We're meeting this girl where she works,' Williams told him.

'She was Lily Bowden's friend?'

'Apparently, yes. Whatever *friend* means these days, though.'

They arrived at a shopping precinct and found a parking spot. While Green got a ticket for the Focus, Williams walked the few yards to have a look at the nail salon where eighteen-year-old Courtney Leigh-Waller worked as a technician. It was a neon-lit unit between two takeaway shops, with an enclosed alleyway to one side. The area was busy with morning shoppers and there was a nice smell wafting out of the Greggs bakery. Green caught up, and they went into the salon. A less-than-pleased mature woman met them; clearly the salon owner. Williams asked for Courtney.

'She's out the back. Can you walk round the side, please? And be quick with her.'

'Certainly,' replied Williams, with exaggerated politeness.

Williams gestured for Green to back up, and they stepped back outside. 'Down the ginnel.'

'Ginnel?'

'Tunnel. The alley. How old are you?'

They emerged at the back of the salon onto a service road, with trees and yet another new housing estate being built beyond. Williams led the way through a squeaky iron gate, finding Courtney there, sorting through a new delivery.

'Courtney Leigh-Waller? I'm DS Williams of Greater Manchester police.'

'Yeah, you called me. What can I do for you?'

Courtney was a white girl with a fabulous fake tan. Her blonde hair was quite big, and she had gone heavy on the eye make-up, making her look like Cleopatra. Green, however, was certainly taken with her.

Williams took out her notebook. 'I just wanted to ask about your relationship with Lily Bowden?'

'Friends.'

Williams saw that Courtney looked sideways when she said that.

'You had a fall-out recently?'

Courtney shrugged. 'Did we?'

'Over a boy.'

'Well, that's normal. Yeah, she was out of order with my boyfriend. Not for the first time. That's all.'

'You threatened her?'

Courtney pulled a face. Then she became emboldened. 'Yeah, I did. So what? I didn't shoot her with an arrow. Is this going to take much longer? I'm busy, as you can see.'

A car stopped, just beyond the gate. Green and Williams saw a teen male looking at the scene from the window of his old VW Scirocco. Williams also saw the slight shake of the head from Courtney, before the Scirocco moved off hurriedly.

Williams actually physically pushed Green in the side. 'Green! Get the car!'

Green bolted away. Williams ran after him, back down the alley. She set off running down the street, barging people out of the way. Green caught her with the Focus within sixty seconds, she jumped in and they roared off. The road behind the shops ran parallel to the main road, so they were hoping the Scirocco was held up even momentarily, and they could catch it up somewhere. Williams was on her radio asking for local assistance.

'There it is!' shouted Green.

The Scirocco was, indeed, trying to squeeze by two lorries, before it got out onto the main road and accelerated away. Green put his foot to the floor and went after it, his blues and siren on. It was a chase, Green's first of his career. Cars and vans got out of his way. It was exhilarating for him. The speeds increased as the Scirocco driver desperately wanted to get away, but Green drove really well to stay with him. At one stage, the Scirocco was on the wrong side of the road, making Williams question the risk of continuing the pursuit, but it came back over and turned into a housing estate, perhaps hoping to shake them off in the tighter roads that the driver surely knew. Green stayed on its tail, and the chase was fairly short lived as the Scirocco failed to take a corner and smashed into a parked Audi. The driver fled on foot, leaving behind his iPod, some coins and his left training shoe in his panic to escape.

Green screeched to a stop and was out on foot, in hot pursuit. He got the man within fifty yards and bounced him off a fence, putting him down. But there was a blade in the man's hand. Green heard Williams scream out a warning, but he had seen it clearly and he jumped on the man's face, before kicking out at the knife hand. The fugitive lost all interest in the fight, let the knife fall away (to be kicked further away by Green) and then he was roughly on his front being handcuffed. From there on, the man was stupidly indignant at his treatment.

'I'm not resisting! I'm not resisting! Why are you doing this to me, man? Aaaaargh.' Passers-by stopped and stared at the scene, and the man appealed to them from his prone position. 'Film this police brutality.'

'Shut up!' said Green.

Williams was on the phone to Octavian. Local patrol cars arrived, but everything decreased in intensity once the officers saw that the situation was contained.

TWENTY-ONE

Octavian hurried downstairs to meet Williams as she entered the reception of the Wythenshawe police station. 'Are you all right, Katie?'

'Fine, Boss.'

'Good. Good. You go upstairs, everyone wants to see you. Where's Green?'

'He's bringing Courtney Leigh-Waller in through the back. I thought it better to speak to her here.'

'Very well done, Katie.'

Octavian made his way through the building. He saw a woman police constable guiding a sullen Courtney Leigh-Waller inside; then Green entered. Octavian gently pummelled the young man in the stomach, like a proud father, having been very worried for him.

'You okay, Lewis?'

'Yes, Sir.'

'Well done. Who is the guy? Darren Kennedy, I heard his name is?'

'Yes, Boss. Local dealer. He had some Class A on him when arrested. DS Williams didn't think he is relevant to the murder enquiry, though.'

'Well, we'll see about that, won't we? Go get a drink. Chill out. Well done, again.'

Green was chuffed to receive praise from Octavian. 'Thanks, Boss.'

The team were excited to hear Williams describe the chase and arrest. There was laughter in the incident room and it lightened the overall mood of the investigation. Green came upstairs and was treated like a returning hero. Knowles tried to bounce him off a filing cabinet and then hugged him. Green was smirking with happiness that he was now fully accepted.

Courtney Leigh-Waller's duty solicitor arrived, so Octavian and Williams got on with interviewing her. The young woman sipped her tea and spoke quite maturely to them; she had nothing to hide, so no need to *No Comment* throughout. She knew Lily Bowden originally online, a friend of a friend in a group. They met, they hung out, she liked her. But Lily had become too keen on Courtney's boyfriend. No, the man in the car was not her boyfriend. So, she liked to do drugs a bit. No, Lily didn't know the drug dealer, as far as she knew.

Courtney Leigh-Waller answered everything Octavian and Williams could think to ask her. They stepped out of the interview room, virtually eliminating her from their enquiries.

Octavian had taken down the boyfriend's name. He had McAlister do a check on him, which came back clean.

The team got back to checking Mercedes owners. Octavian took a phone call, and then left the station. He drove towards Salford Quays. He parked the Golf on a supermarket car-park and walked to a *Starbucks*. He was first to arrive, so ordered a simple coffee (he was not a *Starbucks* regular) and sat down, facing the windows. He shook his coat off, the weather was starting to warm up. He watched the other customers; usual family units, chatting girlfriends, and lone businessmen.

He saw her arrive. Hair in a ponytail, a touch of red lipstick, short leather jacket and pale jeans (were they back in fashion?), black

Doc Martins, one holding the door open as she entered with a big shoulder bag, looking for him. She saw him, gave a tiny smile. He stood up to buy her drink but she waved him back and approached the counter herself.

He stood up again, like a proper gentleman, as Kezia Garswood joined him. She put down her bag, begged him to sit back down, and they settled in. He drank some coffee, trying to ignore the youthful joy that welled up within him, on seeing her. As with the last time he had been in her presence, leaving aside the horrible shock, she did look very changed from his memory of her. But, out of that context, she was a very attractive woman. She looked drained, of course, probably from lack of sleep.

She asked if he had been waiting long. He asked how she was bearing up. They looked at each other. It was so strange, after all those years.

'Tony, I wanted to ask you what's happening with the investigation?'

'I know you do. I can't tell you anything.'

'And I knew you'd say that. I read a lot of crime novels.'

'I remember that you used to like books a lot.'

She half-giggled. 'Yeah, I wanted to be a book editor. Christ. I ended up working as a doctor's receptionist, among other things. Finished up as a single mum to two...one child, living in a flat in Prestwich, on Universal Credit. Oh, you wanted to be a writer. Did you ever do that?'

He smiled. 'Not yet. So, what brought you over this way?'

'Dean. Lily's father. His work was here. Then, coincidentally, some relatives drifted this way. Prestwich's all right. It's not exactly inner-city slum.' She sipped her coffee and assessed him over the cup. 'So, you made it. To the Met and back. DI.'

He didn't remember mentioning London, or even giving her his phone number, but the traumatic events of their recent meeting must have fogged his memory.

'What brought you home?' she asked.

'My wife couldn't stand London anymore.'

'Where's she from?'

'She's from Lymm.'

'Oh, nice. You and me walked around the lake at Lymm, once, remember? One hot summer day.'

The memory of her in white tee-shirt, mind-blowingly smooth legs below tiny denim shorts, and Adidas trainers, without socks, walking ahead of him, glancing back, laughing.

'Yes, I remember.'

'Were you surprised that I contacted you?'

'Yes and no. If our roles were reversed, I would want you to speak to me.'

'Can you at least tell me if you have anybody...what's the term, in the frame?'

'We're following enquiries. Have you anything new to say about Lily's life? No unusual behaviour that you realise now, looking back?'

'No, she was the same as always. Always exactly the same.'

She had crossed her legs, and he could see that she couldn't stop squeezing her knee. Her eyes constantly moved up and down from him to the table. Perhaps she was now on some prescription medication to help her cope. Not for the first time that day, he doubted how wise it was to have agreed to meet, but he really needed to see her again. He had broken up badly with some girlfriends during his youth, but that had not been the case with Kezia. Of course, the drifting apart had seen arguments and moods, but at the end they had expressed love for each other, perhaps both thinking they might only be apart for a year or two.

'Kezia, I'll come and tell you as soon as I have anything for definite.'

'Will you? You promise? I'm going out of my mind. It's so unfair and wrong.' Tears came to her eyes. He held her hand. 'She was only a baby. Just a stupid waste.'

'Yes, it was a terrible waste.'

'What do I do, Tony?'

'You keep going for your son. You leave it to me. Then you deal with whatever comes next in the process. It will become easier over time. I'm sorry, I don't have a handkerchief to give you.'

She sniffled. 'It's okay. I'm sorry, I knew you wouldn't say anything. But I feel safer, somehow, just seeing you. I hope you don't mind.'

'Of course, I don't mind. You've always been with me, you know. You're my Kezia.'

189

'Stop it, you'll have me crying for old times' sake next.'

They smiled. They continued with their coffee.

He stayed with her for another twenty minutes, or so. She told him of the despairing reaction of Lily's father, which was hard to hear. Her family were being great. She was happy to listen to him talk about baby Jack. He told her about his squad. He mentioned Ezi.

'He sounds interesting. You never did take me to Indonesia, Tony? The furthest we got was Ibiza.'

'Sorry about that, I wasn't as in love with Indonesia as I am now. Age, I suppose. We've changed a lot, haven't we?'

'We have. Hey, I should let you get back to work.'

They left the coffee shop. She hugged him, which fairly blew his mind, catapulting him back to his youth, but he kept his face impassive.

'Thank you, Tony. I feel better. I will wait to hear from you.'

'You have my number if you need anything.'

'Thanks.'

He watched her shoulder her bag and walk off. Unlike that time at Lymm lake, she didn't glance back at him. When she was out of sight he headed to the Golf.

TWENTY-TWO

While Octavian was out and about, a big story developed in Wythenshawe, as a fire broke out at an old peoples' Residential Home. Datta heard about it and monitored it throughout the day, wondering if Taheer was involved. She was worried more than usual.

She saw her boyfriend that evening. His crew had been there on scene. It had been one of the worst things he had ever attended. He had personally rescued five elderly people, but sadly four pensioners had been lost before the blaze was brought under control. He had six years under his belt as a firefighter, seeing most things, from child deaths to motorway pile-ups, but that hit him surprisingly hard.

Datta cuddled him in the bath, at one point in the night. He was not weeping, he was just morose, and dead tired. She continued to sponge hot water over his shoulders and kissed his forehead. He kissed her gently on the lips. They looked each other in the eye for many minutes, while *Adele* sang from the living room.

**

It was Maria Knowles's birthday. A game of snooker had been ruled out as a special treat, so Knowles took his wife to her favourite restaurant in Knutsford. They had a lovely meal, pasta and pizza, with wine, dessert, coffee, before taking a stroll through the old, exclusive Cheshire town, home to many a Premiership footballer, and which Knowles believed was the base for some classic novel, from Jane Austen, perhaps. The streets were tight, built for just horse and cart, and the buildings were pretty – what architectural style he did not know. It was a warm evening. They actually held hands as they walked a big circle back towards a bar.

'How are your friends?' she asked.

'My friends?'

'Your work colleagues.'

'Oh, them?' He laughed. 'They're all right. I told you we had the new DS. She's efficient, quite friendly. The PC with us is a good lad.'

'How's Shirley? Is she still single?'

'Who'd have her?'

'How's the Indian fella?'

'Indonesian. He's a good man. I don't envy him with what we have on at the moment.'

They reached the bar. She wanted a cuddle. He obliged.

'Thanks for taking me out, Phil. We should do it more often, like the old days.'

'I'm having a good time. It's beans on toast for the rest of the week, though.'

**

Speight went to the gym for a couple of hours. It was a sparse place, based in an old church, one half given over to boxing training, while the other had running machines and various other equipment. One of the walls had the random, multi-coloured hand and foot holds for climbers, but it was not their night. Everywhere Speight looked, there were fit, tattooed guys, doing what fit, tattooed guys do in gyms. She tried to focus her mind on what she was doing.

**

McAlister and her man stayed in for the evening with a film and various snacks. It was parents' evening at school for Williams and her husband. Green went to the cinema with his girlfriend – being a smart boy, he let her choose what they watched.

**

Octavian put Jack down for the night, then entered the lounge and poured another glass of red wine for Charlotte, and topped up his glass of sparkling apple juice. He was always happy to watch whatever she liked on the TV, as long as it wasn't anything with Ant and Dec in it. He snuggled in with her on the sofa. He kissed the pure skin of her slender neck.

'Will we get away this summer?' she asked, squirming with pleasure.

'Of course. What are you thinking? Stay in England again?'

'Yes. Maybe Abersoch. I know that's Wales, before you say. Jack will love the beach.'

He continued to nuzzle. 'I'll love seeing you in your tiny bikini.'

'Oh, that's not been out since before Covid. I'm not sure I'm still good for that.'

'Don't be silly. You're as gorgeous as ever. All the men will stare at you.'

'Do you want men to stare at me?'

'Not necessarily. It's just a fact. What's on TV now?'

'Ant and Dec's new show.'

He gritted his teeth for a moment; then continued to kiss her neck. 'Okay.'

They turned in early, and made love. They must have fallen asleep immediately afterwards because when Octavian's phone woke him, he was still in Charlotte's sweet embrace. He extricated himself without waking her. The clock told him it was just after 3 a.m. It was Datta calling.

'Yes, Aamina?'

TWENTY-THREE

Octavian drove past the towering domes of the Trafford Centre shopping mall and, soon after, saw the flashing blue lights in the darkness, identifying that he had arrived at his destination. He parked the Golf and walked forward towards one of the bridges over the Manchester Ship Canal. It was a bit nippy at that ungodly hour, so he buttoned up his coat. The road was closed. In the light from a streetlamp, he was challenged by a PC and allowed under the tape, once his warrant card had been checked. In the gloom, the bridge appeared like a sleeping monster, arching up into the slowly brightening sky. Datta spotted him and walked over. She was in a beanie hat and a big brown overcoat. Her face seemed strained, like it had been a shock to the system to be woken in the middle of the night.

'Selamat pagi, Boss.'

Octavian was pleasantly surprised to hear some Indonesian spoken.

'Can we call this morning yet, Aamina? What have we got here exactly?'

'A male victim, looks to be about fourteen. Hanging from the bridge. Dr Shevington, he's down there now, Boss, says maybe for a couple of days.' She held her notebook into the beam from a patrol car. 'Name of Victor Agunbiade, according to his bus pass. Hands tied behind his back, so not a suicide.'

'Who found him?'

'Two local men, walking home from a club. One went down there to relieve himself, which was how the victim was spotted. Can't be seen from the road level.'

'Let's have a look.'

At that moment, Williams and Knowles arrived, separately in their cars, so Octavian waited for them (Knowles yawning widely) and they all went gingerly down the bank together, illuminated by their wavering torches. They found Dr Shevington and the SOCO officers, and, right on cue, a halogen lamp was connected and the underside of the bridge lit up. They had already seen the gruesome shape of the victim as they descended, mainly because he was wearing a white tracksuit, and under the glare of the light he looked an even more tragic and pathetic sight. He was a slim black youth, hanging rigid from an iron girder, perhaps four feet from the bank. A member of the SOCO team took some flash photography, especially of the rope in situ, prior to them attempting to bring the body down.

'Any address?' Octavian asked Datta.

'No, but there is only one Agunbiade family in the local area.'

'You and Phil go there. Okay?'

Octavian and Williams moved forward towards Dr Shevington, but stayed out of the crime scene. The doctor was wrapped up warm with a scarf at the neck and a flat cap on his head. In the strange light he looked quite fearsome.

'I won't say good morning,' growled Dr Shevington. 'This is getting horrendous, Octavian.'

Octavian and Williams climbed back up to the roadway, with her giving him a helping hand for the last few feet.

'Let's hope this new victim is connected to one of the others,' said Williams.

'I bet he's not. What are we not doing, Katie? Are we missing something obvious?'

'I don't think so. Maybe it is totally random, after all.'

'We'll make an appeal for anyone who knows a Mercedes SUV owner. Somebody may know about one that's unregistered, kept in a garage, or something.'

They walked away from the scene.

'Something Knowles said,' started Octavian. 'That the killer is targeting children because he had a bad childhood. Our man on CCTV still looks quite young, so maybe he felt excluded in his teens. Anger. I'll get Beth to look at the internet for anybody ranting about the unfairness of how his life has turned out, etc.' They reached their vehicles. 'Let's head in.'

TWENTY-FOUR

Both McAlister and Speight arrived in the incident room at 8 o'clock, even though it was Speight's day off. Octavian was drinking coffee in front of the white board that he had a strong urge to throw out of the window. He turned to look at them.

'Morning, my favourite police officers in the whole of Manchester. Shirley, it's your day off.'

'Aamina texted me, Boss. And it's not as if I've got a hunky fireman to keep me happy in bed of a cold morning.'

Octavian grimaced at McAlister. 'Did we need to hear that?'

'Worked for me,' laughed McAlister, taking off her coat, while turning all her computer equipment on.

'Beth,' said Octavian. 'When you have settled in, we need to talk.'

'What will the topic be? Hunky fireman again?'

'No. People raging on the internet.'

'Really? How sad. Okay.'

Octavian received a text: Datta informing him that they were with the new victim's family. Williams entered, bidding good morning to her female colleagues.

'It's your day off, Shirley,' she said.

'We've done that, already,' said Octavian, grinning.

Williams brewed up; then was invited to sit with Octavian.

'The one link we have, is that it's random. I'm going to ask Beth to look for local internet ragers. You know, young guys angry that women won't date them, or because Manchester United no longer win anything. That sort of thing. It's a long shot. No pun intended.'

'No, we might get lucky. If there's some disturbed guy ranting about stuff, he might give himself away, somehow. What else can we do, I don't know? Do you want me to do the appeal for the Merc?'

'Do you want to do that?'

'Yes, I do. I will speak to DCI Horsefield, as I know how he likes to bring the media in on things. I'll get that out there today.'

'Thanks, Katie.' He indicated McAlister.

'Yes, yes,' said Williams, getting up and moving away.

'I'm all ears, Boss,' said McAlister.

Octavian told her what he was thinking. She listened, mentioned that she was aware of cases nationwide where people posted rants before going on to carry out acts of violence. She got straight onto it.

Octavian got up and wandered about the office. Lily Bowden's image caught his eye, making him think about Kezia, so he spun on his heels and looked out the window. 'Where's Green?'

'Dentist,' replied Speight.

'My team must have the best teeth on the force.'

Williams had called down and received an invitation for a chat with Horsefield. Octavian nodded at her as she departed.

'More coffee,' Octavian said to nobody in particular.

Knowles and Datta came in. While Knowles sat at his desk and yawned like a resting lion, Datta reported to Octavian, 'Victor Agunbiade's family thought he was with relatives, and that's why they hadn't reported him missing.' She handed over a snapshot, which Octavian added to his infamous white board, writing the name underneath.

'Go on, please, Aamina.'

'Normal boy. No gang connections. A good student. Family members devastated and totally mystified by it.'

'He must have had a problem with someone. Or he was picked at random.'

Green came in, wanting to apologise for his absence, but Octavian waved that away. 'All right, Lewis? Had any treatment done?'

'Just a check-up and clean, Sir.'

'Jolly good. Beth's next for the dentist, but he'll just want to take them all out.'

McAlister turned her chair, playfully aghast. 'Harsh. Harsh but fair. I might have something here, Boss.'

'Internet rage stuff?'

'No, not yet. I was having another look at the Mercedes owners. There's a man called Chris Corbett. He's got form for GBH and burglary. He lives in Benchill, but has previous addresses in... Prestwich and Heywood.'

The mood in the room lightened significantly. Even Knowles stopped yawning and got to his feet. McAlister printed off Corbett's details, and Octavian took a page, handing it to Green.

'Green, get over there. Do a discreet walk-by, see if the Mercedes is at the property. We'll be right behind you.'

'Yes, Sir!'

Green grabbed his jacket and rushed out.

Knowles was having a lightbulb moment. 'Boss, if I'm not mistaken, I think I know this Corbett. Likes to think of himself as a hard man. Hangs around with some of the local proper tough fellas. He'll probably kick off.'

'That's fine by me.' He turned to the others. 'Shirley and Aamina, Beth has something to look at that could do with a lift.'

Speight looked disappointed. 'But I feel like having a barney today.'

'All right, you come along.'

Datta crossed her legs and smiled. 'I'm good here.'

They donned stab-proof vests and left in Octavian's Golf. It was only a couple of minutes away, in one of the older estates, near to Sharston and the motorway. It was starting to rain a little bit. As soon as they parked, they spotted Green ambling along towards them and he spoke to Octavian through the open driver's window, although he had to pause as a truck went by on the main road, right behind the houses.

'There is damage to the Mercedes. It's just up there, maybe ten houses along. Damage is all across the front.'

They all piled out of the Golf.

'It's bloody raining,' complained Speight.

Knowles looked upwards; not calling that rain.

'Boss!' Knowles was suddenly pointing.

A marked police patrol car was stopping, almost exactly at where Green had indicated where the Mercedes was. They all jumped back into the Golf to wait to see what was happening. Knowles found himself squeezed between Speight and Green in the back seat. Naturally, she leant away from him. The officers in the patrol car were taking their sweet time, as expected.

'Who do you support?' Knowles asked Green.

'Sorry? What?'

'Football. Who do you follow?'

'I don't really like football. I don't really like sport, in general. Sport is just new people doing exactly the same things that other people have done before them in the past.'

Knowles tried to digest the sport thing; then asked, 'What are you into, then?'

'I like films.'

'Oh, films are cool. I love the movies. What's your favourite film?'

'*Navy Seals.*'

Knowles had nothing further to say to that. Speight had to stifle a giggle, looking out the side window.

The uniformed police officers finally exited their patrol car and went to an address opposite to where Chris Corbett lived. Octavian and his team realized it was just a coincidence, after all. The officers got no reply, so left a leaflet, probably something to do with a neighbourhood watch scheme. They got back in the vehicle and drove away.

'Let's go,' said Octavian.

They all climbed out of the Golf, to discover that the rain was even heavier.

'Shit,' said Speight.

'Hey!' Green suddenly cried out, shocking Speight so much, by his side, that she instinctively hit his chest with the back of her hand.

A man in a blue hoodie and jeans had left their targeted house and run away down the street. Green was straight after him, with Octavian also in the chase.

'Sod that for a game of soldiers,' laughed Knowles.

Octavian ran along the street. Green and Chris Corbett (he assumed it was Chris Corbett) were off towards the main road. Octavian just got out to the road in time to see Green bolt down the path that ran between the back of the houses and a park.

As the rain got even heavier, Chris Corbett ran along the perfectly straight path, fenced in, with Green in hot pursuit. Corbett was not as fit as Green, who began to catch up. Halfway down the mile-long pathway, Green finally launched a rugby tackle, bringing Corbett down in a big splash of water. Instantly, Corbett was fighting Green, and they were soon drenched and filthy. Punches were exchanged on the ground like a mixed martial art bout, and then Octavian arrived to pile in with his knees onto

Corbett, who almost immediately had had enough.

'There's no need for this,' cried Corbett. 'I'm not resisting.'

It was the same dialogue from the drug dealer that Green arrested in Whitefield. Green just handcuffed the man and got him on his feet.

Octavian and Green frogmarched Corbett back to his home address.

'Nobody else in the house, Boss,' announced Knowles. 'Because this gentleman ran away, we entered and checked everywhere, out of concern for other people.'

'Good work, DS Knowles.'

Thankfully, for Speight's hair, the downpour started to ease off. She and Knowles had been examining the front of the Mercedes, parked on the drive.

'All right, Chris?' laughed Knowles, looking at Corbett. 'Where were you going in such a hurry?'

'I'm a passionate jogger, don't you know? It's DS Knowles, isn't it?'

'What's happened to your car?'

'What do you mean?'

'The damage to the front end?'

Corbett turned his hot face up to the rain for a moment. 'The car's ten years old, Detective Sergeant Knowles. It's had a rough life. Like your wife.'

Knowles laughed even more at that. Octavian, panting hard and resembling a drowned rat, stepped over to examine the Mercedes.

'Where have you been in it recently, Chris?' asked Knowles.

'It's not left the drive for six months,' replied Corbett. 'I've got a SORN notification from the DVLA in Swansea for it.'

'Yeah, right.'

'DS Knowles, do me a favour. Go back over to it. That's it. Now, lift the bonnet.'

Knowles reached with his fingertips and the bonnet lifted up. He and Octavian looked inside.

'Does anything grab your attention?' asked Corbett.

There was no engine.

Corbett laughed. 'Now, you can take that away and your experts will tell you it's not moved for six months.'

Chris Corbett enjoyed more rain on his face before starting to laugh hysterically. Octavian was deflated, and looked like he wanted to knock Corbett out.

Corbett looked right at Octavian. 'You're in charge of the murder investigation. I saw you on the news. You're barking up the wrong tree after me for that, mate. It couldn't be me, I've got a great alibi.'

'And what would that be?' asked Octavian, through gritted teeth.

'It's classic, man! You muppets! I was released from Walton nick only yesterday.'

Chris Corbett proceeded to laugh his head off.

TWENTY-FIVE

Octavian sat in his home office thinking about the case. His coffee had gone cold near to his hand. The file of his Indonesian butler story was open on the computer; he really did feel that writing relaxed him. He didn't know what other detectives did while off-duty; fishing, or watercolour painting, or drinking malt whiskey, but being able to go off into his world of fiction kept him from exploding. He had just written the kidnapping scene of the rich American woman's son in Bali, something that he was surprised didn't happen more often in real life. Now his main character's boyfriend was in charge of handling the ransom request.

'I'm afraid I do have to tell you officially that your son, Mr Rome Lipman, has become the victim of a kidnapping. We have CCTV footage of the moment your son was abducted and there has since been contact, through Mr Finucane, here.'

Margo never took her eyes off Ari. Only her hands, with the gold jewelry, moved into different nervous positions on her crossed thigh. 'Thank you, Mr Syamsul. So, can you assure me that the Bali police are taking a break from robbing tourists, and are seeking to free my son?'

Wow, thought Raja. Didn't see that coming. He looked at Ari, whose face remained the same.

'I can assure you, Mrs Lipman, that the investigation is being conducted at a much higher level than the Bali traffic police. We will do everything in our powers to identify the perpetrators of this crime, secure the release of Mr Lipman, and make arrests.'

'Can I not just pay what they ask?'

'We don't advise that. But it could be an option if we don't make as much progress as we would like.'

'What now?'

'With your permission, my team and I will base ourselves at your property. Perhaps Mr Finucane can continue to converse with the kidnappers, while investigations continue in Bali and other locations.'

'You think my son is no longer in Bali?'

'That's most likely.'

'I want Raja to handle the interaction with these people.'

Ari glanced at Raja. 'I'm sure that will work.'

'Then, shall we go?'

Margo was up on her feet. Everybody jumped up deferentially. They all filed off the yacht towards the vehicles.

The empty snooker room was quickly established as an incident room, with tables and chairs, phone lines, computers, and seven police officers. Raja comforted Mrs Mirdad, the head maid, commending her for handling the situation well. Then she was set to work providing rooms for Ari and his people to use, to sleep between shifts. Mr Roberts threw himself into catering for the extra bodies, just to keep his mind off the drama.

Then everybody settled into a routine of waiting. The phone rang often, as always, but just to do with business, or for Margo's social calendar. The kidnappers' phone line remained open but silent.

It was so strange for Raja – he was used to telling Ari whenever something interesting or worrying happened. Now he was living through such things with his policeman boyfriend. Their relationship was on hold. Raja spent some time in his room alone. He tried to read a novel. He watched a movie, and realized that Rafael Putra Bagaskara had a minor role in it. Raja showered, always listening for the shout that he was needed. It was quite a difficult time for him.

Then London and Harper were brought home by the police. Margo didn't actually rush out to embrace them, but she stepped outside the house to welcome her children home. Raja and Ari stood at the door, watching. In fact, all the staff were looking out from various viewpoints. The girls looked no different. There was no outward sign of distress with either. That was not the case with Harry Rashford, who resembled one of the Halloween party zombies, probably through lack of sleep, and he needed to be supported by the actor man, Rafael. Raja was surprised to see the man still with them – surely his people had advised him to distance himself from the scandal of a kidnapping. But, there he was, arm around the Englishman, and touching London's hand when she looked for him.

The four of them were settled in, and Mr Roberts gave them something to eat. Harry declined the offer of the family doctor, and he went off to sleep, which turned out to last for nearly twenty-four hours. The girls and Rafael kept to themselves. Raja concluded that their privileged upbringing was insulating them against the shock of the event, or they just didn't care, and he left them to their own devices.

And then the first call came in from the kidnappers, and Raja was rushed by a policeman to join Ari in the snooker room.

**

Octavian went upstairs. He was in the action of getting dressed in his bedroom, when he felt the need to sit down on the bed, so demoralized was he with his current situation. Charlotte was sitting there, doing her hair in a mirror. She moved to slide in behind him, to hold him around the midriff.

'We don't have to go out,' she told him. 'I can put Lucy and Gareth off for another night.'

'I'm all right, baby. Just taking a moment. A bit tired, you know.'

'Are you worried about your interview tomorrow?'

'Somewhat, I suppose.'

She kissed his bare shoulders.

'Is the babysitter here?' he asked.

'If by that you mean my mother, then, yes.'

'Where are we going again? Remind me.'

'Well, it's their turn to choose, so it's TGI Fridays.'

'Oh, good, I need a new Collins glass.'

She continued to kiss his shoulders.

He pointed at the dress hanging on the wardrobe door. 'Don't wear that. I don't like it.'

She laughed at his pathetic attempt to be dominant, and she pulled him back for a full-on snog.

**

Speight's throwaway comment about a hunky fireman had some basis in fact, as Taheer had been trying to arrange a double-date with his colleague, Harry, (after being given specific orders from Aamina to keep trying). The only slight problems were that Harry had a girlfriend, until recently, and Harry disliked the police (Aamina excepted) because they once prosecuted him for something he thought only warranted a caution. Harry fancied the trousers off Shirley Speight, having seen her at events like the Fire Station charity fun run and Aamina's last birthday party, but he was a man of principle and Shirley simply had to be denied the joy of Harry love.

'She's recently discovered she's into taking it rough,' threw in Taheer.

'I'll have some of that, mate. Set it up.'

They laughed at Harry's instant change of mind. They were taking a breather while on a shout; dealing with a pub cellar that got caught in a recent flash flood.

'Mate,' continued Harry. 'Always wanted to ask. Does Aamina let you use her handcuffs on her?'

'I've never thought about it.'

'Will Shirley let me, do you think?'

'She'll pepper spray you, if that's what you're into.'

Speight and Aamina got ready at Speight's flat (Speight showing more cleavage than Datta), and they met the men in a heaving and noisy Cheadle bar. Aamina, her hair all black and flowing, looking gorgeous, kissed Taheer. Speight, her blonde hair in a very tight ponytail, and dressed in even tighter clothes, shook Harry's hand, while he complimented her on her appearance. He was in a tight white shirt, and black trousers. The shirtsleeves were rolled up in the warm bar, revealing a full, multi-coloured arm sleeve tattoo on his left arm, which Speight thought looked awesome. 'That's fucking awesome,' she confirmed, stroking it. Harry was bigger than Taheer and very muscled, or maybe that was the tight shirt. He grinned his cheekiest grin at her.

The girls were bought cocktails (non-alcoholic in Aamina's case) and they found a place to settle in at the bar. The music was very loud, but that was helpful for Harry to brush his lips on Speight's ear in order to make conversation.

Speight pulled away, playfully shocked. 'What did you say?'

Datta and Taheer watched on with interest. Harry leant back in to repeat himself.

'Handcuffs?' asked Speight, loud enough for her friends to hear.

Taheer grinned, while Datta acted a bit flustered.

Octavian drove Charlotte away from their driveway. He noticed that the latest builders' skip at the neighbour's house was already full to bursting. 'Seventeen skip loads for that little extension. It didn't take seventeen skips when they built the whole estate.'

'You're getting so old,' she teased.

'I know. I really should learn to chill.'

They headed along the main road from Altrincham towards Manchester. He rested his hand on her thigh as they moved along. She had found a very mellow music station on the radio. Suddenly, and ironically as they were passing the main VW dealership, they were cut-up by a speeding Golf, causing Octavian to slam on the brakes, and blare the horn. Furious with the driver, Octavian started to go after him, until a concerned Charlotte squeezed his thigh.

'Tony, no,' she said calmly. 'It's not important.'

He instantly cooled, and patted her hand.

'Yes, you're right. I'm sorry, baby.'

'I love you, you know.'

'I love you more.'

**

Early the next morning, Williams drove Octavian to Manchester City Centre. She thought it best that he wasn't in the slightest bit flustered or mentally tired by having to drive into the busy city, but in the end, she took a few wrong turns trying to find the Greater Manchester Police Headquarters, and they ended up having the full tour of East Manchester. He joked that he had already seen the Etihad Stadium.

Octavian was relieved when they finally got there with ten minutes to spare, for their meeting with the powers that be, and the serious case review of the recent spate of youth murders. Both of them were in their best uniforms. They were fully prepared, having discussed what to say in the days before, and on the drive in. They waited nervously in an ante-room, until summoned through. But, as it turned out, it was a fairly brief and cordial meeting. The senior officers, while expressing their concern for the lack of progress, did sympathize with the extreme difficulties of the case. They were keen to offer any kind of support they could. Still, however positive the meeting had been, Octavian still felt on notice to get some results, and soon.

He and Williams stopped at a McDonalds for coffee, before making the trip out of the city. Back at the station, the team watched them enter the incident room.

'Anything new happen while we were away?' asked Octavian.

'No, Boss,' replied McAlister.

Knowles cut through the awkwardness by asking how the meeting went.

'Fairly neutral,' replied Octavian. 'At least we've not had a child killed for a week now.'

'Maybe our man has totally stopped,' suggested Knowles. 'Or he's gone away.'

'Right, anyway,' said Octavian. 'Let's get back to it.'

TWENTY-SIX

In the pool club Knowles, Speight and Green had taken a pool table, just below the bar area. They were joined, at one point, by a pint carrying DS Woolaston. Charles Woolaston was in his late forties and had a florid complexion, like a big drinker, so at first glance you might have thought him out of shape, but then you would notice the boxer's bent nose and the rugby player's cauliflower ears, and you could tell that he was still a hard man.

'Evening all,' said Woolaston.
Knowles grudgingly nodded acknowledgement. 'Woolaston.'

Woolaston indicated Green. 'Who's your friend?'

'That's Green,' was all Knowles said.

Green and Woolaston nodded at each other.

'Nothing yet on the child killer?' Woolaston asked Knowles.

'It's... a... bastard.'

They watched Green potting balls.

'The boy is good,' observed Woolaston.

'You should see him with a crossbow.'

A very attractive young woman arrived to be with Green. Everybody in the bar looked at her, and she actually stopped play on the tables. Her blonde hair was in long pigtails down the front of her chest. Her skin was flawless, and she made the simple white tee-shirt and jeans that she was wearing into a fashion event. Two dirty old men, themselves, Knowles and Woolaston stared at her in such a way that made Speight shake her head with sad amusement.

'Would you like to play?' Green asked Woolaston.

'With her?'

'No, pool?'

Woolaston remembered he was too old and too ugly for the girl to even notice that he was there, so took his cue from its case. Green embraced and kissed his girlfriend.

'Oh, sorry, everyone,' said Green. 'This is Joanna.' He unscrewed his cue and held it without a case, ready to walk out with her. 'I'll see you in the morning.'

'Yeah, goodnight, kid,' said Knowles. 'Nice to see you, Joanna.'

Joanna smiled warmly, showing tiny gaps between her very white teeth that only added to her nubile charm.

Woolaston racked the balls noisily. Knowles and Speight watched Green and Joanna leave the club.

'It's always the quiet ones,' Knowles said, causing Speight to laugh. 'Talking about quiet ones, what's this I hear about you and a certain fireman?'

'Early days.'

'And early nights. Aamina said you took him back to your flat.'

Speight grinned like a Cheshire cat.

'You shameless hussy,' said Knowles, shaking his head in mock disappointment, before moving to take on Woolaston, yet again. He mimed to Speight diving headfirst onto the table and she laughed joyously.

Octavian was sitting in a morning tailback along the M56. It wasn't one of those types of hold-ups where people start walking the dog and playing frisbee on the carriageway; he could see the emergency lights in the distance and the Golf was slowly edging forward every thirty seconds. His phone rang, and he wondered, as he always did at that moment in his life, if it was Kezia. It was McAlister, so he explained his slight delay, and she told him that she might have something on the internet rage angle.

'I'll look at it as soon as I arrive, Beth.'

He crawled past the incident, which had the Fire Brigade and the Highways Agency dealing with a lorry fire. He wondered if he was allowed to rubberneck, being a police officer – recently Cheshire police had filmed people passing accidents and sent them fines in the post. Anyway, the motorway cleared and he made better progress.

He had gotten into the habit of driving into the car-park at the station, rather than parking on the road, when the press attention had been moderately high. But now that they had gone a while, without any further murders, the building was no longer under siege. Still, he went in the back way, got a coffee from the vending machine, and joined his team in the incident room.

'No-one at the dentist?' he enquired.

Everyone politely laughed. They were gathered around the TV monitor, drinking tea or coffee, talking about the night before, or about the best schools. Octavian sat himself down next to Datta.

'I just saw some firefighters on the motorway, Aamina. They're such cool people.'

'Oh, they are, aren't they? I thought about joining once, you know.'

Knowles leaned in. 'If only.'

Datta tutted at him. McAlister started the *Youtube* clip she had to show them.

'This man lives nearby,' said McAlister. 'Name of...'

'I can't take another weird name on this investigation,' interrupted Knowles.

'...Name of Richard Hay...'

'Normal enough name for you?' Datta asked Knowles.

Octavian interjected. 'Focus, guys. Please carry on, Beth.'

'Name of Richard Hay. Usually posts rants about how the education system has failed him. Also, not keen on immigrants. Recently just moaning about his local area. Starting to seem more and more agitated, to me.'

While McAlister had been setting the scene, they had watched the man on screen, muted, but clearly disturbed. He was dishevelled, using hand gestures a lot. He seemed the same build as the Chorlton-cum-Hardy killer. The backshot of the video was a messy flat. McAlister unmuted the clip and they listened to him angrily go on about the council and the state of his local area. McAlister paused it.

'That's not his most offensive stuff. It's just to introduce you to him. He's very on the edge, it seems. Now, why have I picked up on him, as there are quite a few similar things in the North West? Well, he does have a record for robbery. He has been in a Young Offenders Institution. He had previously ranted that he stopped having friends at about sixteen years of age, because that's when he started being let down by people. Lastly, he doesn't drive, but he was the last registered keeper of a Mercedes SUV.'

The team relaxed as they processed the possibilities of this man. Williams stood and stretched. Speight re-did her ponytail.

'Doesn't like teenagers,' pointed out Knowles, as he messed with his kipper tie. 'Lives locally, used to have, probably still does have somewhere, our Merc. Would know Peel Hall Park and Palatine Road. But why go out to

Chorlton-cum-Hardy and Prestwich, and bloody Heywood?'

'To avoid suspicion,' suggested Speight. 'Burglars, for example, go to other counties. He might think he would be quickly in the frame if everything was around here.'

'I like that,' said Knowles.

'People who are like him,' put in Williams. 'They get ignored by the authorities, mainly. But some do go on to act on their anger issues. Then we have the usual questions as to how it was allowed to happen.'

Of course, it all depended on what Octavian thought. 'We had no luck with Hallwood, Davidson or Corbett. But, well done, Beth. This guy ticks a lot of our boxes. We need to bring him in.'

A little bit of internet research found that Richard Hay lived in a council bedsit above a Bookmakers in Crossacres, barely a two-minute drive from their location. Speight noted the Bookmakers element, with her own situation, but imagined a very poky, unpleasant flat, compared to her lovely home, which, incidentally still had Harry sleeping in her bed, after he had finished work and joined her. She controlled her thoughts and pointed out to the others that Google Street maps showed just the one entrance up to the bedsit.

With previous ownership of the Mercedes as the primary reason, Williams organized a warrant and some uniformed back-up. They all knew that it was best to hit a property in the early hours, when the target was still in bed, but Octavian decided to give it a visit that afternoon. Uniform were asked to keep an eye out for Hay.

The team carried on with the other tasks they were doing, which was looking into responses to Williams' TV appeal for the Mercedes. Then they broke for lunch. By 1 p.m. they had heard nothing from Uniform, so Octavian decided to make a move. They suited up in their stab-proof vests and packed their tasers. They took two cars, and were followed by two uniformed PCs in a patrol car. They arrived on the rough streets with a small precinct containing a bakery, a newsagent, a charity shop and the Bookmakers. It looked like rain again, which caused Speight to curse like a navvy. She was looking at the concrete stairs up to Hay's flat. She thought it a sad little place to live.

But then it was all suddenly resolved in an anticlimactic rush over to outside the bakery, as Knowles spotted their man. He got there first, detaining Hay and handcuffing him while he still held his sausage roll and doughnut in their paper bags.

'Search him well,' said Octavian.

Richard Hay appeared highly agitated, scruffy, sleep in the corner of his eyes, unshaven, but he didn't resist. He didn't even ask what was happening. He didn't say anything, apart to confirm who he was when Knowles asked him.

Octavian thought the man was on something, either legally or otherwise. He formally introduced himself and told Hay that they wanted him to come back to Wythenshawe police station to answer some questions. Hay was very compliant, even to handing over his keys so they could search his flat.

Knowles and Datta took Hay and his food away.

'Try not to get head-butted,' Knowles said to Datta.

Everyone else headed up the concrete stairs. They were faced with a metal grill across the door, but one of the keys thankfully opened that. Once inside, there was a strong smell of cannabis. The place looked tidier than it had done on the *Youtube* clip. It was one long room filled with a sofa bed and large TV, bookshelves, clothes drying on a rack, small kitchen area, with just old-style hob, microwave and fridge, then his computer set-up. Beyond that was a bathroom that had a black mould problem. Octavian helped with the search – looking for anything at all relevant.

Speight found a small set of scales, a home-made bong and cannabis in a Tupperware box. There were two gruesome hunting knives which Green bagged up. Octavian perused Hay's mail, which all seemed regular, mostly from the council or the NHS. There were newspapers lying around. Octavian noticed that two had front page headlines about Tom Walsh's murder. But there were many other newspapers from different days without any connection to the case.

Green bagged all the keys that he found. Octavian stepped over to him.

'What type are they, Green?'

Green held them out, inside their plastic bags. One seemed to be a spare for the front door. Another was a *Yale* key for a different property, perhaps his parents' house. There was a *Chubb* key for a garage, perhaps.

The search came to a conclusion. They locked up, returned to their vehicles and left the area.

TWENTY-SEVEN

Octavian and Williams had just interviewed Richard Hay. They climbed slowly up the stairs, both deep in thought.

'So, we know now what his keys are for,' said Williams, pausing with the small of her back against the hand rail. 'The *Yale* for his parents' home. Shall I go and speak to them?'

'Yes, take Aamina or Shirley. See if their son ever mentioned wanting to hurt teenagers, and what they think about his recent activity online. Their address is rural, so look about for the Merc.'

'And the *Chubb* lock is for a garage at his brother's address.'

'Which he says is empty. He scrapped his old Mercedes.'

They entered the incident room. Williams only saw Datta sitting there, so that's who she approached. Octavian waved over Green, and then copied out the address for Hay's brother.

'Yes, Sir?'

'Lewis, here is the address for Richard Hay's brother. And the *Chubb* key. Go pay him a visit. Listen, here's a task for you: if he's there, the first thing you do is ask to see the Mercedes, because you're thinking of buying it from Richard. See what response you get. If he's none the wiser, then show your warrant card and just try to see what's in that garage. Be careful.'

'Yes, Sir.'

Green set off, followed out the door by Williams and Datta.

'Where are Phil and Shirley?' Octavian asked McAlister.

'They went to follow up a lead that came from DS Williams' TV appeal. They just walked to Woodhouse Park to look at a scrap dealer's property. Knowles knows the owner.'

'Okay. I'm popping out.'

Knowles and Speight enjoyed the walk in the sun. They chatted about current affairs, sport, wives and boyfriends.

'Oh, one of my cousins lives in that street, there,' said Speight.

'You don't say?'

'He's a student. The last time I saw him he said something to me along the lines of, "I can't be handling the domestics of shopping and cooking. Life should all be about art".'

'The kid's got a good point.'

They walked on.

'How do you know this scrap dealer?' she asked.

'Just from the pub. He's a little bent, of course. You remember when manhole covers were being nicked off the roads, all around the country, and cyclists were getting killed by the accidents it caused?'

'I do, actually.'

'Well, he wasn't involved in that.'

She shook her head. 'You're so bad.'

'But he's definitely bent. I'm not expecting anything here to do with the case. We should have brought your car, though, he might have offered you fifty quid for it.'

'It's my birthday soon. You can buy me a new car.'

'Yeah, right. Fireman Harry can do that for you. So, you're going great guns with him, you say?'

'You're quite obsessed with firemen. Do you secretly want one for yourself?'

'Ah, there might have been a time for that, Shirley, back in about 2005. But not now.'

She looked sideways at him, not sure if he was joking or not. They arrived at the gates of the scrapyard. The portacabin office sat right at the front of the property, and the owner stepped outside as he recognized Knowles.

'DS Knowles, is it not? What brings you here?'

'Hello, Frank. This is Shirley. We were told you've got a dodgy Merc SUV here.'

Frank Kenworthy pulled a shocked face, which made his tanned bald head crinkle up. He politely shook Speight's hand. 'Hello, Shirley. Hopefully he'll retire soon and you can get a better partner.'

'That's the plan,' smiled Speight.

'Somebody's pulling your chain, people. I don't know anything about that. Come on, let's have a stroll around, see for yourself.'

So that was what they did, looked around, chatted with the amiable Frank Kenworthy, and then took their leave of the man.

'Well, that was a waste of an hour,' said Speight, as they headed back.

'Oh, I don't know, we got a bit of exercise and sunshine.'

Octavian drove to Prestwich, in two minds, all the way there. Kezia had telephoned and begged to see him again. He knew he shouldn't, but he really wanted to. She said she was staying at her sister's, which allowed him to decline, at first, but the sister would be at work, so he went.

Kezia invited him into the house where he had left her, on that terrible day of her daughter's murder.

Her hair was up. She was dressed in a white top and cream tracksuit bottoms, with mules on her feet. 'I forgot you were coming,' she said.

'Really? That's no problem.'

'I made a smoothie. Share with me.'

'Thank you.'

They went into the kitchen. It was a small house, but very well done with modern appliances. There was a view of a garden with a trampoline set into the lawn, which looked much better than those with huge net cages around them. He sat down.

'Yes,' she said. 'I'm on something the doctor prescribed. I remember asking you to visit, but briefly it slipped my mind.'

She poured him some strawberry smoothie into a *Collins* glass, which reminded him of TGI Fridays with Charlotte, the other night. She popped what looked like bamboo straws into the smoothies and took the stool opposite him. He tried not to lose himself in her eyes,

'How are you getting along?' he asked.

'Each day as it comes, I believe everyone keeps saying to me. I've not been home, you know. I'm not going back there.'

'I understand that.'

He tried the smoothie and indicated that it was delicious.

'Thank you for coming, Tony. I just wanted to see you, as you're...like...the key for me to move along.'

'I wish I had some news for you.'

'They won't release Lily's body to me.'

'These things take a bit of time.'

'I know, they explained. Have you arrested anybody? Even a suspect?'

'I can't say, Kezia.'

'I know. Silly of me to ask. I know you'll do your best, Tony. Do you want something to eat?'

'No, I'm good, really.'

'I've got chocolate chip cookies.'

The mention of cookies brought Knowles to mind, and what he would make of this liaison.

'Perhaps I shouldn't have come here, Kezia.'

'No, please, it comforts me. I just sit about all day at the moment, fretting. I didn't mean to make you feel uncomfortable.'

Her hand reached out and he took it without thinking.

'I want to be here, Kezia. I want to help you as you need. It's just difficult, professionally.'

'I'm sorry. I'll try not to call you again.'

'Hopefully something will develop soon, then I can call you. Not with details, just to reassure you.'

She finished her smoothie. 'Have you time for a walk? There's a park just at the end of the garden here.'

'A short walk.'

'Good. Oh, I can't go like this. Give me a second to throw something on.'

He found that he was reluctant to let go of her hand. But she left the room and ran upstairs. He wandered about the kitchen, looking out through the window.

She was quickly down again in jeans and a sweater. She put on socks and boots, which he found unusually personal – little things like that that would have gone unnoticed when they dated as teenagers.

She locked the back door and they walked down to the park. There were the usual dog walkers and one or two people in the distance, but they had the path to themselves. It was actually nice for Octavian, to not be thinking about the case. There was a nice breeze that heralded that summer was nearly with them.

They talked about normal things. They even laughed once or twice.

'I often thought about you,' she said. 'I know you probably think I'm a heartless bitch, but I did.'

'I thought about you, too. Of course, life gets busy. There are relationships and career, and before you know it, you're wondering where your twenties went.'

'So, it is good to see you now.'

'Just, you know, really appalling circumstances.'

'Yes.'

'It's a nice park. Your sister's got a good location.'

They took a fairly short circuit around.

'Will you be okay now?' he asked. 'Will you leave it to me and try to not distress yourself?'

'Yes, Tony. I'll try. Could we meet again? Like this, I mean. Just two old friends getting together.'

They were back to the big gate at the back of the sister's property. He let Kezia in, followed her and closed it up.

'If you need to talk, Kezia, I'll be there for you.'

She stepped into his personal space. He both feared and desired a kiss, but she just embraced him.

'Thank you, Tony. I'm happy that you're around again. I know it's only temporary, I'm not completely silly.'

'I'd better get back, or I'll be missed.'

'Of course. Thank you for coming out.'

TWENTY-EIGHT

Green visited the home of Richard Hay's brother, over in Withington, which he noted was quite close to Chorlton-cum-Hardy, where Englebert Dox had been shot dead. Stuart Hay was not at home, but Mrs Hay was, so Green followed Octavian's instructions to say that Richard was thinking about selling the Mercedes. She clearly had no idea what he was talking about and was about to close the door when he formally introduced himself.

'What do you want with Stuart?' Alice Hay asked, suspiciously.

'We've been talking to his brother. It's just some further enquiries. Has Richard ever been here in a Mercedes?'

'I banned Richard from coming here. He's a complete prick.'

'Oh. Does your husband still have contact with him?'

'They go drinking, very occasionally. Here's Stuart now. Speak to him, will you, I'm watching my favourite programme.'

With that, she closed the door. Stuart Hay approached in a fairly confrontational manner, wondering who the man was, disturbing his missus. If it was Jehovah's Witnesses again, he would give the guy a rocket.

'Mr Stuart Hay?' smiled Green, holding out his warrant card. 'Police Constable Green. Could I have a brief chat? It's nothing to concern you.'

Hay softened his attitude a few degrees. He looked like his brother, but was clean shaven and, as far as Green knew, was compos mentis. He was wearing fluorescent orange overalls and boots that he could sway back in.

'What's this all about?'

'We had reason to speak with your brother, Richard, earlier today.'

'What's he done now?'

'Nothing, we hope. Could you tell me if he owns a Mercedes SUV?'

'He used to. I think he scrapped it.'

'So, it's not here on your property?'

Hays looked at his terraced home. 'I think I'd notice.'

Green produced the *Chubb* key. 'What does this open?'

'No idea. Never seen that before in my life.'

Green noticed the shuffling of the feet done by Hay as he answered. The man might as well have said "come this way, officer, and I'll show you.'

'Mr Hay, with all due respect, I don't believe you. It will be best if you tell me what you know about this key, so I don't have to call for assistance.'

'All right, all right. We have a lock-up. Some shady gear in there. But no cars.'

'Show me, please.'

Stuart Hay sighed deeply, but led Green along the street. Green had passed the big row of communal garages on arrival, and now he watched Stuart Hay open up the first one with a key from his own bunch.

The daylight revealed a big grey mass sitting in the garage, which was certainly not a vehicle. Green had to look hard to realise that it was a pile of roof slates. If no Mercedes, then he had been expecting a tonne of stolen wine, or boxes of mobile phones, but not that.

'What church is missing its roof?' he asked Stuart Hay.

'Builders' yard, not church.'

'Oh, right.'

Green felt a sense of what Octavian must be feeling, as every avenue turned out to be a dead-end.

Williams and Datta's destination was out in the countryside, on the edge of posh Wilmslow, which they both knew well. They found the correct little hamlet, and there was no further need to look around, as the first building they saw had Hay Physiotherapy up in bold blue lettering. It was a whitewashed former farm building and it had clinic and office space on the ground level and living accommodation above. Datta looked in to the business premises, but it was all empty, so they ascended an iron staircase at the side and knocked on a barn door with the top portion open.

A small woman came into view, perhaps mid-fifties.

'Mrs Hay?' enquired Williams, flashing her warrant card.

'Yes. Can I help you?'

'DS Williams and DC Datta of Greater Manchester police. We'd like to have a chat about your son, Richard.'

Her face dropped. 'Oh.'

Mr Hay came to be alongside his wife. He wore the white medical shirt, so he was the physiotherapist. 'What is it, darling?'

'The police again, about Richard.'

Williams and Datta were invited in. There was no offer of beverages, they just sat in the very nice apartment, which had the original roof beams on show, and exposed brick at the far end. Mr Hay did all the talking.

'We don't see Richard that often now. Not since he refused to listen to us. We've tried to aid the authorities about his troubling behaviour.'

'Has Richard ever physically hurt anybody?' asked Williams.

'No, I don't think so. He just needs to vent his anger verbally. Has he hurt somebody? Is that why you're here?'

'Not that we know of.' A doorbell rang. 'That will be my next patient.'

'We'll only be another minute.' Williams paused while Mrs Hay left to deal with the new arrival. 'Your son used to own a black Mercedes SUV, we believe?'

'Yes, he did.'

'Do you know where that is?'

'He scrapped it. It was an early model and it had a crash, anyway.'

'You don't happen to know where he got rid of the vehicle, do you?'

'I do. I went with him. I have the receipt somewhere. Shall I look?'

'Please do.'

Williams and Datta shared a look of resignation, while Mr Hay rooted in his cupboard drawers. He turned back to them and offered a document to Williams.

'Do you mind if I photograph this, Mr Hay?'

'By all means, feel free.'

Williams took a snap of it with her phone, handed it back, and then she and Datta got to their feet. Mr Hay saw them out and down the stairs, and they drove away, more than a little disappointed.

TWENTY-NINE

Octavian got home that evening, showered and changed, and checked his emails: three more rejections of his time-travel book. He told himself yet again that many famous writers were constantly turned down at first. But he also remembered those people who are signed to a book deal after their first enquiry letter.

He got an orange juice and went to sit in the garden with Ezi, while Charlotte prepared dinner. Ezi talked about the funeral again, recounting conversations with relatives. Octavian listened, laughing at some of the stories.

'So, Ezi, how did it feel to be back in Jakarta?'

'It was very strange, after being in Altrincham and South Manchester. I was so surprised that we didn't have any power cuts.'

'Yes. Jeez, it was a long flight back, wasn't it?'

'Well, I had a Pakistani man, on this side, he said who he was and everything, and then slept the whole time. On my other side was a girl from Leeds. She was very nice, we had long chats.'

Octavian grinned; finally, the shy Ezi had brought up the topic of the girl.

'That's great, Ezi. Did you get her number?'

'We exchanged details, yes.'

'What's her name?'

'Her name is Poppy.'

'Poppy? That's a fabulous name. Maybe you can get over there. You'll need to get back at your studies, though.'

Ezi sighed into his garden chair. 'I suppose I must.'

Octavian slapped the boy's leg. 'Anyway, it's good to be home, isn't it? Although, now we've got Charlotte's...'

Charlotte had stepped out into the garden. 'Charlotte's what..?' she asked, squinting suspiciously at Octavian, daring him to mock her cooking again. He blew her a kiss.

The investigation continued along its barren path. No more young people were murdered, which was both a blessing and a curse, in Octavian's opinion, as he desperately wanted significant progress – his career record was very good, up to that point in time. He thought the killer deserved to be brought to justice, for possibly up to six killings, not least for Kezia. She was still on his mind. He thought about the exes who came after Kezia and before Charlotte, but they had little effect on his frame of mind. Perhaps it was that old chestnut about first love never really leaving your heart. Or maybe the cruel realities of adult life meant you always wanted to return to that innocent time of youth. He shook the thoughts away again.

Something else would come along soon, some other murder that would have his team re-tasked. Perhaps it would be a clearer crime, compared to the clueless mystery of this one. He caught the glance of Williams across the incident room – she would be relieved of this duty soon.

Everyone was there; they had just discussed the Richard Hay angle, and not felt anything promising from it. Nothing much had come in that was new from the TV appeal. They would have to wait for the killer to strike again and make a mistake. Meanwhile, continue to look at the dwindling list of possible Mercedes owners.

'Listen up, everyone,' called Knowles. Octavian smirked at his DS, wondering what was coming now. 'It's Shirley's birthday in a few days. We need to let off some steam. Can I organize something? A bit of fun. Bring your significant other, although my wife wouldn't like what I have in mind.'

Shirley crossed her legs and her arms and stared up at Knowles. 'What *do* you have in mind?'

'Well, it wouldn't be a surprise, then, would it? It won't be boring. It's a yes, from everyone, right? Green, you can come, too, I suppose.' Everyone groaned at the teasing unfairness to the young PC. 'As long as you bring that fit bird of yours. So, have I got carte blanche?'

'Yes,' answered McAlister. 'Although you know my fella can't be seen fraternizing with the likes of you lot.'

Knowles half turned away, clenching a fist. 'Yes, naked sauna place, here we come. Where did I leave the number?'

Datta and Speight whistled and heckled him.

'I don't want to go Ferrari driving around Donington Park, or anything like that,' said McAlister. 'I don't want to be scared.'

Knowles gave her a withering look. 'A police officer scared of a track day. As it happens, it's not driving. I will tell you where and when. It's Saturday, of course, so shouldn't be a problem.'

THIRTY

The Hummels brothers, Carl and Hans, were both in their early thirties. They originally came from Berlin, but now preferred to spend time with their wives in much warmer climes, such as Florida, Marbella or Bali. Not that they were particularly rich; they were silent partners in a number of legitimate businesses, and also had a few fingers in the drug trafficking trade across Eastern Europe. They were on a few police watchlists in Germany and Poland, for example, but were legit enough to qualify for travel visas, and made sure never to commit any crimes whilst in their host countries – until now.

Both brothers had been boxers in their youth, so were well-built and muscled, with dark hair; perhaps Carl was the better looking one, as Hans had the slight cauliflowering of the ears from too many head shots. This trip, they were in Bali without their good lady wives, enjoying the vibe, the bars and the sea, and generally doing the full tourist bit. They *also rested and waited nervously, as this was no ordinary vacation.*

They had first become aware of the Lipman clan two years earlier, in Miami. The family had then been researched, watched, and a junior maid at the Jakarta house had been persuaded to keep her ear to the ground regarding when the family planned to be in Asia. Through their criminal contacts, the Hummels had recruited a team of Indonesian men – the purpose being to kidnap one of the Lipman youngsters while they were at their most vulnerable in Bali.

Carl and Hans were there when the Lipman party landed at Bali airport, and followed them to their hotel. From then on it was easy to keep track of the group, watching them out at restaurants and bars, or at the beach. Although they all stayed together, clearly no bodyguards were in evidence.

The main associate of the Hummels was an Indonesian man called Bowo Supratno, who lived in Denpasar, Bali, but had his roots in the central city of Yogyakarta, and that was from where he brought in his "firm": his three brothers, actually. Following the directions of the German bosses, Bowo was ready to snatch one of the targets and quickly get them to a safe house in Yogyakarta. Then, one Hummels brother would stay in charge of the hostage, while the other organized the ransom request. Kidnapping in Indonesia was rare, but not unheard of. People tended to pay, rather than involve the authorities. It seemed an easy job for the Hummels.

They continued to watch the Lipman party. Bowo Supratno referred to them as the decadent Lipman party, watching them cavort around. He had no desire to hurt anybody, but he thought they should grab one of the females so that the distressing experience would punish her for being such an arrogant and slutty Western woman. Carl and Hans were more inclined to snatch Rome Lipman, as they had nothing against the girls. In fact, they quite liked the look and spirit of them.

As with all plans, this one went slightly astray for a short period of time, when Carl accidentally found himself at the same bar as the Lipman girls. An arriving Hans saw the situation and did a comedy about-turn to leave again. Carl had smiled at that *performance and called his brother a German swearword.*

'Is that German?' asked Harper Lipman, leaning across.

Carl put his beer down and looked at the woman. She was slightly inebriated, her hair messy, a slight sheen on her temples, but her eyes were stunning, and they were right there, staring deeply into him. Carl's mind was already rushing ahead to getting her outside somehow and beginning the kidnap. But, he wasn't exactly sure where Bowo was, and he was actually amused to have her speak to him.

'Yes, I'm... Austrian.'

'What did you say? I love the German sounds.'

'I was just remembering something. Silly. You're American, right?'

'Yeah! Say something else to me in German.'

In German, he told her what he would like to do to her. She didn't understand a word, of course, but she laughed, so he laughed. They introduced themselves. He was fine with giving her his real first name.

'Who are you with, Carl?'

'Friends. But they are late.'

'I'm with those people, there,' slurred Harper, pointing across the bar at London and the others. 'What do you do, Carl?'

'I'm a firefighter.'

'Noooo?'

'Yes.'

'Where?'

'Vienna.'

'Ooh, Vienna. I've never been to Vienna but I like it there.'

She rested her chin on her wrists and looked coquettishly at him.

'Can I get you a drink, Harper?'

He bought her what she wanted, and they continued to chat. He was in jeans and a tee-shirt, and the way he was leaning against the bar made his biceps bulge. At one stage, she casually touched the vein on his right arm.

'Have you saved many lives, as a firefighter?'

'Of course, many.'

Her black top allowed him a view of her amazing cleavage, and her jewellery was clearly expensive. Just as he wondered if Hans had had the presence of mind to find the crew and set the wheels in motion, she asked to go out for some fresh air. He gentlemanly accompanied her, noting that her sister and friends didn't see them leave.

Outside, motorbikes whizzed by, but it was an acceptable kidnapping moment, and yet Hans was not there. Carl smiled to himself, and then he was helping Harper to stay upright.

'Are you all right?'

'What I am, Mister Austrian firefighter guy, is drunk. Take me to bed or lose me forever.'

'Which way is your hotel?'

'That way. There.' She giggled. 'We can see it.'

Carl put an arm around her and guided her to her hotel room. It was one of the best hotels, but was still tourist basic.

'I make you a drink,' she slurred.

'I think you should sleep.'

'Good plan.'

Harper stumbled around, trying to get her jeans off. He led her to the bedroom. He eased her onto the bed and removed her jeans for her. He enjoyed seeing her little white panties. He had cheated on his wife twice before, so had no qualms about that, but had never taken advantage of a semi-comatose woman before. He put a pillow under Harper's head and covered her with a sheet. He put her key on the table and left her room, but left the apartment door ajar.

Carl went back to the bar. He approached London and got her attention above the music.

'Your sister has gone back to the hotel.'

London looked at the man as if he was telling her the world was about to end. 'Okay.'

'She's very drunk.'

'Okay.'

Carl gave up on the partying older sister and stepped over to the Englishman. Harry was shocked to be disturbed from his dancing.

'Harper was drunk. I put her in her hotel room.'

Harry was surprised to hear this from a stranger, but he reacted better than London. 'Thank you. You think I should check on her?'

'I think that might be a good idea.'

'Jolly good. I'll do that now. Thank you.'

Carl watched Harry leave the bar. Then he went in search of Hans.

The following day, Carl and Hans were watching Rome and Harry as the two friends perused the local shops. Bali was quite busy at that time of year, so the Germans agreed that it needed to be a night time snatch. Hans was still a little disturbed about Carl's interaction with Harper Lipman, and quite confused that he had passed up the perfect opportunity. But suddenly she arrived at the side of them, having spotted Carl through the crowds. She was in denim shorts and a very daring pink boob tube top. She looked refreshed and beautiful.

'Hello, again! I bet you thought I wouldn't recognize you.'

Carl was surprised, but acted as normal as possible.

'Guten morgen, Harper. This is my friend, Simon.'

Hans hardly received a glance of recognition from Harper. She only had eyes for Carl.

'I wanted to thank you for getting me back safe, last night.'

'It was my duty and pleasure.'

Hans watched with mild horror as his brother's face lit up with joy at seeing the

American girl. It was a stupid and unnecessary complication, but it was happening, so he excused himself and melted away.

'Come to the beach with me, Carl.'

'Really, I don't want to interfere with your group.'

'Just with me. Not them. Come on.'

She was leading him away. There was nothing he could do, and he wanted to be with her, anyway. They set off to the beach.

They spent the whole day together, laughing and eating and drinking. As dusk began to fall, and the lights came on the front of the ubiquitous motorbikes, they sat in another bar and she asked for his number. He had a burner cell phone – he gave her that number, never intending to call her, of course. They had already kissed at the beach, and she kissed him again. They had been lucky, he felt, not to bump into any of her group.

'Your hotel room or mine?' she asked.

He thought of his room, probably being used by four Indonesian men to play cards. 'Yours.'

They left the bar, and walked to her hotel. Within minutes, they were making love, and continued to do so throughout the night.

In the end, the kidnap moment arrived on a quiet Bali street, the following evening, as Rome Lipman lingered behind the others while texting on his cell phone. The three younger Supratno brothers rushed Rome off his feet, held a chloroform pad to his face, bundled him into the back of the van that Bowo Supratno was driving, and they were off before the other Westerners could react.

Following Hans Hummel in a hired car, they departed Bali immediately for Yogyakarta. They had Rome there by dawn, and bundled him into a back room of a rural property. Rome was sat down on a bunk, terrified of the masked Indonesian men, who were talking fast and excited in their own language. He could hear a television in the next room and a crowing cockerel outside. He asked foolishly if he could go, and was ignored.

Despite his terror, Rome somehow dropped off to sleep. When he woke, he was given breakfast of chicken and rice. Two masked white men looked in on him, at one stage. They spoke to each other in what he thought was German, and then he was left alone for a number of hours.

Rome was not mistreated in any way. He was fed regularly, and even allowed to watch the television. Finally, the group of obviously violent men split up, and he sensed that the situation was moving along. He briefly considered trying to escape, but then just decided to wait it out.

THIRTY-ONE

Octavian seemed to remember that he used to see the occasional dead grouse, or other game bird, scattered around the edge of the M56 motorway, so there must have been shooting in one of the adjoining farmer's fields. He was glad, then, that Knowles organized a clay pigeon shoot for Speight's birthday at an estate in Frodsham, which was in Cheshire, just south of the River Mersey. Charlotte was keen to give it a try, and he had always wanted to do it, himself, so they engaged the babysitting talents of Joan again, dressed in their most countrified clothes and set off early, Saturday morning.

Charlotte decided on what radio station they listened to: Elvis, Elton John, Barbra Streisand. Charlotte's hair was in a ponytail, and Octavian kept sneaking glances at her beautiful profile.

Williams had a previous engagement, so she had cried off, but everyone else turned up and parked in the car-park in front of a nice Tudor-style pub, with adjoining B&B, which was all part of the shooting set-up. Knowles had come alone, as he had previously mentioned. Speight had Harry with her, both immediately getting into their Wellington boots and wearing flat caps and green waxed jackets. Datta and Taheer were present, although not with any great enthusiasm. McAlister had travelled over with them. She and Knowles were the only members of the group to have done clay pigeon shooting before.

Green and Joanna were the last to arrive. The blonde girl was introduced to everyone, blowing the men away, of course. The young pair were in thick woollen sweaters of the same navy blue colour, and jeans, and Joanna wore a back-to-front *Green Bay Packers* cap (she could get away with anything) with delicate strands of blonde hair escaping.

'That girl is so pretty,' said Charlotte to Octavian.

Octavian, however, was distracted to see John and Lee Paterson, the weapons expert and his architect student son, walking towards them, looking every inch like gamekeepers, with broken shotguns over their arms.

'Oh,' explained Knowles. 'I rang Mr Paterson, Boss. They are members here and he organized a good rate for the group. They'll join us.'

'Great stuff.'

Octavian reached for Charlotte's hand, keen to point out the young Lee Paterson. 'Baby, that's the boy I told you about who wants to be an architect.'

Charlotte was highly interested. The shy Lee Paterson smiled at Octavian, and then he realized that the woman with him must be his architect wife and he strode over.

'Hello again,' said Lee Paterson, looking embarrassed that he couldn't remember Octavian's name.

'Lee, hello,' said Octavian. 'Let me introduce my wife, Charlotte, who I told you about.'

Lee Paterson and Charlotte shook hands warmly.

'Hello,' said Lee Paterson. 'It's very exciting for me to meet you.'

'And for me, also,' replied a smiling Charlotte. 'Tony tells me you're hoping to train to become an architect?'

'Yes, that's my dream.'

Octavian had John Paterson delighted to see him again, so he left Charlotte and Lee Paterson talking shop.

'Hello, Mr Paterson. You're our experienced hand here today, then?'

'Well, I don't know about that. I know the way through the woods. Have you done this before?'

'Never, no. Always liked the idea of it, though.'

'Oh, is that your good lady? Lee will bend her ear off for career advice.'

'I don't think she minds.'

An excitable John Paterson counted up the people present.

'Shall we split into teams?' he asked.

Knowles turned when he heard that. 'If we're having teams, then I want to be on Green's side.'

Everyone laughed at that. Then John Paterson led them through a wooded area towards a clearing that held several log cabins. Spread out before them was, obviously, the shooting zone.

A woman in a proper shooting jacket came out to meet everyone. Sitting on top of her green baseball cap were ear protection headphones. She was smiling, had a little banter with John Paterson, who she clearly knew, and then she addressed the group.

'Welcome, everyone; my name's Natalie. I'll be helping you have fun today. I see everyone is dressed suitably. Please raise your hand if you've done this before.' She noted Knowles and McAlister, while the Patersons didn't bother to raise their arms. 'Oh, mostly newbies. That's how I like it. My colleague will give a little demonstration in a minute, and then I'll take you through the safety rules. So, just chill for a moment. Get your journey here out of your systems, as it's always best to shoot as relaxed as possible.'

Octavian chatted with the two firemen, while keeping an eye on Charlotte, who seemed to be bombarding Lee Paterson with career information and advice, which he was soaking in, as well as perhaps the technical stuff that he himself always tuned out from.

'Have you ever shot anyone, Mr Octavian?' asked Harry, perhaps a little tactlessly.

That got Octavian's attention, making his head turn back quickly. 'Thankfully not. I'm happy with just giving someone a good kicking in the cells.'

The three men laughed.

'At least it's not the real thing here,' said Taheer. 'I couldn't do that. Very cruel.'

'Will we be in teams?' asked Harry.

That was exactly what John Paterson was fussing around. He was saying that he would take on the role of team leader for the boys, while Lee led the girls. Everyone was happy with that state of affairs.

Charlotte moved away from Lee Paterson for a moment to cuddle Octavian.

'We're going to be in competition, darling,' she said.

'Yes. We can include it in any future marriage guidance counselling.'

'I hope the gun won't be too heavy, or bruise my shoulder.'

'I think it might be a bit heavy, baby. But I'll rub your shoulder tonight.'

She grinned. 'Thank you.'

Knowles wanted to gather the boys away from the girls, to increase the fake tension of the event. Usually, whenever playing team sports, like darts or football, his standard battle cry was "We can beat this shit!" but he couldn't do that at the ladies present, especially Mrs Octavian, so he settled for clapping his hands together and telling everyone to get their heads on straight.

Octavian gave Charlotte back to Lee Paterson, and joined the boys to watch a male staff member give a shooting demonstration. Two clay pigeons came up from the left side and he took them both out with quickfire shots. Natalie gave a running commentary on how he achieved the feat. He did it again from the other direction.

Natalie then ran everyone through the safety message, which basically meant that the shotguns were to always face out towards the course, and not be touched without her say so. Like penalty shoot-outs, the team orders were settled on, with Green going up first against Charlotte. The two of them joined Natalie in the semi-circle of a bunker. Natalie asked their names and then formally introduced them to each other.

Octavian had brought along a couple of those little rubber earplugs, which had helped London sleeping when on a night shift, and popped them in. He watched on with great amusement and pride, as his little Charlotte put on the ear protectors and handled the big shotgun. Natalie was alongside her, helping get her settled. The gun went to Charlotte's right shoulder and she said she was ready. Two clay pigeons came across the sky. Charlotte tracked them and fired twice, missing the first but shattering the second one. Cheers and applause filled the clearing. Natalie relieved Charlotte of the gun, and Charlotte turned smiling to look at Octavian, who beamed back at her.

Green was moved into place next.

'Here we go!' said Knowles, confident.

Green looked the part. He was naturally good at all sports. When he was ready, the two clay pigeons appeared across the sky. He fired both barrels, and the targets sailed harmlessly away into the trees. He was commiserated with by most there, jeered by Knowles, and he shrugged at a grinning Joanna.

The shoot continued with great banter and much fun: Taheer versus Datta, Harry versus Speight. Next time around it was Charlotte versus Octavian – they both missed, so it was a smiling draw, and a cuddle once they were away from the shooting area.

Afterwards, with Lee Paterson's team declared the victors, it was decided they would all retire to the café in one of the log cabins for a little brunch. Only the Patersons excused themselves and got off. Octavian shook hands with both of them, while Charlotte and Lee had a little hug, and she again wished him well with his future plans.

The event was being relived in the cosy café when Octavian and Charlotte joined the gang. There was coffee, tea, cheese toasties and ham rolls, or Danish pastries and scones. It was a lovely gathering after a fun morning. Octavian played footsie under the table with Charlotte while he enjoyed seeing his people, and their loved ones, relaxing and letting off steam. He looked to Charlotte, her face all flushed with the activity.

'You made a new friend,' he said. 'You'll have to take him on as an intern, one day.'

'A nice lad. He'll do well, I'm sure.'

'So, your team won, baby.'

'Thanks to Shirley.' Speight had not missed a target. Charlotte raised her mug in salute to Speight. 'Shirley!'

Everyone cheered and Speight actually blushed and fell across Harry's leg.

Octavian brushed a strand of hair behind Charlotte's right ear.

'Are we going now?' she asked.

'We have a couple of hours before your mother returns Jack. What should we do with that time?'

'Supermarket shopping?'

'I was thinking we could find a lay-by on the way home.'

She pretended to be shocked. 'I've heard about policemen like you.'

They got up and were the first to make to leave. There were happy calls and waves from everyone. Octavian shook hands with Taheer and Harry, and Joanna, then told his people he would see them on Monday morning. He and Charlotte waved as they left the cafe.

THIRTY-TWO

Taheer and Harry were on the Sunday late shift together at the Woodhouse Park fire station. After doing whatever chores and procedures were required, they and the other guys ate the nice beef casserole with poppadoms, prepared by Billy, then they could relax a little; wait for any shouts to come in. Taheer played cards with a colleague called Nigel, while Harry sat in the springy IKEA chair to read; he was working his way through the *Jack Reacher* novels. Everyone else watched the wall-mounted TV: a repeat of an episode of *Vera* was on, and Anne-Marie always insisted on watching that.

At 10 p.m. a shout came in for them to attend an apartment building fire in the West Didsbury area. It was not normally their territory, but the local crews were dealing with a big blaze at a recycling centre. Everyone jumped into their boots and threw on their fire jackets. Harry and Nigel got the doors; then climbed aboard the fire engine. Taheer drove them to the scene, which was an apartment fire in a small block of flats, in a very built-up residential area. The orange glow could be seen from miles out. As they quickly got there, Taheer thought about Datta – he found that recently he was thinking about her before a job started, but once he got busy he was fully focused.

There was one engine already on scene, putting water onto the fire. Residents were being evacuated. Taheer, Harry and the team sprang into action. Taheer looked up at the top floor inferno, the roof almost all alight. His crew got another source of water up onto the building, but then there were fears raised of people still inside, so it was Taheer and Harry who got kitted out in respirator gear and headed inside, up the main stairs.

The emergency lights were still on, but the smoke was fairly thick, billowing down around them. They reached the top floor. A disorientated elderly man loomed up at them through the darkness. Harry took a firm hold of him and led him down, while Taheer moved forward, banging on doors and looking down corridors.

Harry quickly returned to be with Taheer. They were as sure as possible that everyone who could get out, was out. They reached the top floor, but could go no further. The fire and smoke was at its most intense there. Taheer signaled that they should descend, when suddenly the floor collapsed from beneath their feet, taking them down in a huge whoosh of smoke and debris and, ultimately, darkness and silence.

Datta got the call at midnight, as she was preparing to go to bed. It was the fire station commander – to calm her instantaneous distress, his first words were that Taheer was alive, but injured and on his way to the Manchester Royal Infirmary. Datta let the adrenalin flood through her in the panic, and then her professionalism took over and she spoke calmly over the phone. She got as much information as possible, hearing that Harry was hurt, too, and then she thanked the man and hung up.

She finished her ablutions, two more minutes wouldn't make any difference, then got back into her day clothes. The shock had perhaps lowered her blood sugar levels, she felt a little shaky and cold, so she drank some milk and ate some dry cereal out of the box. Then she called Speight's mobile, as the relationship between her and Harry was not yet established and she would not have got a call. Speight was still up, and answered the phone as if Datta was going to alert her to another killing. As expected, she had not been informed about the accident. Speight took it calmly, and they agreed to meet at the Royal Infirmary hospital.

Datta drove there in her Mazda. She forced herself to drive carefully. The roads were ghostly and empty. On arrival, the hospital was quiet. She parked in the empty car-park and walked in, finding Speight standing around in reception.

'I've not asked them yet,' said Speight. 'I was waiting for you. So, what happened exactly, do you know?'

'A floor collapsed.'

'Oh, my God.'

Datta did the asking at the reception desk. She was quite prepared to flash her warrant card, if need be, but the staff could not have been more helpful, and she and Speight were soon sitting waiting on a corridor, where a nurse had offered to get them some coffee until the doctor could speak to them.

The same nurse got back to them around 1 a.m. to inform them that both patients were still in surgery. Unfortunately, she had no further details to give them. She padded away down the corridor.

'Should we let the Boss know?' Datta asked Speight. 'We're not going to be in any fit state to go in, this morning.'

'Best if I call Knowles, I think.'

So, Speight went for a walk to use her mobile. A few minutes later, she returned, just as a white-coated Consultant came out to see them.

'You're the police officers?' asked the doctor, who was a mature man of Asian origin.

Datta replied with the introductions. 'I'm Doctor Nguyen. Now, both our male patients have been put into induced comas. Now, don't get upset about that, it's quite normal procedure. They had quite a traumatic fall that knocked them out. They've been scanned fully. We don't think its life threatening. Both have had surgery to repair broken bones in their legs. Actually, almost identical injuries, but one assumes that as they experienced the same incident...'

'Can we see them?' asked Speight.

'Soon, soon. We are just getting them settled. Let's make it brief, shall we, as they won't know you're there. Best if you return in the daytime.'

'Thank you, doctor,' said Datta.

They waited another forty minutes, or so, before a different nurse took them in to see Taheer and Harry, in adjoining rooms. Datta and Speight felt similar emotions; relieved that their man was alive, upset at the situation, both sat and watched their sleeping patients for a while.

They met up again, on the corridor, and hugged each other, very emotional.

'Come and crash at mine for a few hours,' suggested Speight. 'There's nothing we can do until they are woken up.'

Datta started to cry, more with relief. Speight held her again.

THIRTY-THREE

Knowles rang Octavian at 7 a.m. to make him aware of the situation with Speight and Datta. Octavian was deeply concerned for his female team members. He considered going to the hospital, but thought it best to get into work, and take it from there.

Horsefield, McAlister and Green were there at the station when he arrived, all quite shocked by the turn of events.

'Keep me informed, Tony,' said Horsefield, before heading to his office.

'Yes, Sir.'

Octavian led McAlister and Green up to the incident room. Williams and Knowles soon arrived; the latter with no further update.

'It's just awful,' said Williams. 'Poor Aamina and Shirley.'

'We were only laughing and joking with them all on Saturday,' said McAlister.

'Well,' said Octavian. 'Let's plod along. I'll get in touch with them and go to see them when possible. There's nothing else we can do.'

Octavian finally contacted Speight on her mobile. She was heading back to the hospital, but wanted his permission first. He told her it was fine, of course. He would pop over and see her. There was nothing new happening in the incident room, so he headed to the hospital. It was a wasted journey, as he met Speight and Datta on the way out.

'Hiya, Boss,' said a gaunt-looking Speight. 'They're not waking the boys until tomorrow, so they told us not to wait around.'

'How are they doing?'

'They'll know more tomorrow morning,' answered Datta, who looked shattered. 'Also, broken legs and some superficial burns. In quite bad shape, all in all.'

'My God. Hey, they're still with us, that's all that matters. Look, nothing new is developing with the investigation, so you two take some time for yourselves. Catch up on your sleep, be here when you need to be in the morning.'

'Are you sure, Boss?' asked Speight.

'Of course. You're no good to me zombified.'

Both girls managed a little half-giggle. Octavian waved them off.

'Thank you, Boss,' said Datta.

'Keep me informed,' he called.

He watched them walk away, before entering the hospital foyer to pay the extortionate parking charge.

Octavian drove back to Wythenshawe. Returning to the incident room, he reported on the condition of Taheer and Harry, and told the others that they wouldn't have Speight and Datta with them for a couple of days.

'All a bit of a shock, this,' said Knowles. 'Boss, there were three fatalities in last night's fire. Mr and Mrs Scott, who had the flat beneath where it started. And in the seat of the fire, fourteen-year-old Alex Bowden. That's a male Alex, by the way.'

Octavian stared at Knowles simply because of the age mentioned. Not that there was anything suspicious yet about a fatality in a fire.

'Bowden,' repeated Knowles, pointing at the white board.

Octavian looked where Knowles was indicating, seeing Lily Bowden's name in his big felt tip pen writing, then back at Knowles. 'No? Surely not?'

Knowles shrugged.

'When is the post mortem?' asked Williams, intrigued, leaning forward.

'Today,' replied Knowles.

'What if...no.'

'Go on, Boss,' urged Knowles.

'What if the other killings were to put us off the trail, and the targets all along were Lily Bowden and Alex Bowden, yet to be confirmed as any relation.' Octavian acknowledged the doubting expression of Williams. 'But, Katie, we know we would never be troubled by that. But maybe that's how the killer worked it out in his head.'

Knowles was also against the idea. 'Coincidence,' he said.

'I'm never a big fan of coincidences,' said Octavian. 'It's not the second young person called Smith to die recently in the region. It's Bowden. Beth, find out about Lily's father, Dean Bowden. Record, and members of his family.'

'We should wait for the results of the post mortem,' said Williams. 'But I could ring Lily's mother and simply ask if there is an Alex in the family.'

Octavian didn't put off Williams in front of the others. If there was any contacting Kezia, then he would do it himself.

'If there is,' he said, 'She'll be in touch with us. But let's wait a few hours. See what the pathologist says, and to hear from the Fire Brigade. In fact, Phil, let's you and me go along there, see if we can get anything from the horse's mouth.'

Green hitched a ride, not wanting to miss out. The apartment building was a terrible mess, still smouldering from the roof. Crowds were watching from the road. There were two local fire crews on the scene, making sure nothing sparked up again and helping with the clean-up operation.

The first thing they did was to see if there were CCTV cameras near the entrance. They were disappointed not to see any, even though that had not helped them so far in the investigation.

Knowles spotted the Fire Investigation Officer, who he knew from previous crime scenes. He waited until the man stopped speaking to other firefighters and then stepped in to introduce Octavian to him. He shook Octavian's offered hand.

'Hello, sir, the name's Paul Everett.'

'Are you able to say anything yet?'

'An accelerant was used to start the fire. Probably petrol. Started in the hallway of the flat.'

'Thanks.'

Octavian did not suggest that was the primary cause of death. Instead, he thanked Everett again and stepped away – next stop: the mortuary. Knowles shook Everett's hand, then joined Octavian and Green, both looking up at the building.

'The fire was started to conceal murder?' asked Green, feeling a bit puzzled.

'Perhaps something happened and he felt that some of his DNA had been left behind,' said Octavian. 'So, he gets some petrol, goes back and torches the place.'

THIRTY-FOUR

During the morning, Octavian liaised with the police officers who were dealing with the arson attack and resulting deaths. He just wanted to keep them informed that one of the fatalities might be connected to his case. He had also left a message with the Coroner's office, asking to be informed as soon as Alex Bowden's post mortem was complete.

Beth discovered that the Bowden flat was rented to a Jamie Bowden, who was twenty-one years old. Both she and the letting agent were yet to get a reply from the man's mobile phone number.

'Sounds like an older brother,' said Knowles. 'Maybe he was the intended victim.'

'Perhaps he was away last night,' said Williams. 'Let Alex stay there. Or maybe Alex lived there.'

Octavian was suddenly very hungry. 'I'm starving. Anybody want to grab a bite, while we wait this out?'

Knowles got to his feet at the mention of food. 'Let's go, Boss. What, though? The usual sandwich place?'

Beth said, 'No internet presence for this boy. I'll ring round the schools.'

'Okay, Beth. We won't be long.' He looked at Green. 'You hungry? I'm buying.'

'Yes, Sir.'

The three of them went downstairs.

'Is it Subway we're going to?' asked Green.

Knowles laughed. 'You're kidding? It's the café on the corner for us.'

'Oh, it's just that Joanna works in Subway. I was just...'

'She does? Well, seeing as the Boss is paying, we could do Subway for a change.'

They took the Golf in order to quickly get to the far side of Civic Centre and parked in front of a row of shops. They crossed the road for the Subway store.

Joanna was there behind the counter, smiling her pretty and unique gap-toothed smile. She was delighted to see her boyfriend, as well as his colleagues. 'Hello, Mr Knowles,' she gushed.

Knowles was thrilled that she had remembered his name.

'The clay pigeon shooting was such fun,' she said.

'It was, wasn't it? We should all do something again, sometime.'

'Hello again, Mr Octavian.'

'Hello, Joanna.'

The three of them perused the menu board. Green and Knowles also kept eyes on Joanna as she served other customers. Once their minds were made up, Joanna created their brunch, and they took a table by the window. Octavian read a text from McAlister.

'Shevington is doing the post mortem now. We are cordially invited to attend at 11.30.'

'Can I go with you, Sir?' asked Green.

Octavian and Knowles watched as Green demolished his *Meatball Marinara*. Octavian nodded.

Octavian drove Knowles and Green to the mortuary, where a Pathologist Exhibits Officer let them in. Octavian could see a tiny bit of tattoo sticking out from above the man's collar, so assumed that he was one of those fully inked people, but he had a friendly smile and bid them a pleasant good morning, before going off to inform Dr Shevington of their arrival.

'Will we see the corpse?' Green asked Knowles, in a whisper.

'Quite possibly.'

Knowles checked out Green's face to establish if the young PC was showing trepidation or simply continuing with his professional keenness. He decided it was the latter.

'Don't speak in there,' he advised. 'Shevington behaves with insane seriousness in his domain.'

'Okay.'

Octavian checked his phone as a text came in. It was Charlotte checking that he would be home on time, as she was thinking of buying some fresh tuna steak.

'Anything?' asked Knowles.

Octavian shook his head.

They were invited through by the tattooed Exhibits Officer. Octavian looked back to check on Green, before leading them into the examination room, where Dr Shevington was fully kitted out in rubber apron, gloves, surgical bandana and white Wellingtons. The corpse, much to Green's fascination, was still on the slab, although covered with a white sheet.

'Good morning, Doctor,' said Octavian.

Dr Shevington inclined his head in welcome. All that was missing was the outstretched arms. Dr Shevington ignored Knowles, who he found to be slightly unprofessional, perhaps foolish, and he looked with mild contempt at the newcomer. 'Our young fire victim,' he said, indicating the obvious.

'I'm assuming it's not straightforward,' said Octavian.

Dr Shevington pulled back the sheet as far as the belly button of the cadaver. Knowles winced at seeing the skinny corpse of the young Alex Bowden, which was perhaps fifty per cent charred black, but in such a random way, as if it were a terrible skin disease. Added to that were the big post mortem stitches; they always had the effect of unnerving him.

Octavian noticed that there was no reaction from Green. The young man was simply taking the experience as one more step on his career path.

'This young man,' started Dr Shevington, 'died from a blow that smashed the back of his skull. But not before he was in a fairly brutal fight for his life. There are marks on his knuckles that suggest he fought back. There are marks all over him that suggest he was attacked. Finally, the assailant managed to impact the fatal blow. Perhaps a hammer, or a metal object of some kind.'

'So, the fire was started to cover that?' asked Octavian.

'That's not for me to say. One could assume that, I suppose.'

'Has any of the assailant's DNA been left on the victim?'

'Yes. We'll see what that brings, shall we, in my report, due course?'

'Anything else for us, Doctor?'

'Yes. Going back to the damage to the torso. If you look here, below the burning, on the left side of the ribcage. There are old bruises. If I said anything more I would be delving into the world of speculation.'

'Right.'

'That's all I have for you, Detective Inspector. I have quite a full day.'

'Thank you, Doctor. We'll leave you to get on.'

Outside the mortuary, Octavian stood on the pavement with Knowles and Green.

'You okay?' he asked Green.

'Yes, Sir.'

'Let's see what Beth has to say about our latest potential victim, shall we? If she's struck out, I'll contact Lily Bowden's mother to see if there's a family connection.'

They returned to the station. Williams stood watching their entry into the incident room.

'Any new info on Alex Bowden, Katie?' asked Octavian.

'Not yet, Boss.'

'Okay, I'll check with Lily's mother. We need to see if there's a link, or it's just a coincidence. The sooner we get to next of kin the better.'

'Would you like me to contact Miss Garswood with that enquiry?'

'No, thank you, Katie.'

Williams held her tongue.

'I'll get some lunch, then.'

'Yes, Katie.'

Octavian did not just want to call Kezia with the question. If there was no relation to Alex Bowden, then it would be a very brief conversation, indeed. Once Williams had left the station to get lunch, he went out and drove away in his Golf.

THIRTY-FIVE

Octavian drove to the house in Prestwich. Though he shouldn't have been, he was surprised when it was the sister, Emma, who answered the door.

'Kezia has gone into work,' Emma informed him. 'Just for the afternoon. To get back into things. She was stewing here all day.'

'That's probably a wise thing to do.'

'Yes, we thought so. Can I help you with anything?'

'It was just a follow-on question for Miss Garswood.'

'Do you want the work address?'

'That would be helpful, thank you.'

Emma found the address in her telephone book, wrote it out on a piece of paper and handed it over. Octavian thanked her and departed.

It was a short drive to the Doctor's surgery where Kezia worked as a receptionist. Octavian walked in through the front door to be faced with glum, waiting patients sitting to one side, and two receptionists behind a Perspex Covid screen to the other. Neither of them was Kezia, but both were looking at the handsome man in the suit. He picked the elder of the two to lean down to the window and show his warrant card.

'I'd just like a quick word with Kezia Garswood.'

'Poor Kezia, yes, of course. She's in a meeting with the Practice Manager. If you give me a moment, I'll interrupt them.'

'Thank you.'

The receptionist got up as if she needed two new knees and left through the back of the booth. Octavian wandered a few feet away, inadvertently making the doors slide open, so stepped to a different area, aware of all the patients' eyes on him. He was nervous again at the thought of seeing Kezia.

She came out to him. She was wearing glasses; something he was seeing for the first time ever. Her tired eyes looked large with surprise, and he realized that she might presume he had come with good news for her, so raised his hands to calm her. They went outside to the front steps of the surgery. It was not where he would have chosen to speak to her; now the patients watched him though the side window.

'What brings you here?' Kezia asked, in a nice manner.

'Sorry to drag you out of a meeting.'

'It's okay.'

'No fresh news. I just needed to ask you something?'

'You have my phone number.'

'I like being on the go, what can I say. Anyway, I need to ask you if there is a relative by the name of Alex Bowden? A young teen lad.'

'I don't think so. From round here?'

'Last known living in West Didsbury.'

She shook her head. 'Do you want me to ask Dean?'

'Could you? It's just someone of interest and we can't find his next of kin at the moment.'

She had to turn her mobile on. 'Turned it off for the meeting. They just wanted to see how I'm fixed for slowly doing some hours again.'

'That's good.'

They stood awkwardly for a moment, until the Android came alive and she was able to dial her Ex. Octavian looked at her while he listened in to the conversation.

'The police are with me, Dean. They just want to know if you've got a relative called Alex Bowden. Alex Bowden. Right. Are you sure? No. I'll call later. Got to go, they're busy. Laters.' She disconnected the call and turned to Octavian. 'He says no.'

'Right.'

'Does that help?'

'Yes, it does, Kezia. Well, I should let you get back to your meeting.'

He was fumbling for his keys. She was edging back inside.

'Would you like to go for a meal, Tony?'

'Pardon?'

'Shall we go for a meal, sometime? For old times' sake. Just to talk again.'

Surprisingly, it was Williams' face that flashed into his mind, not Charlotte's.

'I'd better go in,' she said. 'Call me if you want to go for a meal or something. Just for me to be able to let things out, I think.'

He acknowledged that without speaking. They exchanged waves, and he walked back to the Golf.

THIRTY-SIX

On the phone, the kidnapper spoke in native Indonesian, asking if it was Arsyanendra Raja that he was speaking to. Ari, listening in, noted that fact, realizing that he was dealing with a professional outfit who knew everything about the Lipman family in Indonesia. The first call was just to say when the second would be coming.

'Is that usual?' Raja asked Ari, after he had hung up.

'Sometimes. Let's just take it as it comes.'

Raja was back in the seat, waiting, six hours later, for the next call. Ari rested a supportive hand on his shoulder. It was brief call, and to the point, saying that they wanted IDR 1.7billion (around $75,000), and that Mrs Lipman had 48 hours to be ready to send it.

Later, Raja and Ari took a walk in the grounds.

'I thought they would ask for more than that,' said Raja.

'Yes, maybe they're hoping for an easy transaction. It's probably an Indonesian gang.

But, tell me, has there been anything unusual recently? Have you noticed anything?'

'I don't think so. Rome had that trouble at the nightclub, but I smoothed it out. And Mrs Lipman had some unpleasantness with Yuri Shipenko over business matters. It crossed my mind that he might arrange to have her shot, he was that angry. But not to go to this kind of silliness.'

'Okay.'

'What will happen next?'

'If we don't catch a break, maybe they will ask you to deliver the money.'

'Me? I have to do that, really?'

'I'll be right there watching you. They will expect to see you drop the package. I won't let anything happen to you, Arsyanendra. Come on, that Mr Roberts of yours said there was roast beef and Yorkshire pudding for dinner tonight. I don't want to miss that.'

Raja smiled at Ari. 'This isn't a hotel, you know.'

'Isn't it?'

The next call confirmed Raja's fears, that the kidnap gang expected him to be the "bag man". They wanted him to put the ransom cash into the back seat of an open car, a blue Toyota Yaris, on a particular street in Yogyakarta, a city five hundred miles east of Jakarta, and probably half way between Jakarta and Bali. Their final call would give a time for the delivery. As soon as the call ended, Ari was on his radio, passing the details to his colleagues.

Raja was not frightened, but did start to feel some nerves. It was suddenly very real. But Ari was back, squeezing his shoulder. Raja imagined it: he would simply approach the vehicle, place the bag inside, no doubt being observed by the gang, and then he would retire away from it. Why would they harm him? Why would it go bad? They knew he was the butler, an Indonesian, just doing a job.

'It will be fine,' said Ari.

'You reckon? So, what now?'

'We get ready to take you to Yogyakarta.'

Margo had more than IDR 1.7billion in the house safe, so that element was covered without any difficulty. In her lounge, she didn't actually thank Raja, but she looked at him with compassion and admiration. The call had come through with a time for the drop-off.

'We'll be going soon,' said Raja.

'Right, Raja.'

'I will call, as soon as we have news.'

'Yes, Raja.'

Raja went to change into clothes that he would normally use for outdoor pursuits; a sweater, jeans, hiking boots, a Helly Hansen woollen beanie hat, and an orange puffer jacket. Ari watched him change.

'Is orange okay, Ari?'

'Fashion-wise?'

'Should I be making myself visible, I mean?'

'I think so. Come here.' They hugged. 'I'm really proud of you.'

Raja giggled nervously.

'Ari, what do I do if it all goes bad?'

'Get that awful puffer jacket filthy by hitting the deck. I'll be right there to you. But you'll be fine. We've been on Google-Earth at where that Toyota will be parked. It's next to the drop of a railway embankment. When they think it's all quiet, they'll be in, and down the slope, probably to waiting motorbikes.'

'Are we going?'

'We're going.'

A police convoy waited on the drive. Finucane had the security gate in the open position. He shook Raja's hand. Then Raja was surprised to have London Lipman come out, together with the actor, Rafael. For a brief second, Raja imagined that she would approach him and say something like, "please do your best to save my brother," but she just seemed to be there to watch the developing drama. Her expression was as cold and aloof as ever. Raja gave up looking at her, letting Ari guide him into the back of a police SUV, and then he was whisked away, with sirens and blue lights, heading towards the airport.

Raja and Ari were taken to Yogyakarta in a police helicopter, which was more like an army gunship, as two policemen pointed their sniper rifles out of both open doors. Raja tried to enjoy the countryside – the green hills, the paddy fields and small villages. He wore a headset but he and Ari did not communicate very much.

At a private airfield, just outside Yogyakarta, they landed and were met by local officers, who seemed, to Raja, to be on an *equal rank with Ari. They transferred to police Land Cruisers and went blue-light to the main police station in the city. Ari introduced Raja to members of his own team, who had gone ahead from Jakarta, or moved back from Bali, and then there began a long wait for the action to happen. There was plenty of fried Gorengan snacks and coffee available. At one point, Raja was shown live surveillance images of the Toyota car, told which door to open, to close the door again and walk back the way he had come. Raja was not party to the details of how Rome would be released after the drop-off.*

Raja's phoned beeped with a message. He would have to make sure to turn it off before he went out. Seeing who the message was from brought a grimace to his mouth: it was from his ex-boyfriend, Melvin, but it wasn't a social contact, with Melvin being a freelance journalist. He wanted the inside "dope" on what was happening. There were rumours and leaks regarding Rome Lipman. Raja replied that he had nothing to say on the matter. Then he switched his phone off.

Ari brought more coffee. He sat with Raja. They were waiting for dark.

'Do you think this will go well?' asked Raja.

'Most do. However this turns out, I'll be happier with you working for a more normal family again.'

'Me, too, Ari. But not many normal families have butlers.'

'That is true.'

A police officer with an awful lot of gold braid on his shoulders and cap looked in. Ari jumped to his feet. There was just a look, and then the man departed. Ari gestured for Raja to stand. Raja felt like it was time for his walk to the place of execution, but Ari was then putting him into a bullet-proof vest.

'Raja, if you hear shooting, throw yourself to the ground. I will come for you.'

'Thanks. I'll try to remember that.'

Night had fallen quickly. Ari talked with his colleagues in the police station control room, from where they would be monitoring events. Then he gave Raja the nod: they were on. They moved out quickly, followed by half a dozen armed officers. In the corridor, Ari was handed a leather holdall, which he moved immediately into Raja's possession. 'Your leaving bonus.'

Raja weighed the bag in his hands, realizing that there was IDR 1.7million in there.

'Ready?' asked Ari.

'Yes. Let's get this over with.'

Ari glanced to see how far behind his colleagues were, seeking a moment of privacy. 'I'll hug you to death afterwards.'

'I hope that's not literally.'

Raja sat in the back of an unmarked van, with the bag of cash at his feet. It was warm, especially wearing the bullet-proof vest. In the darkened cabin, Raja could just about see Ari, facing him, and there were two other policemen, to his side. Through the square windows of the back doors, Raja could make out a fairly normal street in Yogyakarta, with houses lit-up to the right, and parked vehicles to the left, before the void of space where the embankment fell away down to the main railway line.

Perhaps due to the stress of the situation, Raja began to feel fatigued, and his mind started to wander slightly. But then Ari was *slapping his knees, the radios were alive with noise, and the officers in the van were getting ready.*

'It's time,' said Ari.

'Okay.'

'Walk slowly over and make the drop. Remember what I told you. I'll be watching every step.'

Another policeman opened the van from the outside. Raja climbed down with the bag. As casually as possible, he began to walk towards the Toyota. He heard a train go through, and some dogs barking, but apart from that it was a quiet evening. The Toyota was not directly beneath a street lamp but Raja could see it well. With nervous excitement raising his heart rate slightly, he opened the back door and heaved in the bag. As he closed the door, he was suddenly lit up by the headlights of two vehicles, and then a third came from the other side. The quiet street was suddenly as busy as Jakarta in rush hour. Raja felt like the proverbial rabbit in the headlights. He didn't know whether to stand still or walk away, expecting the traffic to pass. But all three vehicles pulled up at the

Toyota, boxing him in. Raja was extremely alarmed. He looked for Ari. He thought about getting down on the ground. Then three drivers, all of Asian appearance, stepped from their vehicles. The men just got out and then did nothing more. They looked at each other, and at Raja, as if to say "What now?"

Raja heard a car door slam and a shadow moved away from the Toyota. Then all hell broke loose. A beam came down from a helicopter. Gunshots rang out. The drivers scrambled away in all directions and Raja threw himself down. A gun battle developed on and below the railway embankment. The beam from above swept the road and blue-lights began to flicker across the scene. Raja tried to crawl under the truck. From that prone position he saw the shadow return up the embankment and let off a stream of automatic gunfire in a yellow flame from the muzzle. He was firing in all directions. The police returned fire, with Raja hearing bullets rip through the shells of the vehicles around him. He held his head, hearing the man continue to fire, until he was finally hit and dropped down with a massive groan.

Silence fell. Raja stayed where he was. After what seemed like an age, Ari rushed to him, gun in hand, dragging him to his feet and hustling him away.

Raja was back in the Yogyakarta police station. He was drinking coffee. The puffer jacket lay filthy and discarded in the corner. Ari sat in the chair, opposite.

Rome Lipman had been rescued from a house in Yogyakarta, a few minutes before Raja made the drop. So, the police were free to engage with the gang members attempting to pick-up the ransom.

'I am very sorry,' apologised Ari.

It was his third apology. Nobody had imagined that any kidnappers would go back up the embankment once the assault began. Everything was supposed to have happened at the base of the slope, near to the railway lines.

'Who were the men who arrived in the cars and the van?' asked Raja.

'Nobodies. They'd been paid to just be there at that exact time, to provide confusion and cover. Quite clever, really. I am sorry,

Raja. I wouldn't have deliberately endangered you.'

'I understand.'

THIRTY-SEVEN

On the Tuesday, Datta was allowed to see Taheer, shortly after he had been woken by the doctors. He was connected to machines and sedated, but he was still her Taheer and they were able to communicate quietly from where she sat at the side of the bed, holding his hand. She assured him that he was going to be fine. He managed to express his love for her. She wept with relief, her head dropping to his arm, then instantly up again as she realized she had landed on his cannula. The watching nurse advised her to be careful.

'I'm sorry,' said Datta.

She looked Taheer up and down again, awfully relieved, seeing his bandaged head, his black eyes, down to the cage under the blankets that protected his broken legs.

'You're going to be just fine, darling. I'll take care of you.'

In the room next door, Harry was being visited by his sister and brother. They had been polite on meeting Speight in reception, respectful of her being a police officer, but they had no idea who she was, so they politely excluded her from Harry's bedside.

Speight sat drinking tea in the hospital café, waiting for Datta to join her. She was being philosophical about it – if the roles had been reversed then she wouldn't have stood aside and let some random woman be with her brother at such a worrying time. She would just have to suck it up, be patient. At least Harry seemed to be out of danger and was talking.

She was surprised when it was Knowles who joined her, carrying a cup of coffee and an iced bun.

'Is this chair free?' he asked, sitting down.

'What are you doing here?'

'Checking on you, of course. I hear the lads are awake and okay. What's he said to you?'

'Nothing yet. He's got his family in with him.'

'Oh, I see.'

'Such is life, I suppose. What's happening with the case?'

Knowles devoured the bun. 'Funny thing. Well, not funny. Coincidentally, the fire was started to destroy DNA left by our man. There was another kid killed in the apartment.'

Speight was speechless and sad.

'I thought that would blow your mind,' said Knowles. 'We might have the DNA, though. Just waiting on the lab report.'

'Victim's name?'

Knowles shook his head. 'It was too normal and boring to remember.'

'Victim's name?'

'Alex Bowden. Yes, but stay calm, there's no connection to the girl in Prestwich. We're trying to find out who the boy's family are.'

'They've not come forward to claim him?'

'Seems he was living with an older brother.'

Datta entered the café, looked around, spotted them and approached their table. Speight stood and the two women hugged firmly.

Knowles watched the female bonding for a moment. 'Cup of tea, Aamina?'

'Yes, please, Phil. That's good of you.'

'I just don't want to have to repeat myself. Shirley can bring you up to speed. I'm delighted about our firemen.'

'Thank you, Phil.'

Speight and Datta sat and held hands across the table.

'Harry's asking for you,' said Datta.

Speight burst into tears. 'Is he? Oh, Aamina.'

Octavian was home in time for tea. It was just soup and cheese on toast, eaten in the kitchen. Ezi was not there.

'No Ezi again?' he asked Charlotte.

'Oh, yes, he texted to say he's gone over to Leeds to see that girl from the flight home.'

Octavian guffawed. 'Has he, indeed? The dirty hound.'

'If he marries an English girl, it will help him get permanent residency, won't it?'

'You're getting a bit carried away, aren't you?'

'Oh, more news. My sister has invited me and Jack up for her birthday.'

'What, the cow thinks we're separated, or something?'

Charlotte tutted at him. 'She assumes that you're busy. You don't much like the Lake District, anyway, do you?'

'Not particularly. I feel it's overrated. When you've seen one lake, you've seen them all. Are you going, then?'

'Well, while I'm still able to, I thought we should.'

'How long for? I'll miss you both.'

'Four days. Can you handle it? I'm assuming that Ezi will return from Leeds; he'll feed you.'

'I'm quite capable of feeding myself, wife, thank you very much.'

They both stretched forward for a kiss.

THIRTY-EIGHT

Speight and Datta both returned to work. Williams, McAlister and Green were extremely happy to see them, gathering around them to ask how the firemen boyfriends were doing, and if they themselves were doing okay.

Octavian now had a photo of Alex Bowden on his despised white board. The boy's family had been traced and made aware of the tragedy. Octavian stood to allocate the day's tasks.

'Morning, everyone. Me and Phil have an appointment to speak with the older Bowden brother. He's finally shown up. Katie and Aamina, would you go visit the parents? It's a bit of a journey, I'm afraid, out to North Wales. Of course, we should ask North Wales officers to call round...'

'No, Boss,' said Williams. 'I want to go.'

'Good. Shirley, you and Green have a chat with the residents of the flats. Beth has a list of their temporary addresses. There's only six, in total, as quite a few apartments were unoccupied at the time of the fire.'

Williams drove Datta south west down the M56. Neither minded the long drive. Their destination was Llandudno, the famous Welsh seaside tourist town. Mostly they listened to music, but their sporadic conversations were about the case, how they met their respective fellas, and Williams' son – specifically her fear that he might be the next young victim. Datta assured her that he had more chance of becoming the Prime Minister.

Datta was first to spot the sea, and called it, making them both laugh like silly schoolgirls.

'Have you been here before?' asked Datta.

'I think as a child, yes. I have a memory of walking on Llandudno's beach with my grandparents.'

'That's sweet.'

'Have you been here?'

'No, no, I was born in Sheffield. We holidayed in Skegness or Scarborough.'

The exact location they sought was on one of the massive caravan parks. They found it eventually, and needed a member of staff to give the final directions through the maze of green or greeny-white corrugated rectangles, down nameless lanes.

They had telephoned ahead, to guarantee an interview. Mrs Bowden was standing outside, waiting for them. She was a plainly-dressed woman in her late forties. She offered them a place to park as if she were guiding in a taxiing airplane. One of the topics of conversations between Williams and Datta was why were the Bowden's still in Wales while their youngest son lay in a Manchester morgue.

'Did you have an easy drive down?' asked Ruth Bowden. 'No roadworks?'

'No hold-ups at all,' replied Williams, putting on her jacket.

'I'm sure you can do with a cup of tea.'

Cups of tea seemed to be an integral part of life as a detective.

'That would be lovely, thank you,' said Datta.

'Please, come in,' said Mrs Bowden, leading the way, before stopping. 'Let me just explain. My husband has COPD breathing problems, so that's why we haven't returned to Manchester. You'll see he's on oxygen, but he can talk to you perfectly normally.'

Williams and Datta shared a look; there was the answer.

They entered the mobile home. Williams had been expecting to see the tacky décor and plush seating of the caravans which she remembered from her childhood, but this was a spacious, pleasant environment. The kitchen was tiny but fitted out with trendy German made hob and stove, and the sink had one of those power jet washes that she didn't even have herself at home.

Mr Bowden was sitting near a switched off television. He gave the impression that it was where he always was. He was connected up to an oxygen tank by a permanent tube up his nose.

'Hello,' he said. 'I'm Fred Bowden. Please take a seat.'

'Hello, Mr Bowden,' said Williams, settling down. 'I'm DS Kate Williams and this is DC Aamina Datta. We're very sorry for your recent loss.'

'Thank you,' said Mrs Bowden, starting to make the tea. 'Do you have any idea who harmed our Alex?'

'I'm afraid enquiries are in the early stages. I assure you we will do our utmost to find out what happened.'

'Milk and sugar?'

Both Williams and Datta said yes please, two.

'You've picked a nice day to come down,' said Mr Bowden. 'Will you see the town before you head back?'

'Most probably not, unfortunately,' said Williams.

Finally, everyone took their tea. Williams and Datta had their notebooks open on their laps.

'Have you lived in Wales long?' asked Datta.

'We came here when Coronavirus arrived,' answered Mrs Bowden. 'Alex was in school here, and there, since he's lived with our eldest son.'

'Has anything unusual happened recently?' Williams asked. 'Had Alex told you anything was bothering him?'

The Bowdens conferred, before shaking their heads, in unison.

'I think he was happy about a girl,' said Mr Bowden. 'His first girlfriend. But then it didn't seem to be so good. I think there was another boy hanging around.'

Mrs Bowden had a little weep at the thought of her boy and his first love. Williams thought again about her only son, saying, 'Yes, it's all very difficult for young people, sometimes. Social media pressure, especially. Do you know the girl's name?'

'I don't think so,' said Mrs Bowden. 'Jamie, our eldest, he will know.'

'What does Jamie do?' asked Williams.

Mrs Bowden looked at her husband. 'A doorman, isn't he, Fred? A bouncer, they used to be called.'

'Oh, that's an interesting line of work,' said Williams, as sincerely as she could.

Octavian and Knowles went to their meeting with Jamie Bowden. He was a well-built unit, the absolute opposite of his younger brother, quite intimidating, in fact. They met in the back courtyard of a shop in West Didsbury, as his girlfriend had the bedsit above it. Most probably that was where he had been during and after the fire.

After the introductions and commiserations, they took seats where they could in the paved space, which made Octavian feel that he was back in Victorian times.

Octavian sat on a low wall, Jamie Bowden on a wooden stool and Knowles sank into a deckchair, of all things. The girlfriend looked down at them from the fire escape, wearing a tiny bra top and shorts, much to the delight of Knowles, until Bowden gestured for her to go back inside.

'This is about Alex, then?' asked Jamie Bowden.

Octavian noted the thick neck; clearly the young man lifted a lot of weights. There was still some acne, too, so maybe he did steroids; Octavian was not an expert. Anyway, he didn't like this man from the off. There was no record on him, but he was young, still. The rent on the apartment which burned down was £800 a month, and his only known job was pub doorman.

'Mr Bowden,' started Octavian. 'Do you know anyone who would want to harm Alex?'

'Absolutely fucking not. Completely normal, innocent kid.'

'Can you think of anyone who would have come to your flat to harm you, but found Alex, instead?'

Jamie Bowden realized that he would need to keep his wits about him. 'I suppose I can. Can't every bloke? I have run-ins with people every night with my job. And I fall out with people socially sometimes. But I can't think of anyone who would be a murderer.'

'Did Alex have anything worrying him? School? Social media? Money?'

'I looked after him well.'

'Apart from leaving him alone on the night of the fire,' said Knowles, comfortable beyond words in the deckchair.

'I liked you when you were silent,' snarled Jamie Bowden.

'Mr Bowden,' said Octavian, deliberately calmly, taking back the man's attention. 'We want to find Alex's killer.'

'Well, you're doing a fucking shit job so far.'

Octavian handed Jamie Bowden a list of names, led by the other victims, and also with people that they had looked at already. His lips moved when he saw Lily Bowden, but there was no recognition on any others.

'You know any of those people? Did Alex know them?'

'No. Who's this Lily Bowden?'

'A coincidence, that's all. You're sure, you never heard Alex say any of those names?'

'I'm sure. He only ever talked about computer games, and Manchester City FC, and some girl.'

'Tell me about the girl.'

'What? Some kid who lived nearby. They went to the movies and McDonalds, that sort of thing. Another boy was butting in. I told Alex to twat him.'

'Did he?'

'No, it just all went away. Kids, you know.'

'Do you know the names of these young people?'

Jamie Bowden was getting red around the neck, infuriated by having to speak to the police. 'Of course not. But, erm, her father does dog grooming. You know, mobile dog grooming. He has a big yellow van. Not hard to find. Is that it? I've not had any sleep.'

Octavian stood up, and Knowles managed to extradite himself from the deckchair. He looked at it lovingly, wanting to take it with him, making a mental note to get one for his garden.

'That will be all for now, Mr Bowden,' said Octavian. 'But we might need to speak to you again at some time in the future.'

'Whatever.'

'Goodbye,' smiled Knowles.

Octavian and Knowles made their way back onto the shopping precinct, heading back to the car. Knowles picked up a couple of sausage rolls from a bakery, and Octavian bought a newspaper to read that evening at home. They drove back to Wythenshawe.

With coffee from the machine, they went upstairs and entered the incident room.

'Beth,' said Octavian, 'I need you to find me a dog groomer.'

She looked straight at Knowles.

'Why did you look at me when he said that?' asked Knowles.

'Any particular dog groomer, Boss?'

'The local man who drives a big yellow van. Anything from the team yet?'

'Nothing yet.'

Octavian and Knowles sat down.

'Maybe the intended victim was the older Bowden,' suggested Knowles. 'He's clearly dodgy. Let's say, the killer was surprised to find Alex there. A struggle happened, the boy was killed, the person set the fire to cover his tracks.'

'So, not one of ours?'

'Perhaps not.'

'I still sense that it is one for us. Someone going to see a thug like Jamie Bowden would be a serious individual. He wouldn't get into anything with the little brother.'

'Unless that was the way to hurt Jamie Bowden. A drug gang punishment.'

'Let's stay on it for now. Let's find this young love triangle. Maybe the male is a bit older than Alex and the girl. Maybe he didn't like competition. Maybe the other victims were in his way with other girls.'

'Lily Bowden?'

'Perhaps she rejected him. Beth, have you found Alex Bowden on the internet?'

'Nothing but a possible empty Pinterest page. His name is mentioned on other places, but it might be another Alex Bowden, of course. As for the dog groomer...' She walked over and gave Octavian a phone number. 'Name of George Georgeou.'

'Yay!' cried Knowles, delighted with the name. 'It's been a while.'

'Greek family origins,' said Beth.

Octavian gave Knowles the piece of paper. 'You ring him. We will go out to wherever he is.'

'Can I have a moment with my sausage rolls first, Boss?'

McAlister heard that and made Knowles share with her.

THIRTY-NINE

Speight and Green spent the morning interviewing the residents of the fire damaged apartment block. Their first stop was to see a Mr Brenton Pugh, who was an elderly gentleman, currently staying with his daughter at her home in the Old Trafford area of the city. Green was excited to spot the stands of Manchester United's ground. There was no time for tea. Mr Pugh didn't even invite them in, although he was perfectly friendly towards them. He had no idea who the Bowden brothers were and did not recall ever seeing them in the building.

'I read in the newspaper that the firemen are out of danger,' said Mr Pugh.

That made Speight smile. 'Yes, they should be okay.'

'I'm happy about that. They helped me down the stairs, you know.'

Speight's heart expanded with pride when she heard that information.

'I'm so pleased you got out safely, Mr Pugh. Thank you for your time.'

Next, they moved on to a Mr and Mrs Sean Jones. The couple had installed themselves in a Stretford hotel, for some reason. Again, no tea was offered, as they met them in the foyer. They all sat in big, comfy chairs, in a semi-circle. Speight explained what they wanted to know.

'I knew the bouncer fella upstairs,' said Mr Jones. 'I spoke to him a few times. Seemed quite civil. Never any noise from up there.'

'Sorry, can't help,' said Mrs Jones, when Speight looked her way. 'Never saw a young person in the flats, at all.'

'Well, thank you, anyway,' said Speight, handing over her business card. 'Do call if you remember anything.'

She and Green made their exit.

'That was short and sweet,' said Speight.

Two sisters were next on the list; Lyn and Jane McConnell. Spinsters, Speight later described them as to Green, but he didn't know what she meant by that term. They were being temporarily homed by their brother in Northenden. Here, they got a cup of tea.

'I remember the young boy,' said Lyn McConnell. 'Unremarkable schoolboy. Came in with fast food, went out with his bigger brother. Nothing more I can say.'

'No trouble,' said Jane McConnell. She was looking quizzically at Green. 'Don't I know you? Is your mother Beryl Green?'

Green beamed. 'Yes, that's right. Do you know her? What a small world.'

'Ohhhh, she's in our church choir. We definitely know Beryl. So, you're her policeman son? She talked about you, I remember. Is she not well?'

'Just a dodgy knee. There's a long waiting list for a new one. It's difficult for her to get around.'

'Oh, yes,' said Lyn McConnell. 'It is a scandal, the NHS.'

'Say hello from us,' said Jane McConnell.

'I definitely will.'

Speight watched on as this domestic drivel played out; then she could get them away, and off to the final name on the list. It was the nearest to the police station.

'This demonstrates my organizational talents,' she joked with Green.

They were parked in the Benchill area of Wythenshawe. Youths looked aggressively at them. Green waved at a passing lady that he knew, then he looked at the street name sign on one of the terraced houses – it took his full attention.

'What?' asked Speight.

'Rings a bell, somewhere.'

She waited, but nothing further came to Green.

'Who are we here to see?'

Green checked their list. 'Jonjo Higgins.'

Speight went up the little path and knocked on the door of the correct property. A man eventually opened the door. It was none other than Alan Hallworth, the man of the e-scooter incident outside the police station.

'Alan Hallworth,' blurted out a surprised Speight.

'What do you want now? Have you come to apologise for my tyres?'

FORTY

Octavian and Knowles found George Georgeou working out of his open van on a driveway of a house on one of the nicer roads of Didsbury. It was certainly a novelty to interview someone while he was shampooing a West Highland Terrier.

'Do they ever bite you?' asked Knowles, genuinely interested.

'Never,' said Georgeou. 'I have a great affinity with them. But Westies are prone to the odd snap, generally. Lovely breed, though. Have you got dogs, gentlemen?'

'No,' they both answered.

Georgeou looked stereotypically Greek, even having the bushy moustache, but his accent was pure Mancunian. He was a genial person, fascinated to know why the police had come to see him.

'He seems to like getting bathed,' observed Knowles.

'She. This is Roxy. So, how can I be of assistance?'

Octavian showed Georgeou a photo of Alex Bowden. 'Do you know this boy?'

'Oh, my God, of course. He slipped my mind. The boy who sadly died. A friend of my daughter's, I think. Although, she's not spoken about him. He was at the house a few times last year.'

'We'd like to speak with your daughter?'

'Why?'

'We're trying to build up a picture of Alex's life and associates. Perhaps she might know if anything was troubling him?'

'You think it wasn't an accident!? Wow.'

'You or Mrs Georgeou would be present, of course. Just a friendly chat, not an interview.'

'I don't see why not. Can I speak to my wife and get back to you?'

'Of course. Here's my card. As soon as you can, though.'

Knowles attempted to pat the Westie before leaving and it went for him. They all laughed.

Back in the incident room, Speight and Green reported to Octavian. There was nothing much to say, until Speight got to the last fire survivor,

Jonjo Higgins, being put up by his mate, Alan Hallworth.

'The loon on the e-scooter?' asked Knowles.

'That's the fella.'

They all looked at each other, wondering if that meant anything.

'We can't start making stuff up,' said Octavian. 'So, a resident where there is a suspicious fire happens to be mates with someone that we've had call to speak with. It's a small town. Almost everybody has some tiny connection here.'

'Well, I don't know about you,' said Knowles, 'But I'm desperate for there to be a connection. Shirley, when you spoke to this Jonjo Higgins, did he have any injuries?'

'Absolutely not.'

'Beth,' said Octavian. 'See if there's anything on this Higgins. When we get the DNA back, who knows?'

McAlister ran the name. 'Handling stolen goods. And... various levels of cannabis warnings. No markers for anything.'

Speight waved her mobile, indicating a message. 'Aamina and Katie are on the way back.'

'When Aamina gets here,' said Octavian, 'do you two need to get off to the hospital?'

'That would be good, Boss.'

'Do that, then.'

Williams and Datta got back to Wythenshawe by mid-afternoon.

Octavian and Williams took a stroll around the Forum area, as she said there was still a vision of moving motorway imprinted on her retinas. It was a lovely, blowy afternoon.

'Was North Wales pretty?' he asked.

'Very pretty. I liked being in Llandudno again. Not a patch on Skegness, though, according to Aamina.'

'So, why haven't the parents come back for their dead son?'

'He has a serious health issue. They seem quite regular people. Their son didn't mention anything to them. There was just a situation with a girl.'

'Oh, yes, we got her through the older brother. Waiting for family clearance to speak to her. Maybe tomorrow. You can lead with that, it's more your thing.'

'Okay. Anything else today?'

'One of the fire survivors, name of Jonjo Higgins, is now crashing at Alan Hallworth's place.'

'Really? What on earth does that mean?'

'Nothing, probably. Unless they're both involved in a series of child killings. But I've never known a murderer kill a boy in the flat above and then set the whole building on fire.'

Williams paused the walk. 'Oh, my head. So many coincidences. If this girl doesn't say anything of interest tomorrow, then I think we are in one hell of a pickle.'

FORTY-ONE

That evening, Charlotte was packing her suitcase for her early departure in the morning to visit her sister in the Lake District. Octavian leaned on the door, watching her. She was in leggings and he loved the curve of her bottom.

'I love the curve of your bottom,' he decided to say.

'I'm pleased that you do.'

'How are you getting to the station?'

'Becky's going to drive us there.'

'I'll miss you.'

She snorted. 'No, you won't. You and Ezi will probably have curry tomorrow night.'

'If he ever returns from his Yorkshire love nest.'

'Oh, he said he'd be back this evening.'

'Right.'

He giggled at a memory.

'What?' she asked, smiling at him.

'Remember the first time we went up to the Lake District? We went looking for Coniston Water, couldn't find it, so just sat on that stone bridge, kissing, and waving at passing Japanese tourists.'

She stood with her hands on her hips, frowning at him. 'That must have been you with your previous girlfriend.'

For a second, he felt a wave of panic, but then he saw that she was teasing him.

'You're such a bad wife.'

She laughed. They heard the front door open. He didn't move.

'Go and see, then,' she chastised.

'It's Ezi.'

'It might not be. It might be a burglar.'

'Well, you go, then.'

He pushed himself off the door and walked downstairs. Ezi was just in the tired action of putting his bag down on the floor.

'All right, Ezi? You dirty stop-out, you.'

Ezi stood up fully. 'Hiya.'

Octavian was taken aback to see cuts and bruises on Ezi's forehead and the bridge of his nose.

'What the hell happened to you?'

'A pub fight in Leeds. It's nothing.'

'Wow, I should have warned you it can get rough over there.'

Charlotte leant over the banister. 'Is that Ezi?'

'Come down, darling,' said Octavian. 'You have to see this.'

Octavian let Williams and Green go off to speak to the Georgeou girl.

The appointment was arranged for 11.30. Williams drove them in her car. She was so proud that the car hadn't been hoovered since she got it, and when she put the wipers on it gave them the feeling that they were on a rally stage, the windscreen was so dirty.

It was Mrs Georgeou who let them in. She was a black-haired woman, late thirties, quite attractive, wearing a pale green sleeveless padded jacket and jodhpurs, no shoes, like she had just come in from being with her horse.

'Why don't we sit in the kitchen?'

'Thank you, Mrs Georgeou,' said Williams.

Green had decided to be silent and to just observe.

'Anastasia!' called Mrs Georgeou.

A younger version of the mother skipped downstairs, also in jodhpurs and socks; so maybe they had a horse each.

Williams waited for the offer of tea, which was not forthcoming. She and Green accepted the directions to sit themselves down.

'Hello,' said Williams, smiling at the girl. 'Can I call you Anastasia?'

The girl sat down. A cat appeared and sought out her lap. Mrs Georgeou sat on a kitchen stool, watching on. Anastasia Georgeou seemed a pleasant enough young lady, without an attitude. 'Sure.'

'I'm Katie Williams, and this is Lewis Green. We're from Greater Manchester police, and just wanted to ask you a few things about your friend, Alex Bowden.'

'That's so bad, that. I was so upset when I heard. We weren't great friends, you know. We just knew each other, and maybe thought about going out with each other.'

'When was the last time you saw Alex?'

'Well, every few days, because my friends all live locally, and I would bump into him a lot. But not really spent time with him since about September.'

'Did he seem okay to you, when you bumped into him recently?'

'He did, yes.'

'Didn't tell you any troubles?'

'No.'

'Anastasia, do you know Alex's older brother, who he lived with?'

'I saw him occasionally. Never really spoke to him.'

'Now, we heard there was another boy on the scene, around last Autumn. Did he and Alex meet?'

Anastasia paused, as if wondering if she was supposed to give a name to the police. 'That would be Bradley Gyollai.'

Green wrote that down in his notebook. Or at least tried to.

'Unusual name,' said Williams. 'Could you spell that for me?'

Anastasia did so. 'He's part Hungarian. Lives nearby. Yeah, he wanted to go out with me. He and Alex had a fight. It got a bit worrying for a few days, but then I didn't want to know either of them. It all blew over.'

Williams put a list of the victims' names on the table for Anastasia to look at.

'Do you know any of those people, Anastasia?'

She perused the list, her eyebrows crinkling.

'No. But I know the Steven McLaughlin name because he went to the same school as me, and we all know who he is now.'

'Okay, Anastasia. I think that will be all. You've been very helpful.'

'All right.'

Mrs Georgeou was pleased that it was all done with. She offered to show them out.

'Thank you, Anastasia.'

At the door, Williams and Green bid farewell to Mrs Georgeou, and headed back to the car.

'My stomach is rumbling,' said Williams.

'Shall we grab something before going back?'

'What was that name? Gyollai? We'll have to try to see him. I'll text Beth to get onto it. Shall we get a barm cake, or something? I'll pay.'

Green was delighted to hear another colleague offering to buy him lunch.

'We should get back first. Do you like Subway?'

Williams thought about that. 'Never had one, I don't think. Are they good?'

'Oh, yeah, awesome. There's a store near Civic Centre.'

'Fine. Let's go before I fall down. Oh, damn, my wallet is back on my desk.'

Green squinted his eyes, having heard that kind of trick from mates before, usually in the pub, but she headed the car back in the direction of Wythenshawe.

'Only take a second to get the wallet,' she said.

Green waited in the car, on a double yellow line, while she trotted into the station for the wallet. She came back with it, but also with Knowles in tow. He got cheerily in the back.

'No, you stay up front,' Knowles joked to Green, who hadn't offered to move.

Green smiled back at him as Williams drove them away.

'I heard Subway mentioned,' said Knowles. 'And, you know me, I don't like to miss out.'

They were lucky to get a spot to park at the shops. It was busy, as always. Williams saw the Spar convenience shop.

'I'll just get some mints, and a lottery ticket,' she said. 'Then I'll come over.'

'It's a rollover tonight,' said Knowles. 'I'll come in with you.'

That worked for Green, giving him a few extra minutes to lovingly spend watching Joanna behind the counter. He jogged across the road. Two customers left, carrying their lunch, and then he entered to find the store empty. She saw him walk in and her face lit up.

'Penguinnnn,' she cried.

He grimaced at her terrible nickname for him. 'Leave it out.'

'You're coming in more than normal these days. Are you cheating on me? Are you? Do you feel guilty?'

'I'd never cheat on you. The bosses keep offering to buy me lunch, that's all.'

She leant on the counter. She must have just been very busy because her face was flushed, with a slight perspiration at her delicate temples. 'Will you be a DC whatever, one day? Earn the big bucks for you and me?'

'I certainly will, I promise.'

A gust of wind heralded the door opening behind him. He stared into her eyes for a moment more, and then started to turn, expecting his colleagues, keen to introduce Williams to the Subway menu. Instead, he was smashed across the back of the head and shoulders with a chair, sending him sprawling.

Joanna screamed wildly, while Green staggered in pain and found himself then being assaulted by a man, with blows raining down on him before he knew what was happening. He tried to defend himself, turning and punching back, but he was in a bad position, taking punches to the face. Joanna screamed again, but before she could get around the counter, or before another member of staff could react from the kitchen area, Knowles was there, rushing in to get hold of Chris Corbett.

He pulled a raging, drunk Chris Corbett off Green and yanked him across the floor. Corbett then went for Knowles, which was a big mistake. Knowles, furious that his young colleague had been the victim of an unprovoked attack, grabbed Corbett by the throat and the groin simultaneously and slammed him with great force up against the wall. That took the wind out of the man, but he still raised his fists to attack, so Knowles knocked him clean out with one punch.

Joanna had rushed to the aid of Green, scrambling on her knees to hold him. Williams just entered in time to see the punch land. She was shocked at the scene, and of the blood on the floor. She checked on Corbett's condition, prone and unconscious; apart from now looking like a broken toy on the floor, he was okay.

Knowles tidied his suit and kipper tie, puffing a great deal from his rush over the road and from the sudden violence. His only concern was for Green, who was bleeding from the back of his head. Colleagues of Joanna rushed over with the First Aid kit. Green seemed okay, reaching for Knowles, and they slapped hands in solidarity.

'I'm good,' said Green. 'I'm good.'

'All right, kid.'

Williams and Knowles looked at each other, and she joked, 'Can't take you anywhere.'

FORTY-TWO

Octavian rushed over to the Civic Centre, where two patrol cars were parked outside the Subway shop and a handcuffed Chris Corbett was being taken away by uniform. Green, along with Joanna, had already been driven to Wythenshawe Hospital A&E by Williams.

Octavian looked about and found Knowles on a wall, a little way along the street, eating his sandwich lunch. He went and sat beside him.

'How is he?' asked Octavian, after a moment.

'He's okay. Needs stitches, I would think.'

'You all right?'

'Yes, Boss.'

'Good.'

They watched the world go by for a few moments.

'This is a bloody nuisance,' commented Octavian. 'Aamina attacked. Now Green. What with the firemen, it's all getting silly. And we're no further along.'

'What's next?'

'Well, when you've finished that, seeing as Katie's not here, we will go see the boy from the Alex Bowden, Anastasia Georgeou love triangle.'

'What's this kid called?'

Octavian took out his notebook. 'Bradley Gyollai.'

Knowles declined to comment. He just finished his sandwich.

Knowles was surprised that Bradley Gyollai lived with his grandmother in a detached bungalow, in a quiet cul-de-sac. The old lady invited them in. There was a pleasant smell of baking, and once they were settled down in the open-plan kitchen/lounge, she produced real coffee in a percolator and a tray of cakes, or "dessert", as Knowles thought of it.

Bradley Gyollai made an appearance and sat in one of the armchairs. Octavian went through the rigmarole of official introductions. Gyollai seemed a sullen youngster, wearing knee-length shorts and a sky-blue Manchester City top from their club merchandise shop. He was a good-looking kid with a sharp parting on the left side of his head.

Octavian leaned forward, giving his reassuring half-smile. 'Bradley, there's nothing to worry about. We just want to ask a few questions about Alex Bowden. You knew him, yes?'

Gyollai nodded. 'Yeah.'

'How did you two know each other?'

'He lives round here. Lived.'

'When was the last time you saw him? To speak to him?'

Gyollai shrugged. 'Late last year sometime.'

Knowles gave an appreciative gesture to the grandmother over the quality of cake and she was pleased. Perhaps it wasn't in the rule book to eat during such a meeting, but he saw no reason to be rude to the lady by ignoring the delicacies on offer.

'Did you have a disagreement with Alex?' Octavian asked Gyollai.

'Yeah.'

'What was that about?'

'Don't know, really. He was bothering Anastasia. You know her?'

'Yes. Go on.'

'Don't know. Me and him just had a go at each other.'

'A fight?'

'A bit. That's all there is to it.'

'Did Alex's brother talk to you after the little fight?'

'No.'

Octavian sat back. 'Well, that seems to be all for now. Thank you, both, for letting us come in. We'll get away now.'

Knowles finished his coffee; then everyone stood.

'Oh, Bradley,' said Octavian. 'Do you know a girl called Lucy?'

'No, I don't think so.'

'Okay.'

Octavian and Knowles took their leave.

'Who is that Lucy you mentioned?' asked Knowles, as they walked down the drive.

'Someone you said about, at the start. Steven McLaughlin was texting a girl called Lucy. I'm scraping the bottom of the barrel now, Phil.'

That evening, Speight and Datta went to the hospital. Taheer and Harry had been moved onto a normal ward, and their beds were alongside each other, as if it were a movie where the heroes should not be parted. Neither woman took any flowers or gifts (there were lots of cards from family and firefighter colleagues), they just wanted to sit and speak with their men in the quiet room, where they looked much better, were both propped up and were not connected to any machines. When the fire casualty topic was touched upon, Taheer and Harry were distressed, but, overall, they had a wonderful hour or so of loving talk, and cross-bed banter. The murder was not mentioned to them.

Speight and Harry spoke about their fledgling romance, and how they would continue to get to know each other. He told her he was a tough guy and would be in the gym before they knew it, getting back into shape for her.

Datta and Taheer spoke about their deep love for one another, and her horror at the thought of going through life without him. He held her hand and promised to always be there for her. She shyly bobbed forward for a kiss, unsure if that was allowed in the NHS. It made her giggle.

'You want to remain a fireman?'

'Of course, baby.'

'There will be a lot of rehabilitation. I'll help you as much as I can.'

He smiled. 'I know. We'll get through it together, okay. I love you, Aamina.'

FORTY-THREE

Ezi made croffles for the three of them; croffles being an Indonesian cross between croissants and waffles.

'That hits the hungy spot,' Octavian said to Charlotte.

'It does, indeed. No more hungy.'

Then Octavian was ready to go to work, and Charlotte would get Jack prepared for the journey north.

Octavian led Charlotte into Jack's nursery and they looked at his little sleeping form. Octavian hugged his wife.

'You be safe travelling.'

'I will, don't worry.'

'I'd better go. Text me as soon as you arrive.'

'Of course.'

He leant to kiss Jack's temple, and then Charlotte went out with him to the car. They hugged and kissed.

'Look,' she said. 'No builder's skip.'

'Hallelujah!'

'You have a good day at work, darling.'

'I wish.'

Another kiss, then he got into the Golf and drove slowly away, looking back and waving.

And there it was: Horsefield seeking out Octavian as soon as he arrived at the station to ask how things were progressing. It had been expected. They were near Horsefield's office, so they drifted into there and sat down. Octavian told Horsefield everything; bad, frustrating, impossible, and what good might still come of the investigation if they got a break. Horsefield didn't say it, but Octavian was almost out of time.

'What about DNA from the latest victim?' asked Horsefield.

'No matches.'

'Well, keep at it, Tony. Oh, there have been two more killings in the Kent region. They are struggling.... a bit, too. Plus, a young person died in Southampton yesterday in suspicious circumstances, but no further information.'

'Thank you, Sir.'

Octavian got coffee and hauled himself upstairs. Everyone was there, except Green, who he assumed to be off, recuperating.

'Any news on Green?' he asked the room.

'He's good, Boss,' said Knowles. 'I spoke to him last night. Bugger didn't thank me for saving his neck, though.'

Green, as if his ears were burning, suddenly arrived. All the female team members rushed around him to check how he was. Embarrassed, he assured them that he was fine.

'Shouldn't you be resting?' asked Octavian.

'I'm okay, Sir. Really, I am.'

Green had something to say to Octavian, but Octavian waved him to a chair.

'Sit down, Green. We're going to have a brainstorming session. Even Phil can join in, if he really wants to.'

Knowles let everyone smirk and point at him. They all took their seats. Octavian drained his coffee cup and set it down.

'Has anybody got any fresh thoughts?' he asked. 'Any ideas how to identify a random killer who leaves no clues, and who has a big black SUV that no ANPR camera or human eye can ever spot?'

Green wondered whether to speak, but Williams had leaned forward. 'As we know, most murders are committed by a relative or somebody close to the victim. If we say, for a moment that this isn't completely random, then one of the victims was killed by someone they knew, and all the others were to mask it. Like you thought about the Bowden's before we found no family connection.'

'Right, Katie. I'm listening. So, we look at the family members again, closely. Maybe check all their phone records to see where they were when other killings happened. Or if their vehicles were in those areas.'

Knowles joined in, 'Sounds like a haystack without a needle, to me.'

Green was impressed with that line, and Knowles nodded at him.

'Does seem very unworkable,' added Speight.

'Is there nobody else like Richard Hay to look at?' asked Datta. 'Other people with a grudge against the young?'

McAlister pulled a face; Richard Hay had been her shot in the dark.

Green had his hand up, getting everyone's attention. 'I just had a call from a colleague, a PC Warnock. He attended the fire scene, and knows the residents. He's been following this case. He said he had cause to speak to Alan

Hallworth and Jonjo Higgins back in November because they were practising with a crossbow at Hallworth's house.'

'Good work,' said Octavian. 'This is Alan Hallworth, who told me he sold his crossbow, over a year ago. And he is best mates with a survivor from the fire that our last murdered child was in.'

'Does Jonjo Higgins have the same build as the Chorlton-cum-Hardy killer?' asked Knowles.

'I would perhaps say so,' answered Speight.

Octavian was reluctant to get interested to any great degree again. 'Wait. Hallworth and Higgins are killing youngsters, with crossbow, firearms and vehicles? What for? For kicks? And what about Alex Bowden? Was Higgins off his head on something and couldn't resist? He went upstairs and battered the boy; then they torched the place?'

'Sir,' said Green. 'What better way to divert suspicion? To destroy your own property, I mean.'

They all took a moment.

'It's as much a possibility as any others we've followed,' said Knowles.

'Maybe they are gamers,' suggested Datta. 'In these violent games you kill by various methods. They could be acting them out in real life.'

'That would at least explain the crossbow,' said Octavian.

Williams asked, 'Any point bringing in Hallworth again for lying about his crossbow?'

'At the very least we need to get it off him,' said Speight.

'Look,' said Knowles. 'We went in on the teacher fella. That suspicion was just down to car insurance fraud. We need to let these two run.'

'Shirley,' said Octavian. 'When you knocked on Hallworth's door, did his arse fall out of his pants?'

'No, Boss.'

'Which might suggest that he's not been worrying about a visit.'

'Or he's too stupid to expect it,' she replied. 'It's all been basic violence. No great master plan, I would say. I like Aamina's theory. Dumb pricks like them might just decide to take the video game outside.'

Octavian picked up his cup, realized it was empty and put it down again. Some of his murder investigations in the Met had been quite simple; threats made in front of witnesses, threats carried through, evidence to place the person at the crime scene. With this, they were constantly chasing their tail. But they had to do something.

'Let's put Hallworth and Higgins under surveillance. We've already lost, with all these names up here on the board, we have to take a chance to get something from it.'

While plans were made for the watching of Hallworth and Higgins, Octavian chatted to Speight and Datta about their firemen. He was relieved that it all sounded upbeat.

Speight grinned. 'When Harry's better in the summer, we're off to Cyprus.'

'Ooh, so far.'

'I know, I know, not South East Asia.'

Datta said, 'We'll just do the house up, when Taheer gets his fitness back.'

'Good. I'm pleased for the pair of you.'

Knowles tried to find the stitches in the back of Green's head.

'What's this 666?'

'Oh, very funny.'

Williams sat with McAlister, identifying what vehicle Jonjo Higgins drove. They also found out that he was a roofer, by trade. More specifically, that he fitted new PVC guttering.

'I had that done last year,' said Williams. 'The workman guy didn't half reek from being up there in the heat of summer.'

'It wasn't our man Higgins, was it?'

'No idea.'

'Happy with the work done?'

'Yes, very.'

Horsefield gave Octavian two PCs to assist with the surveillance, so, with all his people, they could easily keep a close eye on Hallworth's residence. Octavian met the PCs in the canteen; both were in trendy plainclothes. One was a female, by the name of Claire Batty, who was friendly and keen. The other was Green's pal, Dave Warnock. Here was an intense young man who paid great attention to what Octavian was telling him, and if Green liked him, then that was good enough for Octavian. He was not too keen on the messy beard and many visible tattoos, which seemed to have been allowed into the service in recent years – but perhaps that was a positive thing on a stakeout.

Those two officers were given radios and sent out first to keep an eye on the comings and goings at Hallworth's house. A car at each end of the street would suffice, Octavian decided.

FORTY-FOUR

PCs Batty and Warnock spent four hours where nothing happened at all. They were bored and disappointed, but happy when they were relieved by Speight and Datta, who parked behind them in their own cars. There was a brief moment of radio chatter, and then the surveillance watch was officially swapped.

Meanwhile, a late response to Williams' TV appeal came in regarding a possible sighting of the Mercedes. The anonymous caller was adamant that the SUV was in a barn, on a private farm property in the Carrington district.

'Where's Carrington?' asked Williams.

'North of Sale,' answered Knowles. 'It's where Manchester United has its training ground.'

Everyone still there in the incident room, apart from McAlister, set out to take a look.

They took two cars. It turned out to be a large house with enough land to accommodate several polytunnels and out-buildings; a fruit and veg-growing enterprise. There were also caravans, sheds, trailers and the one, large barn.

The main road was slightly elevated from the farm compound, giving a wide view, so Octavian asked Williams to stay with their cars in case anyone attempted to leave while the rest of them were engaged in a search. She had no issue with doing that. She indicated her radio, in case an alert needed to be made.

Octavian, Knowles and Green put on stab vests before walking down onto the property, looking like a Sheriff and his deputies. Disturbingly, they were immediately met by people coming from all directions, from the caravans and from the polytunnels. It was both men and women, and although nobody spoke to them, Octavian thought them to be Eastern European workers – whether there legally or illegally. Octavian flashed his warrant card, and a space was made for an elderly man to step forward to meet them.

'What's all this about, then? My name's Eric Chamberlain. This is my place. Don't mind this lot; they'll take any bloody chance to stop working.'

'Sorry to bother you, Mr Chamberlain. We're looking for a Mercedes SUV. We have reason to believe there's one here.'

Octavian looked around the motley crew of people, not entirely reassured by Mr Chamberlain's statement. Knowles was also quite wary.

'I think we do have one of those vehicles,' said Chamberlain. 'Yes, I seem to remember. Do you want to see it?'

'If you don't mind.'

'No worries. Come this way.' He waved the group away. 'Get back on it, you lazy sods.'

Octavian walked alongside Chamberlain, who was very sprightly for being nearly eighty.

'Do you always wear those things?' asked Chamberlain, tapping Octavian's stab vest.

'We are on a murder enquiry, Mr Chamberlain. So, yes, we tend to.'

Chamberlain made an eek expression, wishing he had not asked the question.

'Is business good?' asked Octavian, indicating the plastic polytunnels.

They were heading towards the barn, so the anonymous information looked promising.

'Can't complain. Mostly strawberries, carrots and kale at the moment.'

Knowles whispered to Green, 'What's kale?'

Green opened his mouth to reply, before he realized that he wasn't entirely sure. 'Like cabbage, I think.'

The barn was made of corrugated metal. A tractor was parked nearby. There were old cars spread about in the long weeds. It was not the tidiest of set-ups.

'In here,' said Chamberlain.

He took them into the barn and switched on the fluorescent lights. They were faced with a dumping ground of scrap metal, wooden fencing, car parts, old tyres, a wall of fertilizer bags.

'This way.' Chamberlain led them through the junk maze. 'This is it.'

There were three vehicles sitting there. One had no windscreen, another had no wheels and the last one was caked in dirt. Octavian was momentarily nonplussed, as obviously none of them was black.

Knowles stepped forward towards the dirty vehicle. 'It's the right model, Boss. Just the wrong colour.'

'Has it been resprayed recently?'

Knowles wiped off some dirt, which had been on the vehicle for months. Still, he examined the paintwork, just to be thorough. Then he looked behind the SUV, to where the grass had grown up; it hadn't been anywhere in a very long time. 'No good,' he just called back.

Octavian turned back to Chamberlain. 'Is this the only Mercedes on the property?' The man nodded. 'Is that definite, Mr Chamberlain? If I have to swamp your property with cops it's going to disturb your business.'

'There's no other Mercedes. Walk about everywhere to look. It's not a big place.'

So, they left the barn and split up, wandering in and out of the polytunnels and buildings. Octavian looked at the land behind the big house; finding nothing of interest.

After thirty minutes, Octavian was sure there was no other Mercedes vehicle on the property. He waved Green to him, and then Knowles reappeared. Octavian looked for Chamberlain.

'We'll get away now, then, Mr Chamberlain.'

'All right, lad.'

'Sorry for the inconvenience. Good day to you.'

The three of them walked back up to where Williams waited with the cars, arms crossed, ponytail moving in the wind.

'Nothing has moved anywhere I could see,' she reported.

Octavian ripped open his vest. 'It was a total waste of time.'

Knowles held up a punnet of strawberries. 'Oh, I wouldn't go as far to say that, Boss.'

In the afternoon, they relieved Speight and Datta at the Hallworth stakeout. Green was sent home to get some rest, much to the amusement of Knowles.

'You're on nights again, kid.'

'I don't mind, actually.'

Octavian stayed with Williams in his Golf, while Knowles took the far end of the street. Octavian got a text from Charlotte saying she and Jack had arrived safely with her sister. It provided a topic of conversation with Williams for a few minutes.

Quite soon, they had activity. Hallworth and Higgins exited the house, and headed in the direction of Knowles. He let them pass him;

then followed on foot, at a safe distance. Octavian and Williams drove up; then got in step behind Knowles. But the two men only went to the local pub.

The cars were moved up, one at a time, and the surveillance resumed. After two hours, Hallworth and Higgins reappeared. They visited a nearby convenience shop; then went back to the house with their snacks and, in Hallworth's case, lottery scratch cards, which proved to be losers and ended up as litter on the road. Hallworth kicked over someone's recycling bin in annoyance.

Nothing more happened. PCs Batty and Warnock came back on for the evening shift. Octavian made sure they both had his mobile number. Then he bid goodnight to Williams and Knowles, and he was glad to be getting home to Altrincham. As Charlotte had predicted, it was going to be curry with Ezi, and it was Tottenham versus Newcastle United on the TV.

Octavian showered and changed. Ezi was studying. It was so quiet, only being the two of them. Octavian went and worked on his new novel for an hour or so, before hunger grabbed him.

'I'll leave the choice of takeaway to you, Ezi.'

'Okay.'

'Have you spoken to the Leeds lass?'

Ezi's expression showed slight embarrassment. 'Yes. She's fine.'

Octavian giggled and left him to it.

During the lads' night in, Warnock phoned twice; to say Hallworth and Higgins had gone back to the pub. Then to say they had a takeaway, back to the house. They looked too drunk to be planning to go anywhere else. Octavian thanked the young PC, let him know that he could keep calling, and what time Green would relieve them.

FORTY-FIVE

Octavian slept through without being disturbed. He showered and dressed, before breakfast was a quick cup of tea and slice of toast, with Ezi already having left for a Uni lecture.

Octavian drove straight to see Green. The young man was tired but still alert. He reported that there had been no movement at the target address. Octavian praised him and sent him home, then stayed watching the house himself. Knowles came along at about 8.30 a.m. He slid into the passenger seat with coffee and doughnuts.

'How do you keep your weight in check?' asked Octavian.

'I'm naturally svelte, Boss. So, are these cretins not doing anything?'

'Apparently not.'

Octavian ate a glazed doughnut.

'Oh, spoke too soon,' said Knowles. 'Here we go.'

The two suspects exited the house. They were dressed for sports activity. They walked off, so Octavian and Knowles got out and followed, on opposite sides of the road.

Hallworth and Higgins went to football training for a local amateur team. Octavian and Knowles watched on through some trees. After a boring hour, the journey was made in reverse. Octavian led the way back to the Golf.

'This Jonjo Higgins is a roofer, right?' asked Knowles, getting settled again. 'He doesn't seem to have much work on, does he?'

PC Batty came over the radio, saying that she and PC Warnock had arrived on the road. Knowles shuffled and scanned behind them, seeing Warnock sitting in his vehicle. Octavian wished them both a good morning, told them to keep their eyes peeled, then drove Knowles to the station. There were no longer any members of the press hanging around, the story having moved away from the front pages, so they parked on the road and walked in the front way, bidding hello to civilian worker, Bill Fitzgerald.

'Bad defeat for the Wolves, last night, Bill,' said Octavian.

'I do hate Wigan.'

'Get them next time.'

The day dragged along, with changing stakeout shifts, and the targets only going out once to the convenience store for cigarettes and bread.

Speight and Datta headed over there, while Octavian drove home. Ezi had cooked meatballs with pasta, topped with mozzarella and put in the oven to brown.

'You really should change your course, and become a chef, mate.'

After the meal, they watched a film; then played a game of chess. Octavian kept his phone at his side, ready to leave if Speight or Datta reported that something was happening.

'Could you not have gone to the lake area?' asked Ezi.

'My sister-in-law doesn't like me that much.'

'Really?'

'I'm kidding. I can't go away at the moment, with the case. Anyway, it's good for a marriage to have some time apart. You'll know that, one day.'

Ezi won the first game quickly; then made coffee for them.

'You keep checking your phone,' he said, on his return. 'Have you got something big on?'

'Just a surveillance job.'

'Can I come out with you sometime? You know, like in that American comedy film we once saw.'

'Sure.'

'Really!?'

'Of course not.'

They started another game. Octavian liked the ornate chess set, as a living room ornament; he could not recall ever beating Ezi.

'I wonder what Charlotte is doing now?' mused Octavian, hunched over his pieces. 'Probably enjoying a glass of wine while looking out at Lake Windermere.'

'Check,' announced Ezi.

Octavian aborted reaching for his coffee, finding himself already under threat. He moved a pawn to cover his King.

'Have you invited Yorkshire lass to visit here?'

Ezi was wide-eyed at that. 'No. Can I do that?'

'Of course.'

Ezi was slowly opening up his attack, bringing his Bishops into play. Octavian steepled his fingers, concentrating.

'What's she called, by the way?'

'Who?'

'The girl in Leeds.'

'Poppy.'

'Poppy? What a wonderful name. Yes, invite Poppy to visit.'

'Check.'

Octavian moved his King aside, starting to feel worried. Then his ringing phone broke the tension. 'Excuse me, Ezi.' He leant back and answered. Surprisingly, it was Green calling. He looked at his watch; it was just after the hour, so Green must have just turned up for the night shift.

'Go ahead, Green,' he said into the phone. 'They are on the move. Right. With bags. Okay. Speight and Datta following on foot. Get yourself with Speight and Datta and don't leave them. I'm on my way.'

Ezi grinned, seeing his easy win having to be abandoned.

'Sorry, Ezi, mate. Call it a draw, shall we? Got to go.'

'Okay. Stay safe out there, please.'

'I always try to do that. What will you do now?'

'Find another film, I think.'

'Okay. I'll try not to wake you when I get back. Ring Poppy, tell her you love her.'

'Pffft.'

Octavian made radio contact with Speight as he sped along towards Wythenshawe, ordering her not to make any contact with the suspects, but to stay a safe distance back. He was there within twenty minutes of leaving his house, finally slowing onto the normal, quiet, dark roads.

Speight's voice guided him to her location, which turned out to be a bus shelter, still in the Brownley Green area. Octavian parked the Golf and joined her. In the glow from the electronic bus timetable on the side of the shelter he checked to see that she had her stab vest on.

'Shirley, what's happening?'

'Boss. They carried sports bags and went into another house. That one, there, where the porch light is on. I think I saw a weapon lifted from the bag as they entered, but I'm not sure.'

'Where are Aamina and Green?'

'In the church grounds, watching from a different angle.'

'So, definitely shady behaviour, you reckon?'

'I think so.'

'I'm going to speak to the others. Back in a minute.'

He walked along the street and, well before he reached the house that Shirley pointed out to him, he ducked through bushes onto the church property. His eyes were becoming accustomed to the darkness and he made out the two figures of Datta and Green.

'You two okay? Got your vests on?'

'Yes, Boss,' answered Green, slapping his chest.

'Shirley has a bad feeling about this. Is that how it looks to you two?'

'They left in a sneaky way,' said Datta. 'Looking about, all nervous.'

'Right, I'll call for armed back-up. Stay on the radio to me. Do not do anything without my say so.'

Octavian returned to Speight, and from there he got on the radio and requested armed response support. Then they waited.

'You cold, Shirley?'

'It's not Miami, I'll say that.'

'Let's hope it hots up soon with these fellas.'

Octavian met the armed response car, ten minutes later, back up the street. He explained the situation to the two officers, who were not particularly interested by the situation, but quickly got kitted out in their RoboCop gear and checked their *Heckler & Kock* submachine guns.

'We'll park out of the way, down that side road,' said one of the officers. 'Let's give these people a chance to start whatever they are planning.'

'Thanks guys.'

Back to Speight, who was sitting in the bus shelter, on the phone to Datta. Octavian was feeling the night chill, so was happy to step out of the wind.

'Armed response is ready,' he told her.

'Bloody good.'

They sat and waited, like a couple waiting for the last bus.

'How's Harry?'

'He's moved in with his sister to start his recovery. She says I can go round anytime. I'm accepted into the family, apparently.'

'That's great.'

'Sorry for disturbing you and Mrs Octavian at home. Dragging you out here.'

'Charlotte's away visiting her sister. I was losing at chess to my nephew. You did me a favour, Shirley.'

'I'm excited, actually. I think this could turn into something. Should we take them as soon as they come out, assuming they will be carrying something?'

'That's what I'm sitting here thinking about. We want them to act, but we can't have the next youngster to pass by getting attacked. I'll make a decision when I see how they come out. Do we know who they are visiting yet?'

'McAlister looked into that and came up with an elderly female. Whoever she is, I don't think she's there at the moment.'

Minutes went by. Octavian's knees began to seize up. Speight started to stamp her feet.

'Knowles is probably tucked up in bed by now,' she grumbled.

Three dark figures suddenly exited the target property and started to walk quickly in their direction. Green spoke a warning over the radio. Octavian turned it down by the switch on the top.

'Are they carrying anything?' Octavian asked Speight.

She was straining to see into the sporadic white light from the streetlamps.

'Yes, I think so.'

The three men were almost up to them, on the other side of the street. Speight rolled herself across Octavian, to give the impression of lovers with nowhere better to go. Octavian looked through her hair, seeing three white faces, inside hoodies, glance at them, and then the men were off down the street, in the direction of the side road with the parked police car.

'Come to us, Aamina,' said Octavian into the radio.

Datta and Green emerged through the shrubbery. The four of them moved off after the three men. The figures walked past a closed pub, then crossed over to avoid a man walking his dog. Octavian led his people in pursuit, without getting too close.

The men got to the front of the late-night convenience store. It was a better-lit part of the area, and Octavian could then observe that all three of them pulled up face masks inside their hoodies and they brought up weapons from their sides: what looked like two with crossbows and the third with a baseball bat. They then stormed into the convenience store, prompting Octavian to break into a run. He got to the road where the armed response unit were sitting and waved frantically for them to move. Their lights came on and the marked BMW shot forward.

'They've hit the convenience shop,' Octavian shouted at the driver through his open window.

Immediately, the blue lights on the roof lit up the neighbourhood and the car went onto the main road and roared the fifty yards or so to stop on an angle, blocking the road. Octavian and his team walked up and watched from a safe distance.

The two armed response officers got out and approached the lit pavement in front of the shop, their sub-machine guns out in front of them. Next, the three suspects burst from the store, stumbling and freezing in the authoritative screams from the police officers. Faced with submachine guns, the men quickly dropped their weapons and the cash and cigarettes they had stolen, and threw themselves down, spread-eagled on the pavement. Two members of shop staff stumbled out after the robbers, and were sharply ordered back inside by the police.

Octavian, Speight and Datta came forward and assisted in the arrest by handcuffing the men on the ground, then sitting them up. The armed response officers lowered their weapons. Octavian unmasked his man, and failed to recognize him. It was Speight who pulled down the facemask of Alan Hallworth, while Datta did the same to Jonjo Higgins.

It had been an adrenalin-fuelled arrest. Octavian looked down at the crossbows abandoned on the floor. They were both loaded with a bolt – thankfully they had not gone off as they were thrown down. He was pleased, naturally, to have foiled an armed robbery, but desperately disappointed that it had nothing whatsoever to do with the case.

FORTY-SIX

'There was me and the wife,' laughed Knowles. 'Matching his and hers pajamas on, cups of cocoa in our hands, watching *I'm a Celebrity*, and you three tackling armed robbers on the street.'

'Didn't need you, anyway,' smirked Speight, making her chair spin slowly.

'It was great fun,' smiled Green. He was still buzzing with adrenalin. He had woken up Joanna at midnight to tell her what had happened. 'Brilliant to be involved in that kind of thing.'

It was the morning after the night before. Williams and McAlister watched on with proud smiles. It had been a good result, but they all felt the same as Octavian had done, that it was another opportunity lost in the bigger picture.

Octavian came in with his coffee and sat down.

'Buggeration,' he said, his face like thunder. 'What do we think, team? These guys moonlight as armed robbers. Are they still in the frame for the killings?'

Speight's expression suggested not. 'Let's see what forensics say about the crossbows we recovered.'

Octavian drank some coffee, calming down. 'That seems our last hope, Shirley.'

'A nasty crew,' said Datta. 'Willing to use a crossbow. So, willing to kill Steven McLaughlin and Lily Bowden with one.'

'Who was the third man, anyway?'

McAlister answered that, 'Name of Wayne Higgins. Older brother.'

'Moron robs his local shop.'

Octavian looked at the carpet, finding that much more interesting than his current prospects of an arrest. It crossed his mind, that if this case had happened in London, then he would most probably not be back up north. Not be a Detective Inspector. Maybe it would have ruined his career.

'I have more Mercedes owners to look at,' said McAlister, almost apologetically. 'But they are much wider spread.'

Octavian didn't even look up. He was not a maudlin kind of man, not prone to feelings of depression, so he took a deep breath and bounced up. 'What's the radius, Beth?'

McAlister was slightly hurried. 'Well, errr, Chester, swinging round to south Yorkshire, up as far as Lancaster.'

'Please get as much information on these owners before we have to start travelling out of the area for routine enquiries. But, if that's all we've got, it's all we've got.'

'We need more help from traffic,' complained Knowles. 'They need to be identifying more of these Mercs and doing stops.'

'They have been doing a lot,' said McAlister, firmly defending that department.

Octavian, Knowles and Green went off to take a look inside Wayne Higgins's house. Apart from discovering that it was a smelly tip, they found nothing of relevance to the investigation.

'What *is* that smell?' asked Knowles. 'It's like rotting soil.'

'Isn't it BO?' suggested Green.

'BO mixed with rotting soil. Nice blokes.'

The forensics on the crossbows was done on the hurry up, and it came back negative. Octavian was given that depressing information from the downstairs office staff, on their return to the station. Horsefield found him there, gesturing him to step to the quieter corridor.

'Tony, we need a breakthrough very soon or it's being taken out of our hands. I'm sorry.'

'I completely understand, Sir.'

'Good work, last night, by the way. Tell your team I'm proud of them.'

'Sir.'

Back upstairs, Octavian told them neither of those things. He glanced out the window at the Forum; then sat down, before noticing that PC Warnock was at the door. The young man was back in uniform; something Octavian imagined himself back doing soon.

'Yes, PC Warnock?'

'Sir, ANPR cameras have picked up a black Mercedes SUV in the Northenden/Sharston area.'

Warnock might have well have come upstairs to tell them they had not won the lottery sweepstake, for all the lack of reaction he received from everyone in the room.

Knowles said the obvious, 'It's the teacher or the wife. The Hulmes. They live in the vicinity.'

'No, Sir,' continued Warnock. 'This vehicle is travelling without number plates. Armed response are already alerted and trying to get across there.'

That had the team bouncing to their collective feet. They rushed downstairs; three cars heading out on blues; Green driving Octavian, Knowles driving Williams, Speight driving Datta. They roared out of Wythenshawe (Joanna would later tell Green that she saw them pass the Subway store). Green nearly collided with a bus at Benchill roundabout, before they were clear and reaching great speeds in convoy.

Octavian was on the radio, following the latest details coming in from the camera operators.

'Up to Sharston,' he ordered Green.

They were soon there. Green gunned his Ford Focus up to sixty, and then had to slow, with obvious congestion up ahead at the junction.

The convoy decreased speed and took to the pavement. There was chaos on the Sharston roundabout, over the M56 motorway.

'Stop! shouted Octavian.

Green brought the car to a halt in a cloud of dust and litter. Octavian was out, looking across to the right side of the roundabout. People were out of their stationary vehicles. One woman was clearly distraught, her arms waving in the air. Even from that distance, Octavian could see a VW Polo, stationary, its windscreen a spiderweb of broken glass mixed with a red colour. A figure was slumped forward onto the steering wheel. He started to cross between the stopped cars, shouting at people to get back in their vehicles. He could see that the mess on the shattered windscreen was blood, and he could tell that the incident was not a traffic accident.

Octavian started to run, followed by the others. He drew his taser and started to run forward towards the incident. Nothing could move on the roundabout, there was a tailback on the slip road, back down to the motorway. People were pointing. Horns were blaring. The distressed woman was being comforted by people. Octavian glanced at the dead person in the driver's seat, who seemed young. He then kept pushing forward, following the frantic waving of lorry drivers and ordinary members of the public.

A figure was fleeing, in a black hoodie and jeans. He was too far ahead to make out any facial features. Octavian began to sprint down the slip road. Panic and exhilaration filled his mind and body. This was it. Surely this was it. He cut between the two lines of stopped vehicles, he was halfway down, the running man was at the motorway. Was he going to try to hijack a vehicle, while the traffic was still speeding by at over 70 mph? Octavian raised his taser, shouting, but he could not be heard, and he was too far back, the motorway was too noisy. He glanced over his shoulder: Green, then Knowles, then Speight, then Datta, then Williams; a line of desperate team members trying to get involved to help him.

The fugitive went out onto the motorway. A lorry sped through; then he was out into lane two. Cars almost wiped him out, before some began to slow, putting on their hazard lights, and he made a dash for it. Hand out to protect himself, Octavian finally got down there and began to go across himself. The man was doing the same on the other, southbound side; then he was running up the other slip road. Octavian hurdled the Armco barrier and continued his pursuit.

Octavian swore through his teeth, out of breath, panting heavily – the man was going back up to the roundabout for his vehicle, and he, Octavian, and his entire team had run after him like headless chickens! Like total fucking novices!

A marked police vehicle arrived, lights flashing, but it was coming along the motorway from the north and could not get up to the roundabout. Its siren added to the awful drama unfolding inside Octavian's head.

Octavian summoned up his second wind for the run up the other slip road. This road was clear because the jam had happened on the other side. He managed to get up there just as his thighs were about to blow up. He saw the Mercedes. So frustratingly he actually saw it, as it was ramming its way through the wall of stopped vehicles. It made its way the wrong way around the roundabout, smashed two small cars out of the way, and then was free to speed away, westwards. Octavian reached the barrier and could only watch the Merc joining traffic in the distance, before it was gone. He turned and slumped down, gasping for air. He managed to radio the direction the Mercedes was heading, and then he almost passed out.

Gradually, led by Green, his team staggered to where he was sitting. Not one of them, and Octavian blamed himself entirely, had tried to secure the vehicle that must have been somewhere in the chaos after the attack on the Polo driver.

FORTY-SEVEN

Somehow, during the excitement, Octavian had not managed to see the big red plastic Learner sign on the top of the VW Polo, or the green L-plate on the bonnet. But he saw it now, in the incident room, looking at the crime scene photographs. Then of the gunshot victim slumped forward, her brunette hair thankfully hiding her destroyed face. The killer must have stopped the Mercedes on the roundabout, run forward to wait for the Polo to approach, and then opened fire with the handgun. The traumatized lady driving instructor had managed to stop the Polo using the dual-pedals. Then had been the moment of his own arrival and the chase across the busy motorway. The chase that had put the final nail in this coffin.

Williams brought him a coffee. She was still a bit shaky. McAlister was there, at her desk, but everyone else was down in the car-park, recovering their senses, breathing deeply and walking about. They had been so close to catching the maniac, and got it so wrong at the crucial moment.

'Thank you, Katie.'

Octavian reverted to looking at the carpet again, as Williams pinned up a photo of the latest victim: seventeen-year-old Natasha Quinn, from the Parrs Wood area.

'You almost got to him, you know.'

'Almost is not good enough, Katie.'

'Shall I write her name on here?'

'Why not?'

She wrote the name in marker pen; then sat down. Her face was still flushed from the motorway incident.

'That wasn't random, of course,' she said.

'I know.'

Octavian looked up and drank some coffee.

'He was there because she was having a driving lesson, and that was the instructor's usual route, to cross the motorway at that point. He waited for that exact person to drive by, knowing she would be slow, coming off the roundabout. A hit.'

'But there's no connection between victims. They didn't know each other. They didn't know the one person who this all revolves around. Anyway, we will be taken off this tomorrow, or the day after. It will ramp up in scale with road checkpoints, the works, and all involved being interviewed again. The area will be swamped with cops.'

'Meanwhile, Boss, we still need to speak to the Quinn family. Want me and Shirley to do it?'

'No, no. I'll go with you. Just give me a few minutes.'

Octavian went to his locker for a clean shirt and some deodorant. In the toilets, he stripped to the waist and had a wash. He looked intently at himself in the mirror. Hopefully, he thought, the Quinn family would say something, anything, that made a connection.

Wearing the clean shirt, and with his hair combed, he exited the toilets, finding Bill Fitzgerald waiting for him.

'Someone here to see you. A DS Woolaston, from the Cheshire Constabulary. I know him, he's a mate of DS Knowles.'

'And he wants me, not Knowles?'

'You, Sir.'

Octavian walked into reception and shook hands with DS Charles Woolaston.

'DS Woolaston? DI Octavian.'

'Sir. Sorry to pop in like this. I wonder if I could have a word?'

'Sure. Come up.' They walked up the stairs. 'You know Phil Knowles?'

'For my sins.'

They sat down in the incident room. Neither Williams nor McAlister were there.

'The girl who was killed today,' began Woolaston. 'My niece.'

'Oh, my God. I'm so sorry, DS Woolaston.'

'My sister is already sedated by the doctor. My brother-in-law is devastated. Of course, you'll need to speak to them, but I wanted to give you as much background as I know.'

Octavian was wary of anything a related police officer had to say about a crime, but he was willing to listen to Woolaston. 'I appreciate that. As you probably know, we can't catch a break on this, as nothing connects up. What do you have to tell me?'

'Tasha. Sorry, I'll stick to her full name. Natasha was a normal young woman. A bit silly, a bit selfish, but a good person, overall. It's her ex-partner I wanted to bring you up to speed on, Sir.'

'Go on.'

'Natasha's Ex was a nightmare. The police were called out many times. Controlling, low levels of violence, a nasty piece of work. I interfered as much as I could, or as Natasha would allow me to. It's difficult with young people, of course.'

'When did they split up?'

'A few months ago. I heard it was a bad break-up, lots of screaming and threats and breaking of windows stuff. But recently it's been calm.'

'You believe this Ex has something to do with today's events?'

'I'm not going that far, Sir. I just wanted to speak to you personally and make you aware of how volatile the relationship was. Hopefully my sister and her husband will only have to confirm this, and not re-live it themselves.'

'Sounds bad for a young girl to get involved with that. Was she at school with the guy?'

'It's not a guy, Sir. It's a woman. I believe she is nineteen now.'

Octavian was surprised. 'Oh, it was a gay relationship? Well, as you know, it was a male today, and throughout our investigations it's been a male we've been after. Do you know any males associated with this ex-girlfriend?'

'No, I don't, Sir.'

'Well, tell me the Ex's details and we will look at her, of course.'

Woolaston brought out an envelope which he passed over. 'All there, Sir.'

Octavian looked inside: name and address. 'Lisa Pham. Chinese?'

'Vietnamese origin. British citizen.'

'Okay, leave it with us.'

'Thank you, Sir.'

They stood and shook hands again.

'Is DS Knowles here, Sir? I might as well say hello.'

'Yes, he's down there, somewhere. Again, I'm sorry for your loss.'

'Sir.'

FORTY-EIGHT

Williams returned to the incident room. Octavian waited for her to sit down; then told her about Lisa Pham.

'A person of interest, certainly,' she said. 'But only for today, surely?'

Octavian popped down to the car-park. Everybody snapped out of their reverie, ready to get back to work, but Octavian shook his head. 'You guys go home. It's been appalling. Be with your loved ones. Everyone is tired after the Hallworth thing, as well. Let's re-group in the morning.'

They all wanted to keep going, but he insisted, so they got their heads around the idea. Octavian touched Green on the shoulder, in passing; then returned to Williams.

'Katie, listen, the Quinn family are in no fit state today, so let's go see if we can find this Lisa Pham person.'

The address from Woolaston was also in the Parrs Wood area, which, with Williams driving, took them back in the direction of Sharston.

'Let's see the place again, shall we, Katie?'

The traffic was minimal. Looking across to the right, SOCO had finished their investigation and there was nothing to suggest anything had even happened there. Williams took the last exit on the roundabout and down onto the motorway. She came off at the next exit.

In Octavian's opinion, Parrs Wood was a crowded, old area, now plagued by an insane amount of traffic calming measures. He remembered being out with friends there, in his teens.

Williams found the Lisa Pham address, which turned out to be a substantial detached property in a quiet cul-de-sac. There were no cars on the drive, but they walked up and knocked anyway; getting no reply.

'Leave a card or try the neighbours?' asked Williams.

'Put a card in, Katie, I'll have a wander across.'

Octavian pressed the doorbell of the house to the right. He showed his warrant card to the elderly lady who answered the door.

'Sorry to bother you, madam. DI Octavian of Greater Manchester police. I don't suppose you know where the Pham family are during the day.'

'He's in. Mr Pham, that is. I can see him exercising in his conservatory.'

'Oh, is he? Right. Thank you. We'll keep trying.'

He walked back to Williams.

'I heard,' she said. 'Let's try going round the side.'

They went down the side of the house, finding the gate unlocked, and then entered the back garden. There was an Asian man in his fifties, in *Adidas* training gear, with headphones in, on his running machine in the conservatory. He slowed and stopped the machine as he realized he had strangers in his garden. Octavian had his card out again for when the man opened the conservatory door.

'Mr Pham?'

'Yes. Who are you, please?'

'DI Octavian, and this is my colleague, DS Williams. Sorry to disturb your exercise session. We were hoping for a chat with Miss Lisa Pham.'

'Lisa? Well, she doesn't live here at the moment. What's it about? I'm her father.'

'There was an incident on the M56 earlier today. It involved someone we think Miss Pham knew. That's all. Just a chat.'

'If you let me ring her...'

'Of course. Very good of you, Sir.'

Octavian and Williams admired the garden, with a very cultured lawn.

'You could putt golf balls on that,' observed Octavian.

'You could. He's coming straight back.'

Mr Pham looked out again. 'Not answering, I'm afraid. Shall I get her to contact you?'

'Perhaps tell us where she is likely to be,' said Octavian. 'We have the time.'

The man hesitated. No doubt he'd had the police there before for his daughter.

'The sooner we speak to her, the sooner we are done,' added Williams.

'She has a part-time job today. You could try there.'

'And where is there?' asked Williams.

'It's a funeral firm, in town.'

That surprised both Octavian and Williams.

'The name and address?' asked Octavian.

'I've got some of their literature here. One second.'

'Perhaps if you could write Miss Pham's current address on the back, as well, Sir.'

Mr Pham left them again. He returned with the funeral firm's brochure, and it had an address for Lisa Pham written on the back.

'Will there be anything else?'

'No, Sir. We'll see ourselves out. Good day.'

They walked back down the drive.

'A funeral firm?' asked Williams, incredulous. 'How does a young woman end up working there? Especially if she's got a bad attitude.'

'Let's go and see.'

Williams had the funeral brochure in her hand. 'Her home address is on the way. Check first?'

'I agree.'

Lisa Pham had a flat, a few streets away. It was in an impressive converted old building that had once been something to do with the railways. But they got no reply from the intercom to her apartment, so they continued on to the funeral firm.

'Passing through the area I grew up,' said Octavian.

'Good wine bars round here.'

It was another old building, that Octavian could imagine the family firm working from in the days when there were only horse-drawn hearses. They walked into the front office, to be met by a small woman, wearing a purple dress and an over-the-top wooden necklace which resembled abacus balls. There was also a badge identifying her as Mrs Sunderland. But she was genuinely friendly, clearly the person who first met bereaved relatives to arrange funerals. Following the full introductions, she sat them down in the front room. Octavian looked about him at the selection of caskets for ashes; oak and ash and something else, and felt decidedly freaked out.

'You want Lisa?' asked Mrs Sunderland. 'I'm afraid we have a funeral on at the moment, and Lisa is on duty.'

Octavian and Williams looked at each other, both thinking, "Should we speak to her in the middle of a funeral?"

'Is it unusual for a young woman to work in this type of business?' asked Williams.

Mrs Sunderland thought. 'I suppose it is. But it used to be unusual for a woman to be a police officer, or a bus driver, once upon a time.

We have Lisa and another girl. They are very professional, in my opinion.'

'We really must speak to Miss Pham,' said Octavian. 'We have some possibly distressing news and we wouldn't want her to hear it from another source.'

'I do understand,' said Mrs Sunderland. 'You will be discreet?'

'Absolutely, Mrs Sunderland.'

She consulted a very tiny watch on her wrist. 'Well, I should imagine they will be arriving at the cemetery very soon.'

Octavian didn't want to stay in that creepy room a moment longer than he had to. 'Right, we'll pop along there. We'll try to speak to her in private. Thank you, Mrs Sunderland.'

'Which cemetery?' asked Williams,
'Southern.'

As they drove along, Octavian had a macabre thought of Lisa Pham being on duty for Natasha Quinn's funeral, but shook it off as Williams looked for a parking space on the road in front of the main ornate gates.

The funeral arrived moments later, the train of cars passing through the gateway and down through the gravestones. Octavian and Williams tried to see the staff in the cars, but the sun was a nuisance of strong reflections.

'Was that a woman driving the hearse?' asked Williams.

They followed on behind.

'I like cemeteries,' said Williams. 'I find them very calming.'

Octavian looked at her as if she were crazy.

Right near the entrance, Williams gestured for them to drift to the right.

'What?' he asked.

'My grandparents are right there.'

'No way?'

The grass had recently had a strimmer passed over it. Williams bent to tidy the grave a little bit. Octavian looked at the two names and dates on the headstone.

'I've not been here for a few years,' said Williams.

They finally continued on. They let the funeral take its course in the chapel, waiting outside. It was the most frustrated Octavian had ever been while trying to interview anyone. Eventually all the mourners headed towards the new grave. Octavian and Williams identified Lisa Pham as the only Asian present, not including Octavian, himself. She wore the black uniform, as did her three male colleagues. She had been the driver – the day got weirder and weirder.

Octavian fully intended to wait until the service was over and people were moving away. Perhaps, with hindsight, looking for Lisa Pham at a funeral had been the best idea. He would not approach the girl until the end, but she had noticed them looking at her. She messed with her black tie, and shuffled her feet, all signs of nervousness. Her mouth was slightly pursed in annoyance. She had a heavy fringe, which she kept pushing away from her eyes. The sides of her head were shaved, but in general Octavian thought she was fairly pretty.

As the service progressed, Octavian sensed the unease of Williams beside him. He was a second or two away from suggesting that they properly step away, go back and wait at the funeral firm, when Lisa Pham closed the gap between them. She walked over calmly, attracting no attention.

'You police?'

Octavian realized that the father must have contacted her on the phone, either at the time, or later, after they had left.

'Yes, Miss Pham. We'd like a word, once the service has concluded.'

Octavian kept his voice low, but Lisa Pham was suddenly agitated, livid; then apoplectic, as if two chemicals had mixed in her brain. Her face went red, she raised a pointing finger.

'Coming to my work!?' It was not a shout, but it was rage-filled. Some nearby mourners noticed. 'My work!? Who do you people think you are?'

'Miss Pham,' said Williams, hoping to keep the girl calm.

'Katie,' said Octavian, wanting to leave before an incident.

'I hate you fuckers!?' More people heard that; there was going to be repercussions, for sure. 'How dare you!? How... dare... you..?'

Lisa Pham looked disgusted at Williams, and then she faced up Octavian; who knew that move. A right-handed punch emerged from the black jacket, which Octavian swerved to avoid. He had not been expecting the instant left as well, which caught him on the right temple. She had clearly done some boxing training. Lisa

Pham had lost it. A shocked Williams attempted to grab her, but the ranting girl was going for Octavian with her nails. Mourners gasped, the service halted, and her colleagues were gobsmacked.

Octavian had no option but to put Lisa Pham down on the floor. From there he kept her under control with his hands and knees until Williams could get some handcuffs on her. The girl was literally spitting mad, her eyes popping, her language appalling.

Despite his best efforts, an embarrassed Octavian could not stop himself taking in the horrified scene of people nearby; not a funeral they would ever forget.

FORTY-NINE

Knowles could not stop himself from laughing.

Octavian sat himself down in the incident room with a coffee. He was extremely tired and had a plaster on his temple where Lisa Pham's left hook had cut him. Williams cradled a cup of tea, sitting nearby at her desk.

'It was so embarrassing,' Williams said to a sympathetic Speight. 'Those poor mourners.'

Knowles checked where his feet were, as if readying for a comment. 'Lisa Pham went full tonto in the middle of a funeral service?' Then he burst out laughing again.

Datta had to giggle, even as she sympathetically touched Williams' shoulder, in passing.

'Oh, my God,' continued Knowles, almost crying. 'That's the best way to quit a job I've ever heard of.'

'So, she's downstairs in the cells at the moment?' asked Datta.

'Yes,' answered Williams. 'We thought an overnight stay would calm her down. Although she was still kicking the door, last time I passed.'

Speight said, 'Shows what a temper she has, then. What a shame for Natasha Quinn to get involved with someone like that.'

'Doesn't mean anything, in relation to our case,' said Octavian. 'Katie, do you want to do the interview with me?'

'Yes, I do.'

They found Lisa Pham's solicitor standing in the car-park, vaping a huge cloud of "smoke" skyward. Octavian liked vaping even less than he did smoking, and it seemed strange from a professional man in a pinstripe suit.

'You ready, Mr Holiman?' he asked.

'Yes, Detective Inspector. Lead on, by all means.'

Lisa Pham sat in the interview room, handcuffed again, to the front of her body. She was leaning to the side, apparently uninterested in any aspect of life. The main reason for her desperately unhappy night in the cell, apart from her rabid hatred of authority, was that she had been told about Natasha Quinn.

Mr Holiman was given the time he wanted with his client before Octavian and Williams joined them and sat down. There was a young female PC standing at the far wall.

'Good morning, Miss Pham,' said Octavian.

Octavian and Williams finally exited the interview room and both found their own wall to lean against. It had been a session of No Comments from Lisa Pham, who had gone from rage to a deep depression.

'What do you think?' asked Williams.

'She's undoubtedly a violent and troubled young woman. But I genuinely don't think she's involved, in the slightest.'

Both of them were tired.

'We know it's connected to the others because we saw our man at the scene,' said Octavian. 'It's not like Heywood, which might be a separate thing. If Lisa Pham was involved in Natasha Quinn's killing, then she has to be involved in all the others. Not for me.'

'So, what, let her go? Charge her with your assault and let her walk?'

'I've no interest in that, Katie. What's the point? Drop that.'

'If you're sure, Boss.'

Octavian found himself looking at the linoleum on the corridor floor, instead of the carpet in the incident room. Williams chose to go the other way, staring at the ceiling.

That evening, there was a barbecue at one of the Woodhouse Park Fire crewmember's homes. The man's nickname was Edge (he was a redhead and vaguely resembled Ed Sheeran). Edge had about fifty colleagues and friends round to his larger than average garden, and this included Taheer and Harry, brought in specially by mini-vans, as both were temporarily still in their wheelchairs. As they arrived at the house, they both tried to start a race down the street, but Speight and Datta ran alongside their wheelchairs and put a stop to the silliness.

Both men were the star guests; they were positioned on the middle of the patio, chatted to, served first, generally fussed over. They were both doing well, and hopeful to start their physiotherapy soon. When they weren't squatting alongside their men, Speight and Taheer mingled with the off-duty firefighters and their partners. It was a fun evening, children running around, music playing from the house, the food was excellent, and Taheer and Harry really enjoyed themselves.

FIFTY

Octavian's evening meal consisted of a bowl of tomato soup and a tuna fish sandwich, from a tin, as Ezi was out somewhere. He made himself a cup of tea. Then he was keen to finish the kidnap part of his Indonesian story, so he could have the family sail away towards their ultimate shipwreck on the desert island.

It had been Bowo Supranto who made the phone calls to Raja. Then he and one of his brothers went with Carl Hummels to the drop-off point. Carl had thought of hiring the local drivers to provide the confusion. While he and the other brother waited on motorbikes on the road beside the train track, Bowo had been the one to go up for the money; had been the one caught in the helicopter spotlight, the one who panicked and returned up the slope during the gun battle, who had fired off his Uzi in all directions. During the firefight with police, only Carl had managed to escape.

Of course, at the same time, the police were raiding the hostage house to free Rome

Lipman. In the ensuing gunfight there, Hans Hummels and another Supranto brother had died, while the last brother had been arrested.

As he rode out of the city, Carl kept trying to reach Hans on the cell phone, before eventually coming to the conclusion that his brother was either dead or captured. By the morning, he learned from a news report that the kidnapping of the American model had been successfully ended by security forces, resulting in the death of three local men and one unidentified foreigner.

Sitting in a roadside café, looking at the TV on the wall, Carl felt no great emotion; he was cold like that. His grief would arrive at some later point, he knew that. With particular German efficiency, he simply rode right back to Bali. Once there, he phoned Harper, expressing his total shock at hearing the news, and also apologizing in case she felt he had suddenly avoided her after their one night together – it wasn't like that.

Harper wanted to see him, but she told him she was with the Bali police. Carl expressed resignation about that, given the circumstances, and even said he would try to contact her once he was home in Austria. He *was wishing the best to her and her brother when she blurted out that she could easily get away from the police, as it was only a lone female officer staying with them in a house. So, they arranged a time and place that he would pick her up on the motorbike.*

Once he had her with him, holding him by the waist, he rode her to a hotel that he already knew (one that he would never take his wife to) and they checked in under aliases. He made love to her with an animalistic fury that she had never known before.

Afterwards, both sweating – she, slightly bruised around the throat, he asked her what had transpired.

'Well, since we reported what happened they just kept us in that house. Then we heard that Rome was rescued.'

'Have you spoken to your brother?'

'No.'

'Oh, well, I'm sure you'll see him soon. You can get home to America and forget the whole nasty business.'

'Will you come and see me, Carl?'

He gave her a snort. 'The good citizens of Vienna need me to get back to work.'

'I'll come to Vienna, then.'

He gave her a look of surprised happiness. 'Okay.'

She giggled and snuggled into his shoulder.

After his rescue, Rome Lipman was actually taken to the Yogyakarta Chief of Police's house, which sat in a secure compound in a village to the west of the city. A still shocked Raja met him there. He could see that the young man was traumatized. He was unhurt, and had been fed by his captors, but the whole thing had left him understandably nervous and quiet. He was able to discuss what had happened with Raja, but it didn't cross his mind to thank Raja for his part in his release.

The Chief's wife, Mrs Susanti, provided them with lots of food, with Raja thanking her each time. They sat in the lounge watching the TV news, while a private flight was being chartered to take them back to Jakarta. Rome had spoken to his mother on the phone, so the family knew the outcome had been what they had hoped for.

'Do you think she has a beer?' asked Rome, indicating Mrs Susanti.

'I doubt it. There will be alcohol on the plane.'

Rome indicated the Indonesian news channel. 'How many kidnappers were killed?'

'They said two, when the special forces came in for you. And two at the drop-off.'

'I counted five at one stage. Do you think the survivors will come after me again?'

'It's not a movie, Rome. They will be hiding like crazy. And you'll be in LA soon.'

'It was so quick, you know. The lights went out. Flash, bang, they were in and shooting.'

'Rome, try not to think about it. We will leave for Jakarta later, and then you can fly to LA.'

Rome looked like he was about to cry. 'Fly? I'm not going on the boat?'

'I didn't think you'd be up for a cruise across the ocean. But, thinking about it, maybe it's exactly what you need.'

'Yes. Yes, I want to be on the boat, with Mom, and you.'

When they got back to Jakarta, the house was besieged by the Press and media. Raja had more messages on his phone from his ex-boyfriend, wanting an exclusive from him, as well as from other journalists and all of the major US networks.

Raja noted that, while Margo and the girls verbally welcomed Rome back to them, none of them hugged him. That was left to Harry Rashford. The Englishman looked so relieved to see Rome safe, perhaps blaming himself in some way for not preventing the kidnap.

Raja received a hug from Paddy Finucane.

'Good to have you back, Raja, mate.'

'Thanks, Paddy.'

Dr de Hoog was waiting to examine Rome. A police doctor had checked him over in Yogyakarta but Margo insisted that Rome be given a medical and then total ongoing care. Actually, he just needed a good sleep, and so wasn't seen again for a day or so.

Raja showered and then slept, too. Then he felt the need to get straight back to work. Margo thanked him for all his great efforts. She promised him an increased bonus, once they reached Los Angeles. That led the conversation to the sailing.

'I suggested to Rome that he fly on ahead,' said Raja. 'But he expressed his wish to sail.'

'Very well. Let's stick to the plan. When can we leave?'

'I will confirm a time today. The Estate Agent wants a meeting with you. I assume that he has offers on the house to present to you. And do you want to release a statement to the media?'

'I will see the Estate Agent. I have nothing to say to the media.'

Raja excused himself and left.

FIFTY-ONE

Getting lost in his story had delayed Octavian's shower. Happy with the chapter, he sat down to relax and watch some TV for a few minutes, but it seemed to him that most of the channels just kept repeating the seven or eight episodes of a series that they could afford to buy, and the news was depressing, as always. He settled on watching some golf from America. But what was that thing that Green had said to Knowles, in the car outside Corbett's house? Sport is just new people doing the same thing that other people have done before. Plus, he didn't particularly like watching millionaires getting even richer just by hitting a little ball around the countryside. He put a music channel on, instead.

When he almost dropped off to sleep on the sofa, he forced himself up and went for that shower. Then he dressed in his best trousers and a tight sweater, put on his newest pair of boots, and went out of the house.

He drove to Manchester town centre. More specifically, to a town centre hotel. He walked

437

into reception, looked about him, seeing two attractive receptionists booking courts for white-clad squash players. He moved on into the bar. It was fairly busy in there, with couples, as well as what appeared to be business conference guests unwinding.

Kezia was sitting at the bar. She turned to watch his arrival. It was almost like that scene from *Pretty Woman*, but instead of a cocktail dress she was wearing an all-black outfit, and had a basket of chips in front of her. She smiled in a kind of pleasant way; it was not a date, in any sense of the word.

'You managed to come,' she said.

'Yes. I made the time.'

'Please join me. Do you still not drink?'

'I still don't drink.'

He climbed onto a stool. The bartender approached.

'Another one of those for the lady, and I'll have a coke, please.'

'Have a chip,' she offered.

'Thank you.'

He was still hungry, so took a couple, before paying for the drinks.

'Are you all right?' she asked.

'A bit frazzled. I'm being kept busy, but there's nothing to say to you yet, I'm afraid.'

'I understand.'

He sipped his coke, happy once again to be so near to her. The ride across had been yet another guilt-ridden, conscience-beating ordeal, with him looking for roads to turn down, in order to do a U-turn, but never actually hitting the indicator.

'How are you doing?' he asked. 'What have you done today?'

Kezia sipped some wine. 'Today, Tony? Today was Lily's funeral.'

FIFTY-TWO

'Oh, Kezia.'

Hearing her tell him it had been her daughter's funeral made his heart bleed for her. Her eyes glanced up at him, before returning to stare at her fingers around the wine glass. Octavian realized that her outfit had been what she had worn all day.

'Kezia, I'm so sorry, I didn't know. Why are you here?'

'I'd had enough of the wall-to-wall sympathy I was getting.'

'Does your family know where you are?'

'No. My son's with his dad. You know, Tony, it was a lovely funeral. All her friends and classmates came. The music wasn't sad at all.'

He took her hand, concerned that she was in a disturbed frame of mind, but she managed a slight giggle.

'Don't look at me like I'm mad, Tony. I'm fine, honestly. I just need to see you at the moment. I don't know why. You make things feel all right. Seriously, I'm okay.'

'Have you eaten? Properly, not just some chips.' He looked about for the restaurant. 'I'll get us a table.'

'No, I'm not hungry.'

They moved to a quieter seat by the window.

'Are you a member here?' he asked, to change the subject.

'No, but my friend works here. If you want a free sauna, anytime, just let me know.'

'I'll keep it in mind.'

'So, have you been to Jakarta recently? I suppose the Covid thing stopped that.'

'I've not been for a long time. We keep saying we must go.'

'You were always my most exotic boyfriend.'

'Good to know.'

A female member of staff approached them, apologetic at interrupting. 'Sorry, sorry.'

'Ellie, hi,' said Kezia. 'Ellie, this is Tony.'

Octavian had already seen the name on the woman's lapel badge, which also said Assistant Housekeeper. 'Hi.'

'Hi, Tony. I just wanted to come over to say hello. I'm late as usual. Kezia, babe, come through and chat before you go.'

'I will do, I promise.'

Ellie started to leave. 'Nice to meet you, Tony.'

They watched her depart.

'Where were we?' she asked.

'You were saying how I was the most exotic boyfriend you ever had.'

'Oh, yes. There was an Australian fella. He wasn't exotic, but he's from further away, isn't he?'

'An Australian? What *were* you thinking?'

'I know. Anyway, you look well. A bit tired, as you said. But you've aged well. I can say that, can't I? We've passed beyond the polite age. Life is what it is. It's not about nightclubs and shoes anymore.'

'You've aged amazingly, Kezia. But I knew you would. My father once advised me to look at your mother...'

She giggled. 'Pardon?'

'To see how you would turn out. I was well impressed with your mum, back in the day.'

'I'll be sure to tell her. She'll be well chuffed. Yeah, I'd heard that theory.'

'But the theory only applies if the two people stay together for life.'

'Yes.'

Suddenly the fire alarm sounded. As always in those situations, nobody bothered to move, just waited for it to stop. But it carried on.

'I don't quite believe this,' said Kezia.

A Manager called for everyone to briefly go out to the car-park. Octavian and Kezia followed the couples and the conference delegates out through the fire exit, where everyone lingered around.

'At least it's a nice evening,' she said.

'It's probably a false alarm. Nobody seems bothered.'

'Have you been in some dangerous situations, Tony? You must have done, with your job.'

'One or two. Violent drunks. People who didn't want to be arrested. That sort of thing.'

'Have you got any medals? From the Mayor of London?'

He laughed. 'Absolutely not.'

After a couple of minutes, a sole fire engine rolled in. They watched the crew go inside the hotel. Soon after that, the firefighters left again, and the Manager invited everyone back inside the hotel.

'I told you,' said Octavian. 'A false alarm. Or a chef got a bit careless with his pasta.'

They returned to the bar and he got them more drinks. They decided to sit outside on the terrace.

'Are you sure you don't want to ring your sister? Tell her where you are.'

'I might do, later.'

'I can take you there, whenever you want.'

'I might stay here tonight. Ellie will sneak me a room key. Oh, don't arrest her for that.'

'I'll just give her a verbal warning.'

'Why don't you stay with me?'

Octavian looked off to the trees that bordered the hotel grounds. It was an awkward moment. But she did not follow it up with, "Sorry, that was silly of me to suggest". She just drank her wine and observed his face.

'For old times' sake?' he finally said.

'If you like.'

'No.'

'Okay. I just thought it would be sweet.'

'No.'

She smiled softly. 'I hear you.'

His phone beeped with a message, making his mind go straight to thoughts of Charlotte (not that she hadn't been lingering around in there all evening). 'Excuse me a second.' He brought the phone out of his pocket, seeing that it was nothing, just something from his service provider.

'Is work going to take you away?' she asked. 'Like in the movies?'

'No, it's not important. Let me take you back to your sister's.'

'No, it will still be full of relatives. I think I'll get a room, just to rest for a few hours. Then I'll get a cab back.'

They sat quietly for a few minutes.

'These are the moments when I wished I drank,' he said.

'Maybe that's why you're still so handsome. Not drinking alcohol. Anyway, I'll go and get a key from Ellie. Then I'll come back to say goodnight. Will you wait a bit?'

'I'm comfy here. I'll wait to say goodnight, Kezia.'

She walked through the fire door. Octavian watched a group of women in their leotards walking to their cars. A barmaid took the empties off his table, so he smiled up at her.

Kezia returned quickly. Octavian saw the big key fob dangling off her fingers. He looked at her gorgeous face.

'I'll say goodnight, then, Tony. Thank you for coming to see me again. I appreciate you being so good to me.'

'You have a good rest, Kezia.'

'It's room number is 219. I'll leave the door open.'

He found the tree line of interest again, and then she was gone. He sat there for several minutes, which turned into fifteen, as he really was comfortable and no new customers came out there to disturb him.

Finally, he hauled himself up, and walked back through to reception. Instead of going to the right for the exit, he went left for the stairs. Upstairs, the corridors were cool, and the carpet plush underfoot. He padded along until he found 219. The door was, in fact, ajar. He pushed it softly and entered quietly. The room had the curtain closed and was lit by lamps. The TV played a music channel, quietly. He didn't encounter Kezia. To his left, the bathroom was empty. He took a step forward, and saw her bare legs through the mirror, as she lay reclined on the bed. Her toes were rubbing together. That's all he could see, her stunning legs. The best years of his young life rushed back to him as he enjoyed the sight of the smooth flesh. He wanted to move forward and join her so much, but, instead, he backed away silently and slipped back out of the door. He walked back along the corridor, down the stairs and left the hotel.

FIFTY-THREE

It was dark by the time Octavian got back home to Altrincham. Ezi was sitting there in the lounge, just coming off his mobile phone.

'Good evening,' said Octavian.

'I just invited Poppy to visit, like you said.'

'Excellent!'

Octavian stood there. It was very quiet without Charlotte and Jack. He noticed that an episode of *The Sweeney* was on the TV. Regan and Carter were trying to pull a couple of birds.

'Have you eaten?' he asked Ezi. The youngster shook his head. 'Let's go out and grab a bite to eat somewhere.'

They went to an Indian restaurant that Octavian knew, in nearby Hale; one of the really posh areas of Greater Manchester. They sat facing each other across the table, with their feast spread out before them.

'Last time I was in here,' said Octavian. 'Three United players were at that table, there.'

'Thank you for this.'

'Is Poppy excited to visit?'

'Yes! What should I do with her, when she's here?'

Octavian grinned over his poppadum, and Ezi blushed.

'Apart from that? Where should I take her?'

'Plenty of places to take her while she's here on the cultured side of the Pennines. She'll be happy just hanging out with you, anyway.'

They enjoyed their meal. Octavian found it fun to be out with his nephew.

'You were late tonight,' said Ezi. 'Still on that stakeout thing?'

'No, that came to a conclusion. Same case, but that came to nothing.'

'You know these murders...?'

Octavian watched new customers being sat at their table, before looking back at Ezi. 'Hmmm?'

Ezi had a mouthful of naan bread, by then, so Octavian had to wait.

'These murders. You've looked at Contract Market, of course?'

Octavian paused, fork in mid-air, staring hard at Ezi. 'Pardon? The what?'

'Contract Market, on the internet.'

'Tell me more about this.'

'It's a place on the dark web where kids can pay to have other kids hurt. It's a joke place, I think. The money is exchanged when the job can be verified. Usually, it's a beating up or a smashed window. But there are really bad ones on there. Those are the ones that aren't taken seriously.'

Octavian was absolutely gobsmacked, not least because it was the most his nephew had ever said in one go, since coming to England. He put his fork down and reached for his wallet. He took out all the cash he had on him, sixty pounds, and placed it in front of Ezi.

'Finish your meal, pay, and get a taxi home.'

'Where are you going!?'

Octavian grabbed his coat off the back of the chair and walked quickly out of the restaurant.

Octavian got the Golf onto the M56, heading towards south Manchester, trying to remember how to get to the Cheadle area. As he came off the motorway, he remembered the way to McAlister's house. It was close to 11 p.m. when he pulled onto her road, slowly cruising along until he recognized her parked car.

A light came on as he walked up the drive. He rang the bell and then stood with his face up to the security camera. DCI Neil Horsefield answered the door, in his pajamas. He was not unduly disturbed to see DI Octavian show up at his house, late at night.

'Sorry to disturb you at home, Sir. And so late. I need to see DC McAlister.'

Horsefield waved him in.

McAlister was in her dressing gown, ready for bed. She was surprised to see Octavian arrive so late.

'Boss?' she said. 'Come to my office.'

'Sorry about this, Beth. I need to discuss something with you urgently.'

They crossed the hall and entered her home office.

'Do you want some tea?'

'No, no. Let's sit. Please turn your computer on.'

'I think I know what you're going to say.'

'Do you?' he asked, intrigued.

'It's been troubling my logical brain. What the link is. It's something to do with the internet, isn't it?'

'Looks like it.'

Octavian went home at around 2 a.m. Then he took the following day off. He had to leave McAlister alone to deal with the IT boffins before anything could move forward. Of course, his mind continued to turn it all over again and again, so he went for a long cycle ride around Tatton Park, and he went food shopping, and he managed to watch a full F1 Grand Prix race – not just the start.

The whole team gathered in the incident room at Wythenshawe. Octavian was on his feet, animated. The words Contract Market were written boldly on the white board.

'Beth's been burning the candle at both ends on this, so, thanks to Beth. You've all seen the email you were sent. All our victims are on that dark web site. The reason we don't have any more victims is because there are no current jobs, in the North West. Whatever the reason for our victims being on there, or who paid anonymously: this is our link.'

Everyone was still in shock. All had been woken very early. Knowles acknowledged the importance of the moment by using his hand to shield a yawn.

Octavian continued, 'Beth informs me, after hours talking to the IT department, that trying to track the killer through the site would be impossible. It's too complex. But at least we now have something to go on.'

'Yes, but what, Boss?' asked Speight. 'I read about these sites, and most are just scams for morons to lose money through Bitcoin.'

'Most are, yes, Shirley. But this one seems to have active participants.' He raised an email print-out and read it aloud. 'Tom Walsh was knocked down for just £250.'

'So, what's our next step?' asked Williams.

Octavian sat down; he had not slept much since the breakthrough moment.

'We need to set a trap for our killer,' he said. 'We need to commission a hit.'

Speight was incredulous – she knew the Boss liked to step outside the box, a bit, but setting a trap was completely not by the book. 'How?'

Octavian saw what her face was registering. 'I know it's wacky, and I've not even asked Horsefield yet, but we create, or Beth creates, an account on this site, and then we pay for a murder.'

There was a stunned silence in the room. After a moment, Knowles laughed.

'What's funny?' asked Speight.

'Computer stuff is funny. It's all nuts. One of my nephews was talking to me the other day. He met a Malaysian girl on a penpal site and she wanted to video call. They were explaining their lives to each other and she then played the piano for him. He said she was fabulous at it, but it went on for about eight minutes.' He laughed so hard that tears appeared in his eyes, and everyone smiled at the story. 'He wondered if she was ever going to stop. Anyway, I digress. Who are we going to get killed?'

Octavian pointed a finger at Green, who waved and grinned.

'Me,' said Green. 'Well, my younger brother, actually.'

'Can anyone look younger than you?' asked Knowles.

Everyone laughed again.

'My brother has just left for New Zealand. He says we can borrow his social media. So, it's not like we make something new up. The killer can see a real person. He looks like me. I'll be him, in your heads, as the trap is set.'

'Let me get this straight,' said Datta. 'Is Green going to be out there as the next victim?'

'No, Aamina,' said Octavian. 'He won't be in any danger. It's if we need anything new. If we need to place him wherever we decide. And just to give us a focus. It will be a fictional target. We just let it be known where he could be attacked and let Armed Response be waiting.'

Knowles made a lot of facial expressions, taking it all in. 'Where do we try to tempt the killer to?'

'That's what we need to think of,' said Octavian. 'Somewhere away from the public, with only a couple of ways in.'

Williams said, 'I'm concerned that all we end up with is arresting our man while going equipped to commit a crime. What's to link him to the murders if there's no forensics?'

'That's a valid argument, Katie. But we've had nothing because there's no connections. We have to get him before he strikes again. Then we throw everything at finding a forensic link.'

'What guarantees that our man goes for it?' asked Datta.

'Nothing,' answered Octavian. 'He might have finished. But, he's only been going for the local jobs. Green will be very local. If Beth sees anything else posted, we will pick up that person and offer protection until this is over.' Octavian looked around all their faces. 'Are we agreed this is the way to go?'

Everyone agreed.

'So, we have our target,' said Knowles. 'Which is Green. We will put a contract out on him. The killer will come for Green, but find Armed Response, instead.'

'You catch on quick, Phil,' said a grinning Speight.

Knowles nodded at her. 'Thank you. What we need is an enclosed space that the killer has to come into. I'm thinking a multi-storey car park. Green can be on duty there as a member of staff, according to his social media.'

'You're forgetting that Green is a child,' pointed out Datta. 'He can't have a job in a multi-storey car park.'

'We need a house in a remote area,' said Williams.

'Boss,' said McAlister. 'My brother is a property developer. He has some almost finished apartments in Wythenshawe. I'm sure we could take it over for a short time. Have Green excited on his social media about recently moving in there. We can have Armed Response staying inside, with full surveillance.'

Octavian liked that idea. 'Good one, Beth. Can you set up a meet with him? We need it to be the right place. Okay, let's take a break. Then we can work on the plan.'

Everyone drifted to the canteen. Octavian got a coffee and sat with Williams.

'Katie, why don't you speak to our nice Mr Anstead, down in Kent? Let him investigate this angle for his killer there.'

'Yes, I'll do that.'

They drank their coffees.

'Are you thinking what I'm thinking?' she asked.

'Maybe. What were you thinking?'

'People like Lisa Pham, Bradley... Hungarian kid, Courtney Leigh-Waller. If these people were the ones who paid for these hits, when do we go after them?'

'That's exactly what I was thinking!'

They both laughed.

'We focus on the fake Green thing?'

'Yes,' he said. 'Plenty of time to go after those people afterwards. There's nothing they could tell us about the killer, anyway. They don't know who he is, either.'

FIFTY-FOUR

Octavian and McAlister stood on a new, rabbit hutch estate in Wythenshawe (so new that the road was still to be laid and the manhole covers stood proud) and looked at a small development of only four apartments.

'Are you all right?' he asked her.

She looked at him, crinkling her eyes from the sun. 'Yes, why?'

'You're out of the office. I thought you might be feeling a bit dizzy.'

She tutted, then pointed at an arriving *Jaguar XF*. 'My brother, Zack. I filled him in on things last night.'

The man parked, got out and walked towards them. Octavian saw that he was in a better suit than his own, and his expensive brown shoes were very shiny. He carried his mobile, ready for all new business. He wore a goatee beard, greying slightly. His outstretched hand shook Octavian's.

'Zack McAlister. How are you?'

Zack McAlister gave McAlister a little brotherly hug.

'This is DI Octavian,' she introduced.

'Yes, yes. I'm here to help you as best I can.'

'Very good of you, Sir,' said Octavian.

'Zack, please. No worries. Beth has cost me money throughout my entire life.'

'We're just waiting for Inspector Oxlade-Flynn. Her armed response people will be inside the property. She has the final say on the plan.'

'Oh, right.'

Right on cue, an unmarked BMW pulled up, and the unsmiling, serious career policewoman joined the group, putting on her police hat. She had on one of those chequered cravats on top of her white shirt, which Octavian always thought ridiculous. After the introductions, Zack McAlister took them into the property. There were no carpets yet, but each apartment was going to be high-spec when completed. Octavian especially liked the marble-effect walk-in shower. Inspector Oxlade-Flynn looked at everything; at the stairs, at the door, and the view out from the windows. She even looked at the walk-in shower, and Octavian thought he noticed her eyebrows raise slightly. But she was not forthcoming with an immediate decision.

Back on the street, they all shook hands and went their own ways. Octavian would have to wait for his trap to be given the green light.

After knocking on Horsefield's office door to bring him up to speed on matters, Octavian left Wythenshawe early that day. Charlotte and Jack were coming home. He met them at the Altrincham tram interchange. Charlotte wore a black head scarf that, in his happy opinion, made her look like a French woman. Following lots of hugs and kisses, then more hugs and kisses, he drove them to the house, talking non-stop to Jack in the rear-view mirror, as he sat happily in his child seat.

They hauled the luggage in and then relaxed in the garden with tea and milk and biscuits.

'What have you been up to, then?' she asked.

'Huh?'

'Done much on the new book?'

'Not really. My genius can't really flow without you being nearby.'

Octavian was delighted to see his wife and son again, and listened to Charlotte go on to

463

talk about Lake Windermere, and a day trip to Barrow-in-Furness. Part of his concentration, though, was churning over the possible surveillance on the apartment building, and how best to work it. It was not like the Hallworth stakeout, which was just trying to see if they were up to anything; this would mean full commitment, maybe even getting a camp bed in his office. Once the contract was placed, he and his team would be on it round the clock. Maybe McAlister would like to get involved. Perhaps he could get PCs Warnock and Batty again.

'Wait a minute,' he said to Charlotte. 'Back up a bit. Did I hear right? You went to Barrow-in-Furness? What on earth did you go there for?'

'Because that's where my brother-in-law is from. Have you forgotten?'

'Oh, right. Was it nice?'

'It was nice to see his relatives.'

Octavian lifted Jack on to his lap. 'Jack, lad, tell me, did you enjoy Barrow-in-Furness?'

The following morning, Octavian received a text from Horsefield. His plan had been given the go ahead and he would get full cooperation from Armed Response.

He and Charlotte went out to walk Jack in his stroller around the local park.

'You seem invigorated,' she said. 'Amazing what a few days away from the wife can do, huh?'

'Noooo. You silly billy.'

She giggled and linked his arm firmer.

'A beautiful day,' he said. 'Shall we run along with Jack?'

'You can do that, if you want to.'

'Listen, babe, I'm about to start on a busy phase of the case. It will mean long hours and nights.'

'I understand. All I want is for you to stay safe.'

They stopped walking and kissed tenderly. 'I love you,' they said in unison.

Early afternoon, the team gathered in the incident room. McAlister's desk was the focal point, as they all wanted to see what she had done on the Contract Market, and with Green's social media presence.

'Green is excited about moving into his new family home,' said McAlister. 'He's taken more photos than an estate agent.'

Octavian wanted their attention. 'Listen up, everybody, please. So, we will split into two teams. Our job, and our job only, is to spot the suspect arriving, and report to the officers on duty in the property. Armed Response will have their own covert surveillance, so we should have it covered. Oh, we've got Warnock and Batty patrolling in an unmarked car for some of the time, so that's extra eyes on the location.' Knowles raised a hand. 'Yes, Phil?'

'Do I have to be on Shirley's team? She's extraordinarily boring on a stakeout.'

'Here are the two teams,' continued Octavian. 'Myself, DS Williams and PC Green. Then we have DS Knowles, DC Speight and DC Datta. You three go and get some sleep because you relieve us in eight hours' time.'

Williams pointed to three yellow tasers on the desk. 'We will have these. Just pointing that out.'

'And everyone, wear your stab vests,' said Octavian. 'Now, we have a minibus to use for the surveillance. I don't want us in separate cars. Any questions?' Nobody had any. 'Okay, then.' He looked at Knowles, Speight and Datta. 'See you three in eight hours. I don't want any heroics. Do you hear me? If you spot anyone suspicious approaching the apartments, get on the radio. Good luck to us!'

The minibus was parked fifty metres away from the entrance to the apartment block. There was a locked play area to the left side, so they only had to worry about an arc to the front, right and rear. The windows of the mini-bus were dark tinted, so Octavian, Williams and Green could not be seen from the outside.

They were three hours into the first shift. Octavian had been in radio contact with the lead officer inside the building, but they had not seen any movement, whatsoever. Octavian moved his legs, conscious of deep vein thrombosis, like he was on a plane. Williams was eating mints, while Green, on the back seat like a schoolboy, slurped the last of a McDonald's milkshake.

'Right, that's favourite movies and books covered,' said Octavian. 'What's the next topic?'

Tell us about Indonesia,' Boss,' said Green. 'Why did you decide to be a policeman here, and not there?'

Octavian laughed quite loudly for the enclosed space. 'I wanted to be a policeman who didn't take bribes.'

'Oh,' said Green.

'You lived in Jakarta, right?' asked Williams. 'That's very exotic.'

'It is an amazing place, Katie. Have you been to Asia yet?'

'No, not yet. The furthest east I've been is Turkey.'

'I lived in Jakarta because my mum, who's English, was a teacher there. But I was born in my dad's home town of Jogjakarta.'

'Me and Joanna will go there for a holiday, next year,' announced Green.

'I hope you do. I'll give you some addresses, so you won't have to pay hotel prices.'

'Thanks, Boss.'

The shift drifted slowly along. Some of the properties on the estate were already occupied, so they saw a few residents coming and going, and there were always dog walkers, wherever you were. A postman, in shorts and with both calves tattooed, came along with some late mail. Octavian had been to McDonalds, and Williams had brought sandwiches and a flask of tea; the bus seats were padded, so it wasn't the worse stakeout, in the history of stakeouts.

The nights were getting lighter, so the sun was still visible, reflected on the apartment windows, when it came time for a shift change. Williams did a yawn and a stretch. A radio call came in from Knowles; they were on site.

'Okay, I'll slip away,' she said.

'Right, Katie.'

Williams left the mini-bus on the sheltered park side and hurried off. Octavian and Green waited in silence. A few minutes later, they were joined by Knowles, carrying a bag, no doubt full of supplies.

'Hello, campers. Nothing happened yet?'

'Not yet,' replied Octavian. 'Okay, Green, off you go.'

'Good luck, DS Knowles,' said Green, before jumping out and scuttling off.

'It's like *The Great Escape*,' laughed Knowles, picking a seat. 'You know, when the prisoners escape the tunnel at intervals.'

Octavian passed over the walkie-talkie. 'I'll relieve you at 6 a.m.'

'Okay.'

The door slid open and Speight hauled herself in.

'I'll go as soon as Aamina arrives,' said Octavian.

She was there within two minutes. 'Hello, Boss.'

'Hiya, Aamina. Have a good one. Goodnight, people. Keep sharp.'

A police car dropped Octavian, Williams and Green outside the police station.

'Lewis, do you need a ride anywhere?' asked Octavian.

'No, Sir. Joanna lives just round there. Goodnight to you both.'

'See you in the morning, Lewis.'

Octavian and Williams gained access to the car park and walked towards their vehicles.

'Goodnight, Boss. See you in the morning.'

'Goodnight, Katie.'

FIFTY-FIVE

Nothing happened overnight, and Octavian was back on time to relieve Knowles, Speight and Datta at the mini-bus – they left exactly like Knowles had earlier described, scooting away at intervals like escaping prisoners of war.

Williams and Green soon joined him and they settled down to watch the area again. Williams had brought a couple of newspapers, as every second of the shift didn't need all of them on look-out.

'Here we are again,' she said, cheerily.

'I forget, Katie, are you married?'

'Yes, I am. He's actually a property developer, like Beth's brother. But no way would he lend you a building.'

Octavian laughed.

'Green, is it McDonalds for lunch again?'

'If you're paying, Boss.'

'So, what do you think about doing surveillance?'

'It's a bit tedious, to be honest. But I'm enjoying it.'

They all saw movement from a side street, but it was just a resident walking his dog. Octavian checked in with the officers in the building; he was still to see any movement at any of the windows. He scanned the street. There was normal movement of people in the distance, and there was the sound of building work coming from the far side of the estate, which was still to be finished.

Williams said, 'They are building everywhere. I don't get it. Soon, everybody in the country will have a small home, but no job.'

'Don't get me started on that topic,' laughed Octavian. 'This estate, for example; soulless, without any extra infrastructure, just pouring more people in cars out onto the main road.'

'Yikes, I'd better not go there again.'

'Can I tell you news about Joanna?' asked Green.

They both looked back, wanting to hear it.

'She's been offered a modelling contract.'

'That's fantastic,' said a smiling Williams. 'Is it a reputable company?'

'Definitely, yes. It's going to be work around Manchester, at first, but maybe London, one day.'

'I'll call the Met,' said Octavian. 'Tell them you're on your way.'

Green smiled and blushed.

The day panned out just like the previous one. It was too early for negative thoughts to creep into the minibus; thoughts that the killer wouldn't take the bait. During his time in London, Octavian had been involved in surveillance operations that lasted weeks before the suspect showed his face. He felt it was like how a war felt for a soldier: hurry up and wait.

They all talked of their families. Green accepted a wad of cash and went off to McDonalds for them all. That restaurant, virtually opposite the new estate, was their comfort break place, and Octavian had already squared that with the helpful manageress. Green told them the plot of a Danish series he was starting to watch.

'I can't do subtitles,' said Williams. 'My brain's not wired that way.'

A number of times, a red Vauxhall Zafira cruised past them, with Warnock and Batty circling the estate. There was no shared acknowledgement through the windows. The shift proved uneventful, and they were relieved by the others by mid-afternoon.

Octavian went home to try to get some sleep, before doing his first night shift. The house was empty, with a note saying Charlotte had gone food shopping, and Ezi had a lecture to attend. Octavian reappeared in the kitchen by early evening. Charlotte asked if he was hungry, but he just wanted coffee.

'Ezi tells me his girlfriend is coming to stay,' said Charlotte.

'Is she his girlfriend now?'

'Well, whatever, female friend, then. That will be nice.'

He leaned in for a much-needed hug.

'You're a great hug,' he told her.

'I've not been told that before.'

'I want that Welsh beach holiday with you.'

'Oh, yes, my bikini. Will you be able to go?'

'Here's hoping.'

'Oh, before the holiday, I got those tickets to that architectural exhibition in Manchester, next month. Do you think you'll be able to go with me?'

He would love to be anywhere that Charlotte was, although an architectural exhibition was low on the list of things to do together. 'I'm sure I will.'

FIFTY-SIX

Octavian returned to the stakeout early, so he could flag down Warnock and Batty and have a word with them. He chose a quiet, little through road to step out in front of their Vauxhall, to get their attention, then went around and spoke through the open driver's window.

'Anything, you guys?'

'Not seen anyone fitting the bill, Sir,' said Warnock.

'How long are you on for?'

'We were told until midnight, Sir.'

'Okay. Keep circling. And, listen, you two, remember you are just to call it in if you see anyone. Do not attempt to challenge. This man possesses firearms.'

'Yes, Sir,' they both said.

He let them drive on; then walked to McDonalds for three coffees. From there he headed to the minibus, where Knowles, Speight and Datta looked about ready to kill each other. Perhaps in a couple of days he would change the teams, as Knowles did tend to get on the girls' nerves, after a while.

'I'll get away first,' said Knowles. 'Man United's on the TV tonight.'

Octavian sat at the back, placing down his tray of coffees. They let Knowles disappear.

'Anything at all?'

'Nothing, Boss,' answered Datta. 'Delivery drivers, a few builders wandering about, and that nurse who lives over there came home. No lone males checking the place out.'

'Okay, Aamina. You make a move. See you in the morning.'

'Goodnight, Boss.'

Speight got the door for her. After two minutes, Speight was ready to leave, herself.

'Off you go, Shirley.'

'Goodnight, Boss.'

'Goodnight.'

Once Williams and Green turned up, the three of them settled into their first night shift together. It was overcast, so went dark early. There were street lamps but virtually no light emanating from any properties. Green expressed the opinion that it now felt weird to be sitting in a dark van, but he continued to watch every vehicle passing; it was still an experience for him.

As it went fully dark, the cars became bright headlights and then red tail lights, which they watched from arrival to departure, and the dog walkers hopefully had something flashing on the collar, or a fluorescent dog coat. Nobody else moved on the estate – Octavian had his first inkling of another failure, but on a grander scale of time and manpower.

'Joanna is definitely up for Indonesia,' Green suddenly said from the back.

'Good,' replied Octavian. 'She'll love it.'

A car approached. Once the glare had gone by, they could make out a dark SUV type vehicle.

'What was that?' asked a drowsy Williams.

'Might be our man,' said Octavian. 'It turned the corner and stopped. Look, you can make out the brake lights on the opposite building.' He reached for the walkie-talkie and spoke into it. 'Possible suspect just pulled up.'

'We have visual,' came back from the leader of the Armed Response team. 'Please wait.'

They sat in silence in the dark minibus. Seconds felt like minutes.

'False alarm,' came over the radio. 'Elderly resident in a Toyota SUV.'

Green sighed audibly and the tension calmed.

'Shall I go for coffee?' asked Octavian, making them both jump a bit.

Octavian slipped out of the minibus on the side adjacent to the park and walked quickly away. His route to McDonalds took him past the now parked Toyota. He controlled the urge to put its back window in and walked on. Perhaps he was tired, or just lost concentration, but suddenly there was a male youth walking towards him, with a big bag on his back. Octavian slowed, and the young male slowed. Then the young male changed direction to avoid passing Octavian, so Octavian changed direction to follow him. The young male was casual around a bend, but then he was off running. Octavian went after him.

'Police! Stop!'

The suspect kept running.

'I'll send the dog! Stop!'

The suspect carried on, but the weight of the bag allowed Octavian to close the gap.

'Police! I have a taser! Stop!'

The young male came to a stop. Octavian, pointing the taser, approached carefully.

'Put the bag down! Get on your knees.'

Octavian's heart was pumping with adrenalin, not from the quick chase, but at the thought that his worse ever case might end quickly and easily like that. The stop had happened halfway between streetlamps. He came forward very carefully, concerned that the suspect was armed. The suspect obeyed and got down on his knees.

Octavian then realized that the young man was black, and his heart emptied with disappointment, as their man, from what slim information they had so far, was not a black person.

'What are you doing out in the middle of the night?'

'Going to my mate's.'

'Tip out the bag, slowly. The taser is still on you.'

The suspect tipped out the bag onto the pavement, causing a metallic clatter. There seemed to be a selection of screwdrivers and a big crowbar.

'Save us both some time,' said Octavian. 'What are you really doing?'

'All right, man, I'm looking to do a bit of house breaking.'

FIFTY-SEVEN

Octavian handcuffed the young male and searched him, finding no weapon. Then he walked him and his bag to McDonalds. That was where he got a uniformed patrol to meet him to take the youth into custody.

With the coffee, Octavian returned to the minibus. He told Williams and Green what had happened. His eyes were accustomed to the dark, so he could see their shock and surprise.

'Another coincidence?' asked Williams.

'Probably. Unless our man is actually a double-act. But this guy's only weapons were screwdrivers and a crowbar, nothing more professional.'

'Unless it was his job to gain entry to Green's home for the other man to enter.'

'We'll interview him later today. We can keep him as long as possible.'

'If he is a co-conspirator, then we're blown.'

They finished their shift. Williams and Green went home for some sleep. Octavian briefed Knowles, Speight and Datta, before getting a lift back to the station. Normally, they closed at night, but with the major operation on, there was a sergeant and a PC on duty. Octavian found Sergeant Neagle on the front desk.

'Evening, morning, Sergeant, whatever it is.'

'Sir.'

'Is our man cosy?'

'Just gave him a cup of tea, Sir.'

'Any ID yet?'

Neagle referred to a clipboard. 'I've never come across him before. Name of Clinton Warner. Form for burglary.'

'Thank you, Sergeant.'

Octavian went to the cells. He peaked through the hatch on the first door, seeing the seated form of Clinton Warner, who declined to look around at his visitor. Octavian closed it up. He got a coffee from the vending machine and went up to the incident room. He had a camp bed set up there. He sat down on it, sipping the coffee. Then he set his phone alarm for two hours' time.

'Just some local scrote,' said Williams, as they exited the interview room, after talking to Clinton Warner.

Octavian was slightly surprised by the language Williams had used; maybe she was over-tired.

'I hate burglars,' she continued. 'How dare they think it's okay to break into a person's home? It's such a violation. Anyway, that's all he seems to be.'

'I agree with you. He showed nothing when we went at him with the heavy stuff. But we'll keep him as long as we can, just in case.'

They went upstairs. McAlister had just arrived. Octavian sat with her at her desk and asked her to do a thorough check on their Mr Warner.

'I'm sorry we didn't hit the jackpot,' said McAlister.

'Me, too, Beth. Maybe tonight.' Octavian looked at Williams. 'Ready for another evening shift, Katie?'

'Yes, Boss. Must we have McDonalds again?'

'No.'

Octavian rang Green, and had the young man meet them on the High Street. The three of them visited Subway, to get nice sandwiches for their supper, later. It was great to see the love between Green and Joanna. It briefly reminded Octavian of his days with a young Kezia, but, once again, he shook that from his mind.

'Congratulations on your modelling contract,' Williams said to Joanna.

'Oh, thanks! So excited about that.'

Octavian said, 'Yes, best of luck with that, Joanna.'

They got to the stakeout minibus. Octavian went forward first. Knowles was gutted to see the Subway bag, but nothing for him.

'Anything?' asked Octavian.

'Absolutely not a thing,' said Knowles. 'I'm in love with the nurse at number fifty-three, though.'

Octavian had already phoned to bring them up to speed on the Clinton Warner arrest and subsequent interview, so there was nothing more to say; his tired crew slunk away at one-minute intervals, to be replaced by Williams and Green, in due course.

'Something's not right,' said Octavian.

'What's not right?' asked Williams, pausing mid-sitting.

'I'm banned from McDonalds.'

She smiled. 'Just for today.'

They settled into the routine. Octavian said hello, via the walkie-talkie, to the Armed Response team leader, who was a woman, that shift. Two JCBs trundled by, with hard-hat wearing drivers. The postman walked along late again. The nurse at number 53 went off to work. They had their soft drinks from Subway early on, but saved the sandwiches for later.

'Warnock and Batty approaching,' said Green.

They watched the Vauxhall go slowly by.

'Someone should phone the police about those two dodgy characters,' joked Octavian.

Knowles' father had been a policeman, so he remembered having to be quiet, as a kid, whenever dad had been on nights. He woke and looked at the clock. His wife was banging about in the kitchen.

Speight and Datta only had a little sleep, as they both wanted to spend time with their men. Datta took Taheer for a hospital check-up, as his right arm had been quite badly burned in the apartment block fire. Speight took Harry to the gym, just so he could do some upper body work – he was worried about losing the muscle strength in his arms. Both men still had to take things easy, and they were several weeks away from having their casts removed.

After the hospital, Datta wheeled Taheer into a KFC restaurant. He was very pleased with that. After the gym, Speight drove Harry back to her flat and made love to him. He was very pleased with that.

After his latest shift, Octavian drove home to be with Charlotte. They had a late supper, before turning in for the night. He would relieve the team in the morning; then do another night shift, before swapping things around. Unless Horsefield finally pulled the plug on him, that is.

Octavian's next night shift with Williams and Green was the one that really started to worry him. No traffic moved around that unfinished part of the estate, they saw no late-night dog walkers, and didn't even spot the nurse coming home from the hospital.

Knowles, Speight and Datta were sombre creatures when they relieved him, the following morning. Even telling them he would change-up the teams didn't spark any life into them. At least Knowles called after him, 'Put me with Green. He needs eight hours of football education.'

'Will do, Phil.'

Octavian walked off the estate and jumped in the waiting patrol car for the brief ride back to the station. All three of them were tired. They were dropped off outside the station car park. Octavian could see it on their faces that they thought it all a wild goose chase. Octavian looked across the road to where the Earlestown market was being set up.

Williams yawned. 'Well, I'm off to my bed.'

'Yes,' said Octavian. 'I've never liked nights.'

Octavian watched Williams use her fob key to open the security gate. He turned to say good morning to Green, but the young man was no longer a few steps behind him...

Instead, he was down on the floor with a crossbow bolt sticking out of his chest. Blood was oozing quickly through his jumper and he was gurgling for air.

'Noooooo!' screamed Octavian, dropping to the boy.

Williams let out an audible gasp of despair as she collapsed to her knees beside Green's head.

'Get help!' shouted Octavian at her. 'Get help now!'

She was already on her mobile, with her free hand applying pressure beside the bolt. Octavian jumped up, scanning the area in a maddened panic. The bolt must have come from the chaotic market scene. Drawing his taser, Octavian sprinted across the road, causing a car to slam on the brakes, and then market traders had to jump aside. He could see a fleeing figure, heading towards the shopping precinct. He ran in pursuit, cutting in and out of the market stalls.

Octavian ran down the road behind the Forum. He could see his target, running onto the doctors' car park. There was the black Mercedes. The person climbed in, gunned the engine, and bounced out onto the far road, leaving Octavian distraught, impotently waving his hands about as he slowed his sprint. He took out his phone, desperately trying to alert traffic cops in time.

All Octavian could do was jog back to the station. A crowd of officers were around the stricken Green, with Bill Fitzgerald doing CPR. Williams couldn't watch that, turning away in a flood of tears. Octavian hurried to hold her. An ambulance arrived. Bill Fitzgerald, also weeping uncontrollably, looked at Octavian as he gave way to the paramedics. He shook his head, telling Octavian that Green was gone.

FIFTY-EIGHT

A couple of hours later, Octavian managed to drive home, though he could not remember doing so. He found Charlotte in the back garden, with Ezi helping to take the washing in off the line. She was aware of the incident; he had called, so she rushed to hold her husband. Ezi took the washing into the kitchen, leaving them to be alone.

'Has he passed?' she asked softly at his ear.

Octavian could not help but weep onto her shoulder. 'Yessss.'

'Oh, my darling man. I'm so sorry.'

She held his head while he let it all out. After a number of minutes, he regained control of himself.

'You need a cup of tea,' she said. 'And something to eat. Maybe some sleep.'

All he could do was mutely agree with her.

'How's Jack?' he asked.

'Jack's perfectly fine, baby.'

Octavian showered and then fell asleep on the bed. When he woke, the nightmare was still real, and he was still stricken with guilt over the murder of PC Green. He was also suspended, pending an enquiry, but that was beside the point.

He only moved when Charlotte brought him a cup of tea. She covered his nakedness with the bedcover and tried to tidy his messy hair.

'Sorry, darling,' he said, sitting up. 'Nights are like jetlag. I'll get my head back on soon. I'll come to terms with it.'

She could see that he was trying to be stoic. 'Don't apologise. Just take as long as you need. I worry about you.'

'Hey, maybe we won't need a nanny now. I can be a stay-at-home dad. You can get back to earning the big bucks.'

'Wait to see how it pans out. It wasn't anyone's fault.'

'What are you doing today?'

'Supermarket shop. Deep joy.'

'Want me to come with you?'

'No, you rest. Ezi will go with me. He's worried too.'

'Tell him not to be. I'm okay.'

'No, he's worried that he should cancel Poppy's visit.'

Octavian became a little indignant. 'Certainly not. You tell him. She should visit and things should be right here. I don't want anything to change at home because of this. Tell him.'

'Okay, baby, I'll tell him.'

'Very well.'

Poppy Smith arrived from Leeds three days later. They decided not to tell her the situation – she would just have to say to her family after her holiday that Charlotte was lovely, but the policeman uncle was a bit morose, and not at all like Ezi had described him.

Poppy was brunette and small, a lovely girl, very polite. She was obviously into Ezi in a big way. She settled into Ezi's room with him, which had been the big worry for her. Then they spent quite a lot of time out, visiting Manchester, for shopping, and Liverpool, for the culture. Ezi had arranged his schedule, but when he had an important lecture, she would happily wander around the Arndale Centre, or wait for him in a nearby café. Also, Charlotte took Octavian and Jack out quite a bit, to the park, and to Chatsworth House in Derbyshire (having just watched the Pride and Prejudice movie again – with Octavian making sure to stand in the exact spot where Keira Knightley had been filmed). It became as normal to wonder if Ezi and Poppy were home, as it had done with just the Indonesian boy.

FIFTY-NINE

The morning of Green's funeral came around. Octavian put on his best dark suit, and Charlotte did his black tie for him. Ezi and Poppy looked up shyly from the breakfast table as he entered the kitchen.

'Morning, you two,' said Octavian.

They both bid him good morning. Ezi had already explained to Poppy that a police colleague had been killed in the line of duty.

Charlotte came in. 'Are you sure you don't want me to drive you?'

'No, baby. I'm just going to the church. Then I'll come away.' He looked at the young lovers. 'What are you pair doing today?'

'We're going to Blackpool for the day,' said Poppy, smiling.

Octavian spluttered. Ezi held up his hands, to say that it wasn't his choice.

Poppy did a sweet giggle. 'I know, I know, Ezi says it's not very nice. But it's a famous town and I've always wanted to go there. I want to go up the Blackpool tower.'

'Okay, you have a good time.'

Charlotte took his hand and led him out. It was a beautiful, clear morning. They kissed on the drive, and then he got into the Golf and drove away.

The church was in Woodhouse Park. A large group of members of the public were watching the funeral, and there was a local TV news crew filming for the evening bulletin. Octavian parked on the road and walked in. It was a big turn-out, but of course his eye was taken by seeing the Top Brass waiting at the entrance, in their best uniforms. Horsefield stood with them. Nearby were Green's former colleagues, lined up, looking very smart.

Octavian spotted his team and walked across to them. Speight was holding Datta, both tearful. He hugged them both and kissed their cheeks. Williams shook his hand, while McAlister touched his forearm, at the same time. He shared a nod with Knowles. Knowles had clearly been crying. Perhaps, Octavian thought, he had just missed an outpouring of grief. Knowles was in a shiny black suit, with a big black tie that only went halfway down his white shirt. Octavian shared a look with Knowles; they both knew that, even though he had teased the young PC a bit, that he had really liked the man.

Behind this group stood Bill Fitzgerald, with his wife. Fitzgerald winked at him and Octavian nodded warmly back. Then Octavian settled into the group.

'Lots of people,' he said.

'He had a big family,' said Knowles. 'And was a popular chap.'

Then Octavian saw the black feathers on top of the horses' heads as the hearse came slowly along the road. It turned up the drive, followed by three limousines. Green's immediate family got out of the cars; the mother and father, sisters and brothers, and then there was poor Joanna. Her blonde hair was striking against her black dress. She looked completely heartbroken, and Octavian welled-up, having to look away.

Octavian came downstairs one morning and put the kettle on. He still felt odd not to be going to work. He looked aghast at morning TV before the kettle was ready. Charlotte came in, in her dressing gown, hugging him from behind.

'Darling, I was thinking,' she said.

'Steady now.'

'I know it's such a difficult time right now. But we could use the free time to make that Indonesian trip. I know Jack won't know anything about it, but he should be shown his other home.'

He turned in the embrace, kissing her.

'I like the plan,' he said.

After breakfast, they went food shopping again.

'Little Poppy doesn't half eat,' he joked in the car.

Charlotte got the trolley. Octavian had Jack strapped to his chest – something that he had always thought completely naff, before becoming a father, on a par with those mad cyclists who towed their children behind them in a little buggy with the flag in the air, but it worked for them. The aisles were fairly empty of shoppers. Charlotte got the proper food while Octavian focused on the snacks. He picked up a packet of biscuits.

'You know, I remember when these were twice the size and half the price.'

'It's the government trying to reduce obesity.'

'No, it's not. It's corporate greed. It just means people have to eat the whole packet instead of two biscuits.'

Charlotte put a different product in the trolley.

'Why are you getting those?' he enquired.

'They're Ezi's favourites.'

'Look at the price. That's shocking.'

Charlotte grimaced at having her husband doing the food shopping with her.

They headed through one of the checkout tills. Octavian talked to Jack while Charlotte packed the bags. He looked at the total on the screen before Charlotte paid.

'Is that acceptable?' she asked, grinning.

'I suppose so. In Indonesia that would be ten million rupiahs.'

Octavian now had all the time in the world to work on his new novel, and it progressed nicely. He had a radio station playing music through the computer speakers. Charlotte brought him coffee, hugged him; then left him to it.

Margo accepted an offer for the house. Raja saw the Estate Agent out again. Raja had briefly considered becoming an Estate Agent, when he heard what the man's commission would be, for doing so very little. The two men smiled and shook hands at the gate, both glad that the deal was completed.

There was an air of closure around the mansion. The family was ready to go. There was no television or radio noise. The servants were all thinking about their immediate futures elsewhere.

Daring the mosquitoes to bite her, nearing dusk, Margo took a stroll around the garden with Raja. It was just one last time, to remember the old days with her husband.

'He did so much to this garden, you know, Raja.'

'He certainly did.'

'Well, he did well out of Asia. I suppose it's just the end of a chapter.'

Their big loop headed them back towards the house.

'Early start tomorrow, Mrs Lipman,' said Raja. 'We are scheduled to set sail at 7 a.m.'

'I assume the paparazzi will follow us all the way to the boat?'

'Yes, but we are promised a police escort.'

'Is everything done here?'

'I think so, Mrs Lipman.'

'Good. Thank you, Raja. Then that's it here. Goodnight.'

'Goodnight, Mrs Lipman.'

He watched her walk into the house, before heading off to his own quarters.

Mr Roberts was up at 5 a.m. the next morning, keen to get going. He made breakfast for himself and his fellow travellers, as and when Raja managed to get them up. Then he and Raja gathered Mrs Mirdad and all the staff to thank them for their efforts and wish them well with their new positions. Raja handed everyone an envelope containing a generous bonus.

The cars were packed with the luggage. Raja and Mr Roberts took two trays of coffee down to the press men and police. Raja looked for Ari, but his boyfriend was not yet there.

'We're going soon,' called Raja, bringing cheers from the press. 'Let's not have a stampede to the docks, boys.'

People tried to ask him questions about Rome, even as they keenly accepted the coffee.

'No comment. No comment.'

Finally, the Lipmans and their two guests, all wearing casual clothes and dark sunglasses, came out to the waiting cars. Finucane and Mr Roberts got in. Raja waved a goodbye to the staff, got in beside the chauffeur, and they were on their way.

The paparazzi were snapping away, before, during and after the departure. Raja imagined the hundreds of magazines worldwide reporting that kidnap victim, Rome Lipman, and his family were departing Indonesia for LA. Raja finally saw Ari's car, as part of the convoy. With media vehicles at the back, they drove to the docks.

'What a to-do,' said a giggling Paddy Finucane.

'A to-do?' asked Raja.

'Never mind. Lost in translation, pal.'

'Are you sorry you're not coming with us, Paddy?'

'Raja, mate, nothing in this world would get me on that boat.'

Raja laughed.

'Mr Roberts is looking forward to having a rest. Aren't you, Mr Roberts? Apart from his little battles with the chef on board.'

Mr Roberts pulled a face. 'Don't call that man a chef, please.'

At the docks, thankfully, the press pack were held back by the police, leaving the Lipman cars and Ari's vehicle to park, quite a way into the facility. Raja had not spoken to Ari recently. He wanted to have a nice farewell, so approached his boyfriend. Ari half-smiled. They walked together in the direction of the yacht.

'I'll call you as soon as we arrive in Honolulu.'

'Okay.'

'I wish I could kiss you goodbye, Ari.'

'No, it's too public.'

The Lipman group were being welcomed by the Captain and his First Officer. Raja did not really watch them, as he needed to give all his attention to Ari. But he glanced when Ari said something unpleasant about them all. Raja could make out crew members, standing on the lower deck, holding a tray of champagne flutes that glinted in the morning sun. The passengers started to go up the gangway, while the luggage was loaded by another.

'I suppose I'd better go,' said Raja, with a grimace.

'I'll think about you for every mile.'

Raja was almost brought to tears at hearing that. 'Thank you. I will not stop thinking about you saying that.'

'Say something nice, back, then.'

Ari crossed his arms at Raja pretending to struggle with that concept. Raja thought for a moment. 'I want to be the snow outside your window.'

They both burst out laughing.

The second gangway was being taken up. Stevie was about to cast off from the dock. Raja and Ari hugged like two male friends, not lovers. Then Raja jogged to the yacht and hopped up the gangway, followed by Stevie, who then dragged it aboard. The engines moved the boat slowly sideways, churning water below where Raja stood at the rail, watching Ari. They both waved, and then the yacht began to depart.

Once the dock was behind them, Raja looked at the scene, onboard: the youngsters were lounged around on the lower deck, drinking champagne. From his position he could only make out shorts and trainers, legs crossed, not a care in the world. Melancholic over leaving Ari, Raja briefly hated them. Margo came back up, having checked her cabin and luggage. She took a glass of champagne and reclined down. Mr Roberts was on the bridge, enjoying the technical exercise of leaving port.

The yacht sailed slowly out of the harbour. Raja and Margo exchanged a glance, then he went down to his cabin for a lie down, having to squeeze past Jack, in passing, both laughing and Raja patting his chest.

'We're off, then, Raja!'

'Yes, Jack. Wake me when we get to Hawaii.'

Jack laughed. 'Will do.'

Raja's cabin was a small single, but very luxurious. He had a square porthole that showed...the Java Sea. His bunk had Egyptian cotton sheets on it, his en-suite bathroom had a marble sink top and the most modern fixtures. There was a TV, and when he opened his suitcase, he had his favourite novels and *his MP3 player with him. On the yacht, he had fewer responsibilities, Margo was separated from the world, so he could relax. He lay down and was instantly asleep.*

Octavian checked his emails; there was the usual nonsense, but also a nice one from Williams, simply checking on his wellbeing. Speight and Datta had recently texted him, and Knowles would ring to speak to him every few days. He saw there was an email from a London literary agent, the one who had requested the full manuscript, all those months ago. Octavian read it on auto-pilot, expecting yet another polite no, but he gradually realised that the lady really liked his time-travel book, and she was offering representation, and she wanted him to telephone her. He was stunned. If it had come at any other time in his life he would have been jumping around the house, running to Charlotte and swinging her around. But he just sat there, quietly satisfied. 'Well,' he said to himself. 'How'd you like them apples?' He would telephone the lady, but in his own good time. He got up and went to tell Charlotte the amazing news.

SIXTY

While having breakfast with Charlotte, Jack, Ezi and Poppy, Octavian received a text from Kezia Garswood, asking if she could come to see him. Charlotte was busy feeding Jack, and Ezi was busy looking at Poppy, as usual, so Octavian didn't have to make a flippant comment about it. He looked at Poppy; if the girl knew about him seeing his old flame, then that would really put the cap on her opinion of the disturbed policeman.

Octavian read more of the text: Kezia had remembered something about Lily that she needed to tell him. He realized that he no longer had that nostalgic urge to be with Kezia. She could now reside in a nice corner of his memory. But, although he was off the case, he was not going to ignore it. He waited until he was alone, then texted back that "We'll be in touch." He then rang Williams with the information.

Williams and Datta went to see Kezia. She was back at the flat in Prestwich, but when they arrived there, they could see that she was in the process of packing her belongings.

'I've got a place near to my sister,' explained Kezia. Then she looked over the shoulders of the two women police officers. 'Is DI Octavian not with you?'

'DI Octavian is unavailable, I'm afraid,' said Williams. 'We understand that you have new information for us, Ms Garswood?'

'Yes, yes. Come in. I can't brew up, the electric's off. Sit where you can.'

Williams sat between cardboard boxes on the sofa. Datta leant on the windowsill. Kezia sat on the floor and crossed her legs.

'Errrrm,' started Kezia. 'I saw one of Lily's friends, the other day. She asked me if anything had been done about the Lucy person who had been texting Lily.'

'Lucy who?' asked Williams.

'Well, I'm not sure. I remember hearing the name Lucy. At the time, I assumed it was another girl. But, according to Maya, that's Lily's friend, this Lucy was a woman teacher. Now I'm wondering why an adult was texting Lily privately. It might be nothing, but Tony... DI Octavian did say I should be in touch if I remembered anything at all.'

'No, you were right to contact us,' said Williams. 'It sounds interesting. We'll look again at your daughter's social media. Do you remember anything else, while we are here?'

'No, I don't think so. It was just that.'

'Okay, thank you. We'll look at that, I promise.'

Williams and Datta returned to the station. Knowles was on holiday, touring Scotland with his wife, Maria. Speight was off, going to the gym with Harry, their relationship progressing nicely, and his fitness almost fully restored. There was only McAlister there, who Williams went to sit with.

'Beth, Lily Bowden's mother says there was an adult female, name of Lucy, contacting her daughter prior to her murder.'

'A Lucy does ring a bell. But I thought it was just another teen girl. Let's look again, shall we?'

'Me and Aamina have that pub fight killing to get on with. I'll check back with you later.'

'Okay.'

There had been a death outside a Benchill pub the previous evening. They had a man in custody, and were still to decide if it was a premeditated attack or a spur of the moment thing, which would decide between a murder or a manslaughter charge. Williams and Datta went down to meet the arrested man's solicitor.

McAlister found Williams later in the day, near to the drinks machine. They both sat down with cups of tea.

'I've got a handle on this Lucy woman. Lucy Wiley. She's a teacher of Reiki.'

'I beg your pardon? Of what?'

'You know, the new-age wellness thing. Head massage and stuff, I think. She's forty, but quite attractive. She was quite persistent in trying to get the attention of our Lily Bowden. But nothing overtly worrying in the tone of her contact.'

'So, just an old lesbian wanting a young girl?'

'Well, this woman is divorced, with a twenty-year-old son. But who's to know?'

Williams finished her tea. 'So, probably a waste of time?'

'Ah, well, you know me, I went on looking. Her son has recently left the British army. I also looked at the socials of our other victims again. Steven McLaughlin, the original victim, was in contact with this Lucy Wiley person.'

'Really!? Grooming, perhaps?'

McAlister pulled a face. 'Chatting, liking, showing interest in the same things. Nothing that went to the grooming stage.'

'What did the son leave the army for?'

'I'm waiting to hear back on that.'

'So, she's not talking to any of the other victims?'

'Well, not openly as herself.'

'Surely not another coincidence? A reiki weirdo...Okay, no reason to think that's relevant...but an older woman trying to connect with youngsters, who end up murdered, and a squaddie son recently back on civvie street.'

Horsefield came near to them. His eyes glanced lovingly over McAlister; then went to get himself a coffee. He joined them and Williams invited him to sit down. She then ran the new information by him. He mulled over the idea of a predatory mother and a violent son.

'It's not the worst thing I've heard in my time,' he said. 'Remember, though, Katie, because of Lewis Green and this case, if you decide to go there, make sure to take back-up.'

'Will do, Sir.'

The team, minus the holidaying Knowles, headed out at the crack of dawn the following day. They travelled in convoy with the armed officers who would be gaining entry to Lucy Wiley's home in the Cheadle Hulme area.

Wearing their stab vests, the team stood on the corner of the road and watched their colleagues approach the property. It was a large bungalow, in a nice area, but none of them worried about that, in regard to a murder enquiry. They saw entry being gained without the need to use the big red battering ram.

'Oh, dear,' said Datta. 'They never like it when they can't smash a door in.'

'We don't have Knowles with us again,' pointed out Speight. 'Maybe we should move him out. Pension him off.'

Williams grinned at her. 'You miss him, really.'

A thumbs-up came from the leader of the entry team, who resembled a paramilitary soldier in his black riot gear. Williams led her team along the road. They entered the bungalow, finding a disorientated Lucy Wiley sitting on her sofa in her dressing gown. Williams introduced herself and told the woman that they were investigating the murder of Lily Bowden.

'Oh, God,' said Lucy Wiley.

Williams pulled up a leather footstool to sit on, looking at the blonde, still attractive Lucy Wiley.

'Am I being arrested?' asked Lucy Wiley.

'I don't know. Should you be?'

'Oh, my God.'

'What?'

'Armed police looking like that coming here. I'll never live it down.'

'We have to be careful, you understand, Ms Wiley. One of my colleagues was murdered investigating this case.'

'Yes, I read about that.'

Williams looked at the armed police still in the hall. They would not leave until she said they could.

'Where's your son?'

'In his room.'

'Is he a heavy sleeper?'

'No, why?'

'He's ex-army, is that right?' Lucy Wiley nodded. 'Why did he leave the army? Was he thrown out?'

Lucy Wiley took offence to that. 'No! He most certainly was not.'

'Well, here is my warrant. We will have a look around. I'm afraid I'll have to get your son out of bed. Then you and me can have a little chat about your interest in Lily Bowden.'

Speight was already looking through the kitchen drawers, while Datta had found the spare bedroom. Williams got to her feet and walked down the hall. An armed police constable held a bedroom door open for her. She stepped inside, expecting a cheeky ex-squaddie to give her some choice barrack-room language. Instead, she was faced with what looked like a hospital room; bed with railings, monitors, oxygen cylinders. On the wall were a couple of signed Liverpool football shirts. Sitting up in the bed was a young man who had clearly undergone some kind of major trauma. His gaunt eyes simply looked at her. He didn't seem able to speak, let alone give her any attitude.

'Oh,' said Williams, deeply embarrassed. 'I'm so sorry. Please forgive me.'

The suspended Octavian found that he had the time to make strawberry, Oreo cookie milkshakes. The last time at TGI Fridays he had been invited up into the "back bar" area to watch his being made, and so he tried his best with crushed ice, milk, and then the strawberries and biscuits. It was not a sign of premature senility, he had his team coming to visit, and he felt like offering them something other than tea or coffee.

Poppy and Ezi came home and saw him sitting in the garden with four women, drinking milkshakes. It was just another anecdote for Poppy to tell her family.

'My cousin, Ezi,' introduced Octavian. 'And his girlfriend, Poppy.'

Williams, Speight and Datta and McAlister all waved cheerily. The young couple smiled back before disappearing into the house.

They had been discussing Octavian's upcoming hearing, in Manchester. They were all keen to speak on his behalf.

'Where's Phil, did you say?' he asked.

'The Scottish Highlands with the missus,' answered Speight. 'This milkshake is awesome.'

'I thought they were separating?'

'Trying to give it another go, apparently.'

'Thank you all for coming to see me. It means a lot to me.'

'How's Charlotte?' asked Datta.

'She's great. She's going back to work soon. We might need her to.' That caused an awkward moment. 'Hoping to get an Indonesian nanny for Jack.'

'A lovely home you've got,' said Williams. 'Is this Bowdon?'

He laughed. 'Charlotte wishes it was Bowdon. No, this is still Altrincham. So, Katie, the Lucy person was of no interest?'

'Not really. The son was injured in a training accident. Nothing at all to suggest her involvement in anything. Questionable behaviour on her part, regarding the young people, but nothing to do with the investigation.'

'Have you informed Ms Garswood?'

'Yes, I've told her it was a dead end. Not about the internet communications.'

'Okay. So, that's the end, then.'

They all sat quietly, accepting the collective failure to solve the case.

'Oh, I didn't tell you!' Octavian's guests all sat up, suddenly intrigued with what he had to say. 'I've got a London agent who wants to represent my book.'

SIXTY-ONE

The day came when Ezi had to let Poppy go back home to Yorkshire. It caused him to mope around the house. Octavian and Charlotte were sensitive to his distress. They were willing to drive the pair to the train in Manchester, but Ezi wanted to do that on his own – he was Poppy's man. So, there were farewells at the house, with Poppy promising to return, at Christmas, perhaps. She thanked them for allowing her to stay, and for all their hospitality. They watched the young couple walk off, with him pulling her suitcase behind him.

'That's so sweet,' said Charlotte, feeling quite emotional.

'Freedom,' joked Octavian.

Octavian and Charlotte went into Manchester, the following day, to the architecture exhibition that she had tickets for. Octavian drove them through Sale and Stretford and Old Trafford.

'Some wives take their husbands out for a nice pub lunch,' he said. 'Or a walk along the canal tow path. What do I get? I get an architecture exhibition.'

'You'll enjoy yourself.'

'What even is an architecture exhibition?'

'You'll see.'

They were heading to the Manchester Central Convention Complex Centre, which used to be Manchester Central railway station. They parked in a multi-storey car park and began to walk across. It was a sunny day, with lots of people out on the streets. They reached the magnificent, old Victorian building.

'There is one good thing about today's outing,' said Octavian.

'What's that?'

'Your ponytail. I love that.'

'I only put it up for you.'

'Mwah. My incredibly beautiful wife.'

Just after midday, Octavian and Charlotte, arms linked, walked happily away from the conference centre, and he had been entertained, after all, although he still wanted to tease her.

'Well, that's three hours of my life I won't get back.'

She hit him with a brochure she had brought away with her. 'Shush. I know you were interested.'

Many other visitors were leaving all around them, fanning out towards cafes and restaurants, or back to wherever their cars were parked.

'Yeah, it was good. Shall we get some lunch?'

'Yes, but not in town. Closer to home.'

'Okay. You decide where.'

Still with other exhibition visitors nearby, they walked towards the multi-storey car park. They jogged up the mildly pungent concrete stairs and approached the Golf.

'Shall I drive back, darling?' Charlotte asked.

He took out the car keys. Then he stopped dead. Octavian looked down the low, gloomy car park. Standing near to a black Mercedes SUV, a male figure, carrying the same brochure that Charlotte had, was staring at him. Octavian grabbed Charlotte so hard that she squealed. The male figure rushed to the Mercedes and the engine soon started up.

'I love you,' Octavian said with great intensity to Charlotte. 'Get a taxi home.'

Octavian jumped for the Golf's driver door.

'Tony!?'

'Get home!'

Octavian started the Golf and wheel-span away down the car park. He had to drop down one level, badly scraping the left front side. Then he followed the exit arrow, gunning the Golf hard. The exit pole had just descended after the Mercedes, so Octavian smashed right through it, and bounced out onto a Manchester street, with pedestrians staring aghast at him.

The Golf, blue lights flashing in the grill and the siren blaring, pursued the Mercedes at speed. Octavian grappled for his phone and managed to dial the number for Knowles. He shouted into it. 'Phil! Octavian. I'm on him. Leaving Manchester city centre. Yes. Wait.'

The two vehicles sped along, swerving around normal traffic. They were headed south out of the centre.

'Phil! Heading towards the A34. Yes, call for backup. Do it! Yeah.'

Octavian stayed in touch with the crazy driving of the Mercedes. It flew straight through red lights. If it had been any other circumstance, then Octavian would have backed off, fearing for the safety of the general public, but he could not stop.

They flew down Oxford Street, onto Oxford Road, before the Mercedes took a left. in between some Manchester University buildings. Students stopped and watched from the pavement – one of whom was Ezi, with his friends.

The Mercedes got onto the A34, still going at a crazy speed. Octavian's brain handled the fast driving, trying to remember his training. He reached for the phone again. 'Still south on the A34. Phil, it's got number plates on but it won't be registered.'

The chase raced along through the southern suburbs, freezing horrified pedestrians and forcing cars to get out of the way. Octavian drove very well, trying to make the overtaking moves only when it was safe to do so. Then it got onto the Kingsway dual carriageway, with speeds touching 100 mph.

The reckless Mercedes created a gap. Octavian was forced to go faster. He could see less traffic ahead. Greenery flashed along in his peripheral vision. After each curve, Octavian expected to see the Mercedes wrapped around a bridge, but there it always was, in the near distance, barrelling along. Suddenly Octavian realized where they were heading to.

'Gatley!'

He was shocked by the realization behind that fact.

He reached for the phone. 'It's Gatley, Phil! Gatley.'

The Mercedes overtook a lorry speed, narrowly wiping out against the side of a bus. Octavian had to slow to get around safely, and the Mercedes was out of view. But he knew where it was going. He got off Kingsway and drove onto the road where John and Lee Paterson lived, and hit the brakes. Of all the places, the Mercedes had crashed here, halfway into a hedge, in a cloud of steam, opposite the Paterson house.

Octavian jumped out and rushed to open his boot. There was no time to don the stab vest, as there was Lee Paterson re-emerging onto the road. The young man's face was impassive. Octavian grabbed his taser, and then stepped out from behind the Golf. Lee Paterson looked thin and nerdy, but he was panting from the crazy car chase. Octavian realized that he had something behind his back.

'Armed police! I have a taser! Get on the floor! Get down!

Octavian didn't think he was near enough to fire the taser. He had to move forward.

'Armed police! Drop the weapon! Drop the weapon!'

Lee Paterson brought a crossbow into view. Octavian moved from side to side, even did a quick squat, trying to put Lee Paterson off his aim, while all the time attempting to close up enough to make the shot with the taser.

'Put it down, Lee! It's over, Lee!'

Lee Paterson let the bolt fly.

There was the sound of police sirens in the distance. Octavian moved forward, as if it were a duel. He fired the taser, hitting Lee Paterson in the chest. Lee Paterson convulsed with the 50,000 volts and then collapsed to the ground, completely incapacitated. Police cars entered the street and officers jumped out, screaming and aiming their firearms at both Octavian and Lee Paterson.

Octavian sank to his knees, dropping the taser. Only then did he look to see that his left side had been impaled by the crossbow bolt.

Printed in Great Britain
by Amazon